THE KILLABLES

THE
KILLABLES

Gemma Malley

HODDER

First published in Great Britain in 2012 by Hodder & Stoughton
An Hachette UK company

First published in paperback in 2012

1

A CIP catalogue record for this title is available from the British Library

B format paperback ISBN 978 1 444 72280 2
A format paperback ISBN 978 1 444 72281 9
eBook ISBN 978 1 444 72279 6

Printed and bound by Clays Ltd, St Ives plc

Hodder & Stoughton policy is to use papers that are natural, renewable
and recyclable products and made from wood grown in sustainable forests.
The logging and manufacturing processes are expected to conform to the
environmental regulations of the country of origin.

Hodder & Stoughton Ltd
338 Euston Road
London NW1 3BH

www.hodder.co.uk

For Diggory

With advances in neuroimaging technology such as MRI, neuroscientists have made significant findings concerning the amygdala in the human brain. Consensus of data shows the amygdala has a substantial role in mental states, and is related to many psychological disorders.

In a 2003 study, subjects with Borderline personality disorder showed significantly greater left amygdala activity than normal control subjects. Some borderline patients even had difficulties classifying neutral faces or saw them as threatening. Individuals with psychopathy show reduced autonomic responses, relative to comparison individuals, to instructed fear cues.

In 2006, researchers observed hyperactivity in the amygdala when patients were shown threatening faces or confronted with frightening situations. Patients with more severe social phobia showed a correlation with increased response in the amygdala.

Similarly, depressed patients showed exaggerated left amygdala activity when interpreting emotions for all faces, and especially for fearful faces. Interestingly, this hyperactivity was normalized when patients went on antidepressants. By contrast, the amygdala has been observed to relate differently in people with Bipolar Disorder.

A 2003 study found that adult and adolescent bipolar patients tended to have considerably smaller amygdala volumes and somewhat smaller hippocampal volumes. Many studies have focused on the connections between the amygdala and autism. Additional studies have shown a link between the amygdala and schizophrenia, noting that the right amygdala is significantly larger than the left in schizophrenic patients.

Wikipedia, January 2011

1

Dirt, dust and grime in her eyes, in her nose, choking her. A hand around hers, pulling her on, reassuring her. A rock catches her unawares and she falls, her face pressed into the ground; she lifts her head and wipes her forehead – there is blood on the back of her hand. Her lip begins to quiver but before tears can come she is swept up; her arms wrap around a familiar neck and the journey continues.

The rhythm of his walking calms her; she feels safe. His body is warm; she nestles into him. She can smell him; sweat, hunger, determination, love. 'Nearly there,' he murmurs into her ear. 'Nearly there, my darling.'

She closes her eyes, and when she opens them again she is somewhere else, somewhere sunny, surrounded by grass, the bright light making her squint. A face leans towards her and she smiles, reaches out. 'We're here,' he murmurs. 'We're here, my darling . . .'

Evie opened her eyes and sat bolt upright. She'd had a nightmare again, a dream so vivid she checked around her quickly to make sure that she was alone, that she was in her bed. But of course she was. Quickly she knelt down at the side of her bed and started to whisper, 'I cleanse my mind of bad thoughts. I cleanse my brain of evil. I look to the good, I strengthen my soul, I fight the demons that circle me day and night. I am strong. I am good. I am safe. I am protected and protector.'

She repeated the mantra five times, then, trying not to notice that her sheets were drenched in sweat, Evie made her way to the small bathroom next to her bedroom, the only bathroom in the house – why would you need more than one? – and stood under the cold shower, washing herself, washing away the smell of the man holding her. The man whose face she never saw, but she knew who it was. Every night she went to bed telling herself that she wouldn't see him again; every night she failed in this resolution, and every morning she woke fearful, wishing she could purge herself, wishing she could be like everyone else, wishing she could be good, free from the nightmares that plagued her, that marked her out as strange, as dangerous.

The dreams never felt like nightmares. They never felt dark and scary; they felt warm, happy.

But that just made it worse.

She was depraved. That was the truth of it. The man represented the evil within her, trying to tempt her, to make her reject good things; she knew that because her mother had told her so. He was evil, and her longing for him told her that she was weak, that she was a failure, that she was corrupt and dangerous. But she could fight it, if she tried hard enough. That's what her mother said. And the way she said it always suggested that so far Evie hadn't tried hard enough, that the dreams were her fault, her choice.

Which was why Evie was relieved to find her mother busy in the kitchen that morning when she walked in; absorbed in cooking porridge on the stove, scrubbing down the work surfaces. Hard work, cleanliness of thought and deed, chastity, charity and order – these were the ways to virtue, this was how life should be lived. Her mother was a paragon of virtue, much lauded by the Brother. A good woman, he would say as his eyes fell on Evie, with a slight shake of the head.

Her mother nodded to Evie's place and put a steaming bowl in front of her daughter, then returned to her work. 'It's nearly seven,' she said abruptly. 'You need to get a move on.' She walked back to the cooker, then turned again. 'You . . . shouted out in your sleep again last night,' she said, her tone suddenly cold.

Evie's heart thudded. Her mother had heard her. She knew.

Their eyes met, and Evie suddenly felt a strange but intense longing to share her fears, to tell her mother everything, to have her comfort her, reassure her, wrap her arms around Evie, to recreate the cocoon that had felt so intoxicating, so complete in her dream. But she knew it was impossible, knew that her mother would never understand, would never reassure her. She would judge her, she would blame her. And deservedly so.

'I . . .' she started. 'I . . .'

'You have to stop, Evie,' her mother said flatly. 'You have to fight your evil impulses. In spite of everything you have a good job, a good marriage on the horizon. Do you think you can marry if you cry out in your sleep? Do you think people will look at you in the same way if they find out? How will they look at us? What will people say?'

Evie looked at her uncomfortably. 'I keep reading the Sentiments,' she said, biting her lip, her hand inadvertently moving to the small scar to the right of her forehead, her fingers tracing around it to reassure herself.

Her mother looked at her for a moment, her face twisting slightly as she did so. Then she let out a long breath. 'Reading the Sentiments is not enough. You dream because you allow yourself to dream,' she said, her eyes narrowing. 'Because you invite the dream in. It shows that you are weak, Evie. Imagination shows an ability to lie, to pretend the world is different than it is. So you'd better be careful. Now eat your porridge. Don't waste good food.'

Evie started to eat, but the food felt dry and alien in her mouth. Her mother was right, though she didn't know the half of it. She was weak. She was a deviant. She tried to chew and to swallow the oatmeal, but it was impossible – it was as though her stomach was rejecting it, as though it knew that she didn't deserve it.

Even her stomach couldn't follow the rules of the City properly, she thought to herself miserably. Rules that led to a good life. Rules that everyone followed without question. Don't waste food. Don't allow emotions into your heart because emotion is the door to evil. Work hard, follow the rules, obey your parents, do not ask questions, listen to the Brother and heed his teachings, accept your label but strive to improve it, be fearful of evil because it is pernicious, opportunistic, because it never sleeps and once it takes hold of you, you will never be free . . . To everyone else it seemed so simple, so easy. To Evie the rules felt like a straitjacket, forcing her mind and body into a shape that was unnatural to her. And the only explanation she could come up with was that evil had already taken hold of her, that it was the evil within her that rejected the rules established for her protection, for everyone's.

Eventually she gave up, put her spoon down and pushed her bowl away. Her mother shot her a long stare, then shrugged. 'You'd better get to work. You don't want to be late.'

Evie left the kitchen, brushed her teeth, put on a light coat, then left the house and started her walk to work. She would work harder, she told herself as she marched forward. She would not allow destructive thoughts into her head any more. She would be a better person. She would follow the City's rules, even if she found them restrictive. She would follow them *because* she found them restrictive, because she had to fight the evil within her, had to rid herself of it once and for all. Because the City was all that stood between her and self-destruction; between their fragile society and the darkness that longed to destroy it and everyone within it.

* * *

The City was where Evie lived, where everyone lived – everyone who was good, anyway. Its high walls protected them from the Evils who scavenged outside, who wanted to kill them all and fill the world with terror, just as they had before.

It had been Evils, or their ancestors, who had nearly destroyed the world some years earlier. Evils who had brought about the Horrors. Before the City, the world had been filled with Evils, humans with no capacity for love, for good. Humans were not all destined to be evil; only a few had distorted brains that made them unfeeling, selfish, bent on destruction. But others were easily influenced, and the psychopaths were convincing, twisting minds, making good people do terrible things and thinking that they were good.

The Horrors had started as a small war, but they turned into a huge one that went on for years. Millions of people died in terrible ways, all because people couldn't agree with each other. But the one good thing about the Horrors was what had come out of them: the City. Like a phoenix, the Great Leader said in his Sentiments. Outside the City walls, evil still reigned and men still fought with each other for everything – for food, for shelter. There was no order and no civilisation. There was no peace.

But Evie didn't have to worry about the world

outside, because she was one of the lucky ones, one of the ones inside the City's walls.

The City was the only good, safe place in all the world, and that was why it was always under siege. That's why its citizens had to understand how fortunate they were and had to work as hard as they could to keep the City secure – to do everything they could to remain virtuous, to remain worthy of the City's protection.

Because it only took one bad apple to ruin the basket.

The road to work was long and wide; before the Horrors it had been the financial district of the City of London, a place where evil had flourished, where all that mattered was the collection and multiplication of money. The City didn't have money; workers received tokens for goods which provided them with everything they needed.

But whilst money and its servants had not survived, the road had, and some of the buildings. Including the hospital – although now it was the Great Leader's headquarters. It had been to the hospital that he had fled as the final hours of the Horrors had unfolded; in the hospital that he had convinced others to follow him, to believe in him, and to seek another way of living. A good, peaceful way.

There were five departments in Government Block 3 where Evie worked: Unit 1 – technology. Unit 2 – data. Unit 3 – label changing. Unit 4 – intelligence. Unit 5 – research. Evie worked in Unit 3. It was an airless room in a grey building, a new one, built in the centre of the City just minutes from the City Square, where a statue of the Great Leader stood proudly. Most of the government buildings were new; the ground on which they were built had been cleared of the rubble and old buildings left after the Horrors. The Great Leader had seen them as a new beginning, a chance for the City to establish itself as different from the cities that had stood before, with their corruption and deviants. Not everything was new; resources were limited and where buildings still stood safely and securely, they had been incorporated into the City's design, exorcised of their previous inhabitants and allowed to be part of this new, good place. Just as its citizens had been allowed a second chance; a new, better future.

As Evie approached the building she was already taking off her coat, ready to place it quickly and efficiently in her locker before walking up to her Unit. Loitering was not condoned in the City; busy, focused minds were good minds, the Sentiments said. Standing around, gossiping; these were the breeding grounds of evil, of temptation.

But as she got to the steps that led up to the building's door, she hesitated, her cheeks flushing slightly. It was Lucas.

'Evie.' Lucas smiled formally, his blond hair made almost white by the early morning sun, his clear blue eyes so striking in colour but so emotionless that Evie sometimes wanted to hit him just to see if they were capable of tears. But that was because she was a terrible person. Only a terrible person would have such a thought about the man they were going to marry. 'Good morning. How are you today?'

He walked towards her, hand outstretched for a formal salutation, his gold watch glinting as he did so. She held hers out too, forced herself to smile, reminded herself how lucky she was that Lucas had chosen her. Marriage matches were made by both partners, both partners' families. But everyone knew that someone like Lucas could have had his pick. Evie still wasn't sure why he had chosen her. 'I'm well,' she said. 'And you?'

'Very well.' A smile. Then an awkward little raise of the eyebrows. 'Well, better get to work.'

'Absolutely.' Evie nodded, trying to project herself into a future where they were married, where they slept in the same bed, where they spoke to each other with an easy familiarity instead of in stilted, awkward sentences punctuated by even more stilted, awkward silences. But she couldn't see it, couldn't imagine what it would be like.

He turned, and her eyes followed him as he walked back to his brother, who was waiting for him on the other side of the steps. Lucas was never far from Raffy, who looked so different from Lucas it was as though he was his negative: dark, dishevelled hair, dark thunderous eyes.

They said that where Lucas looked like their mother, Raffy looked like their father – and it was more than just looks. They said that was why Lucas rarely left Raffy's side: because he wanted to watch over him, check up on him. Because he didn't trust him.

Then again, no one seemed to trust Raffy much.

Silently, Evie watched as Lucas and Raffy walked towards the building; then, just before they disappeared, Raffy turned and their eyes met for less than a second before he turned again, Lucas looking at him quizzically before they were hidden from view. Lucas would be going to the first floor where the senior managers worked; Raffy to Floor 3 where the male Units were situated. Evie herself was on the fourth floor, in one of the female Units.

From the age of eight, boys and girls were all segregated to prevent impure thoughts. From then on, they were educated separately, even worked separately when they left school at fourteen. As Evie made her way to the stairs, she found herself trying to remember when Lucas had started being a presence in her life, when his visits had become visits to her and not to her parents. Not that they were ever left alone. Not for long. As far as marriage was concerned, their parents arranged meetings between them to find a match. She wasn't sure who had been more surprised – herself or her parents – when Lucas had made the match formal by asking her parents for her hand. Even then he barely spoke to her. Even then it felt like something that was happening to someone else.

Sometimes Evie wished it was.

And then she wondered why she couldn't be like everyone else, grateful for what she had. But even as she wondered, she knew the answer. Because her mother was right about her. Because she was the bad apple in the basket.

'Morning!' Christine, who sat next to Evie, smiled at her as they arrived together. 'How are you?'

'Really well. You?'

'Great!' Christine smiled again, then turned back to her computer.

Christine was the closest Evie had to a girl friend, but they didn't talk all that much – a few words after the weekend, a smile in the morning. It wasn't that Evie didn't want friends. She just found it hard to make them when her head was full of secrets and longing that she could never reveal, not to anyone. And anyway, now that they were working there wasn't much opportunity. Talking was frowned upon during work hours, and after work they were both expected home to help their mothers and meet with their matches or, in Christine's case, potential matches that her parents had deemed suitable. So Evie found it easier not to share at all; to keep her head down, keep herself to herself. It wasn't hard; the City didn't encourage close friendships, after all. Friendships created loyalties that might conflict with the City's needs. Friendships might become awkward if things ever changed. Like Labels.

Evie made her way to her desk, stopping first to pick up ten reports from the supervisor's desk at the front of the room. Ten reports at a time; once finished, another ten would be taken until the reports had ended or the day had finished. At least that was what the managers used to say, but the reality was that usually the day ended before the reports did, and usually everyone worked a little bit late in order to finish them off.

The government building that Evie worked in was known as the System building; it supported and enabled the System, which regulated everything within the City walls and kept order.

Evie's job was Label Changer; it was her first job and she had been doing it for three years, since leaving school. Their teacher had introduced the various trades and apprenticeships open to them. Seamstress, carpenter, grower, farmer, builder, technician, electrician . . . the list had seemed endless, some of the roles so inviting, like Growers – to immerse her hands in earth every day, to create food from small seeds, nurturing crops until they were ready to harvest.

But Evie's mother was a seamstress; if she were to take any apprenticeship, it would be at her side, pricking herself with needles, her clumsy fingers failing to copy the small, delicate patterns that her mother so expertly produced. The choices seemed wide at school, but daughter followed mother and son followed father; that was always the way. Unless they did very well at school. Unless they were good enough to work for the City itself.

And so Evie had chosen the government, an office job, considered a coup because it required tests to be passed, interviews to be endured. More importantly it had persuaded her mother to drop the idea of Evie becoming a seamstress, convinced her that Evie wasn't letting the family down in any way. Once she was married, their job would be complete. They thought they had done a good job, too, on the surface. Evie was a good citizen to all intents and purposes. Her grades were good; she could recite the Sentiments, every single one. She was a B, a good label; she had never been in any real trouble. Lucas, a senior manager, a respected citizen, was to be her match. She had done well. So far.

She looked at her reports. The first one: a change from B to C. Not life shattering, but an unhappy message to receive. In her mind's eye Evie could see the letter arriving with its official stamp, the yellow ribbon accompanying it which would replace the blue 'B' ribbon, to be worn at all times on the lapel. She could hear the whispering of neighbours as they craned their necks to see, could feel the humiliation of the man concerned – Mr Alan Height – his fumbled apologies to his family, his shoulders hunching slightly as he left the house the following morning. Labels were how the System looked after everyone, looked after the City. People were given labels of A, B, C or D. As were the best – they were pure-thinking, truly good people who always helped their fellow citizen, who never thought about themselves, who were courageous and honourable and just. B's were next best; they were also good, but not quite as good as A's. They were trusted members of society; they held good jobs, ran community functions. C's were okay. Most people were C's. C's were good on the whole but were open to temptation; sometimes had bad instincts; were easily led. C's had to be careful; during the Horrors it had been C's who carried out most of the carnage, dropped most of the bombs, co-ordinated most of the atrocities. Not because they were bad but because they'd fallen for the arguments of the evil ones. Of course they didn't have labels back then; they thought people were just people, all the same. And if they didn't, then they didn't say anything in case they offended someone. But it wasn't an offence to warn someone that they were vulnerable. It wasn't an offence to look after them, to make them aware, to monitor them and make sure they were safe. That's all the labels did. It was easy to see physical differences between people: who was strong, who was weak, who needed protection from the sun, who needed to eat less and exercise more. Everyone accepted that people were different physically. But inside? Inside, they were different too. You just had to know how to tell, what to look for.

Evie started to process the label change, inputting the relevant codes, checking and double-checking that everything was as it should be. It was irrelevant and nonsensical to feel for someone whose label had changed, she knew that. As Sentiment 26 explained, a label change was neither happy nor sad, just self-induced fact. But Evie couldn't help herself; she could not forget the look on the face of her neighbour, Mrs Chiltern, when she had gone from C to D. She carried the shame with her long after her label had changed back to C; had never again spoken to Evie over the garden fence, or popped round to their house for tea. She wasn't welcome; Evie's parents had made that much clear, but even if she had been, Evie knew she wouldn't have come. D meant deviant. D meant dangerous. Evie never knew what Mrs Chiltern had done to deserve such a label, but it didn't matter. The System knew, and that was enough.

The System knew everything.

Evie had nearly finished Mr Height's label change. Downward changes were always easier than upward changes – fewer checks and double checks, fewer codes to input again and again to ensure that changes were correct. Every day, the System would assess all the citizens of the City; every week there were hundreds of changes to ensure the equilibrium, to ensure that society was regulated, that goodness was valued, that order was maintained. Because order meant peace, goodness kept out evil, and because the City was predicated on community, on society, on the group not the individual.

But it wasn't the several thousand strong City community who got the labels, it was its individuals, Evie often thought to herself. It was its individuals who had to break the bad news to their husbands and wives, individuals who were shunned on the street if their label had changed for the worse.

But such thoughts weren't allowed. To question anything about the City was to suggest that you knew better than the Great Leader. And what could be a greater sign of selfishness than that?

Methodically Evie keyed in the codes and made the change, writing the System code onto the paper report when she had finished. Her problem was that she thought too much, she told herself. Even when she was asleep her brain kept working when instead it should be resting, trusting, accepting. By thinking too much she was as bad as the people who had doubted the Great Leader. The people who had brought about the Horrors. The people who lived outside the City walls, waiting to destroy everyone inside.

'Evangeline, are you staring into thin air again?' Evie looked up with a start to see Mrs Johnson, her supervisor, looking at her, and she reddened.

'No,' she said quickly. 'I mean, I'm sorry.'

Mrs Johnson raised an eyebrow and Evie took out her second report. C to D. Forcing her eyes to look only at the screen ahead of her and not into the immediate future of the report's subject, Evie started to type.

2

As usual, Evie was late home. An hour this time. Sometimes it was more. It didn't matter; her parents would wait for her. Everyone worked hard in the City; everyone was productive. Busy minds were happy minds, the Great Leader said. Productive individuals meant a happy society. And hard work meant less thinking time, less opportunity for evil to flourish.

But when Evie opened the front door and went straight to the kitchen, just as she always did, she saw that they were not alone that evening; there, sitting next to her father, a large glass of wine clasped in his hand, was their Brother, the Great Leader's appointed one, their mentor and guide. The Great Leader himself was old now, rarely seen; he himself had chosen the Brother to lead his people, to see that evil was never allowed within the City walls.

'Evie!' He smiled at her, his watery eyes not quite meeting hers, his flaccid cheeks rosy from the warmth of the kitchen and the alcohol in his blood. 'And how are we today?'

Evie returned the smile, but it didn't reach her eyes. They were not due a visit from the Brother. He had come for a reason. Because he knew something. She felt the familiar feeling of dread creep up on her. 'I'm well, Brother,' she said nervously.

'Then sit down. Eat. Your mother has prepared a pie. Such a wonderful cook, your mother. You should be very proud.'

'I am proud,' Evie replied quickly. 'And grateful.'

'Of course you are, of course you are,' the Brother said, nodding. Then he looked at her, right at her, the way he used to when she was small, when he was teaching her about the Horrors that had torn the world apart and a past that was full of people who thought only of themselves. People who created religions only to use them to fight other religions, who allowed evil to roam amongst them because they wouldn't listen to the Great Leader, because he wasn't the Great Leader back then, just a doctor with an idea.

'I hear you had a bad dream again.'

Evie's eyes widened. 'I had the dream, yes,' she said fearfully, looking from the Brother to her mother to her father, her voice wavering. 'But I didn't mean to. I tried not to. I read the Great Leader's Sentiments. I—'

'You dreamt of a man you think is looking after you? A man you think is protecting you?' the Brother cut in.

She nodded anxiously. 'But I know that he represents evil. I will fight him, Brother. I will fight . . .'

The Brother sat back in his chair, his brow furrowed. His pink cheeks were now glistening with a thin layer of sweat, beads of which had collected on his nose. 'Yes, well, that's interesting,' he said thoughtfully, his eyes not leaving Evie's. Then he leant forward. 'You know that the brain is a dangerous thing. You know that it will lead you into darkness if you let it? That like riding a horse, we must keep a tight reign and stay utterly focused if we are to get to the destination of our choosing?'

Evie nodded again. She knew all this. She knew it. The last time she had seen the Brother he had shouted at her, told her that her dreams were brought to her by the evil inside her, that if she didn't rid herself of the lies in her head then she would be punished by the System. She had cried, desperately, had begged him, had told him that she would dream no longer, that she would be strong and she would not let him down. She clasped her hands together; they had become slippery under a veil of sweat. Was this the judgement day she had feared for so long? Was everything over?

'And the subconscious brain is the most dangerous of all,' the Brother continued. 'That is where darkness resides, where desire and greed and envy roam freely, unfettered by our conscious minds. We are pure of mind, but the New Baptism cannot protect us for ever. Our brains are predisposed to have a weakness for evil; after the New Baptism it is up to us to remain good.'

'Yes, Brother. I know that,' Evie said, full of shame, wishing she were someone else, someone good, someone who wasn't tormented by terrible thoughts and dreams.

'Yes,' the Brother replied. 'Yes, you do know. But I have consulted the Great Leader. I have thought deeply about you, Evie. And I have come to a conclusion.'

Evie closed her eyes. The Great Leader? A conclusion? It could only mean one thing. He was taking her away.

She took a deep breath. She was ready. She had been ready all her life. It was better this way, better that the truth was finally exposed, that everyone could hate her just as she hated herself. Evil had found its way into her brain. That's why she did bad things. That's why she had bad thoughts. She opened her eyes again. 'Yes, Brother?'

The smile was returning to the Brother's face.

'Finally I think I understand. And I realise that there is no need to worry. The man in your dreams is the City,' he said.

Evie stared at him uncertainly. She didn't understand.

'The City.' Evie's mother nodded firmly. 'You see, Evie? There's nothing to worry about after all. Is there, Brother?'

The Brother flashed her a little smile. 'No, Delphine. You can stop worrying.' He turned back to Evie and his smile broadened. 'The man in your dream is not the Devil. That is why you haven't been able to push him away. The man in your dreams represents the City, carrying you towards goodness, saving you from evil. This great City, which looks after us all, which has our best interests at heart – that is what the man represents. That is the comfort you feel. That is why you return to the dream again and again. You are not evil, Evie. You are not evil after all.'

'But . . .' Evie's mind was racing. Nothing made sense. She stared at her father, who smiled at her.

'The City,' he said, sharing a glance with the Brother before smiling at her again. 'Doesn't that make you feel better? There's nothing to worry about, Evie. Not any more.'

Evie managed to nod. It didn't feel right, not at

all. But she recognised that this was a way out, a door opening – an opportunity to stop the questions and end her parents' suspicious glances.

'Thank you, Brother,' she said, trying to look grateful, to look good.

'You're welcome,' replied the Brother. 'I'm glad we don't have a candidate here for a second New Baptism. Aren't you, Evie?'

Evie nodded. A second New Baptism. The ultimate recourse for a lost soul. 'Yes,' she said quietly. 'Yes, Brother. Thank you. May the City watch over me and the System reward and reprimand me.'

'Indeed,' said the Brother gravely. Then his eyes left Evie, his expression changing as he turned back to her mother and father, his eyebrows rising, his eyes glinting slightly. 'Although I think the System is more interested in reprimanding Mr Bridges from Road 14. You've heard the news, have you?'

Evie's father frowned. 'What news? Mr Bridges is in trouble? He always seemed a nice man. Learned.'

'Learned indeed. A researcher,' the Brother said, his eyebrows still raised. 'Research that he was using to disguise his true agenda of deviancy, I'm afraid. He has been labelled a D by the System. I would urge you to stay away from him lest his dangerous thoughts infect this community.'

Evie's mother gasped, but Evie suspected from the look in her eye that she already knew. The letter would only have arrived with Mr Bridges today; the notice would be outside Mr Bridges' house tomorrow. But word spread on report changes ahead of the signs, which were replaced on an almost daily basis. And whilst Evie's father steered clear of gossip, her mother considered it part of her responsibilities as a City citizen. 'That despicable man.' She shuddered. 'Only the other day he was in the cloth district buying clothes. We will not sell to such a man, Brother, you can be sure of that.'

The Brother nodded sagely. 'I think that's a good idea, Delphine. Whilst the Sentiments tell us to leave punishment and retribution to the System, when we clearly have evil in our midst it is our duty to hound it out, to show others who are tempted by evil that we will not tolerate it within these walls. Do you not agree?'

'Wholeheartedly,' Evie's father said firmly, banging his hand down on the table. 'We must be on our guard. All the time. Every minute of every day.'

'You are so right,' replied the Brother. Then he pushed his chair back and patted his belly. 'So, Delphine. Pie, wasn't it? I think we are all ready now. I think it is time to eat. Happy now, Evie?'

'Very,' Evie lied, and they all started to eat.

*　　*　　*

The Brother left at 10 p.m. after patting his stomach and refusing thirds of the pudding Evie's mother had made. Her parents saw him to the door; he embraced them both, smiles on all their faces. Then Evie's father disappeared into his study and her mother returned to the kitchen, the smile gone, a scowl replacing it.

'That is the last time,' she said, 'the last time that the Brother calls at this house because of you. Do you understand, young lady? You are not a child any more. You will be married soon. And until then, until you leave this house, you will do nothing more to worry the Brother. He has enough to worry about. He is a very important man, Evie. Do you understand?'

She was staring at Evie; Evie reddened and nodded. She wanted to point out that she had not asked the Brother to come, that it was her mother who had made the request – or so she suspected – but she remained silent. She had learnt long ago not to argue with her mother.

Her mother sat down at the table and sighed. 'Well? Are you going to clear away the dishes? You don't think it enough that I cooked the food?'

Evie jumped up and started to clear the table. 'Of course not,' she said quickly. 'I just know that you don't like things cleared away until—'

'Until the meal has ended. Until the guests have

left. Yes,' her mother barked. 'But I think it's clear that the evening has come to an end.'

Evie stacked the plates, ran the water and took out the scrubbing brush and started to scrub. She wasn't sure when she'd become such a disappointment to her mother; what it was exactly that she'd done to incur her wrath. All she knew was that she was a burden that her mother had to carry, and she did not bring her mother happiness.

'Did you see Lucas today?'

Evie turned. 'Yes Mother.'

'When you marry him,' said her mother, 'then you will be his responsibility. Make sure you do nothing to vex him, Evie.'

'I won't,' Evie said hotly. 'I mean, I wouldn't.'

'And yet you vex me without a second thought?'

Evie put down the scrubbing brush. 'I don't mean to vex you,' she said cautiously.

Her mother half laughed. 'You don't mean to? Don't tell lies, Evie. You do mean to vex me. Otherwise why would you behave as you do? Why would you cry out in your sleep? Why would you insist on working for the government instead of following me into the seamstress quarter where I can keep watch over you? Why would you have a look in your eye that is so furtive, so secretive, as though you are inviting evil into your life instead of pushing it out?'

Evie stared at her uncertainly and took a deep breath. She had to stay calm. She had to resist the urge to get angry, to argue, to prove her mother right about inviting evil in. No one argued in the City. Certainly no one argued with their parents. But Evie sometimes wondered if that was because no one else had Delphine as their mother. 'The Brother explained about my dreams,' she said, when she was sure she could control her voice. 'And I thought you were happy that I worked for the government. I thought—'

'You thought? No, Evie. You just did what you wanted to do without thinking. How do you think the other seamstresses view me when my own daughter won't work beside me? How do you think that looks?'

Evie regarded her mother carefully. 'You've never said that to me before,' she replied. 'You said that you were pleased I had a job. A job that is respected and—'

'I said I was pleased because your father was pleased,' her mother cut in. 'Because he likes to see the best in you, Evie, and I don't want him to be disappointed. But I know the truth. I know that you're hiding something. I've always known. So don't think you can fool your mother. Don't think I'm not watching you.' She gave her daughter a sharp look, then pushed back her chair and stood up. 'The sooner you marry Lucas the better,' she said, as she walked out of the room. 'Then I can stop worrying that you're going to bring shame on us, Evie. Let us hope that he is as easily fooled as your father, shall we? Let us hope that he doesn't see through you before it's too late.'

Evie watched her as she walked through the door then slowly turned back to the dishes, anger welling up in her like an avalanche. Anger and sadness and frustration and all the other things that she wasn't meant to feel, because in the City everyone was safe and good and there was no place for such emotions. It was anger and sadness and frustration that led people to do evil things – that had led to the Horrors – and that had to be kept out of everyone's heart at all costs.

But Evie couldn't keep them out. She didn't want to. She was angry with her mother, with herself, with everyone and everything that had conspired to make her feel so helpless and hopeless. But her anger had nowhere to go. Not right now. And tonight of all nights she wanted to be left alone. Tonight she needed her parents sleeping deeply in their beds. So she let the anger and the sadness and the frustration simmer deep inside her where they couldn't be detected, then she finished the dishes and went to bed.

*   *   *

She checked her watch. Midnight. Her parents had been asleep for nearly an hour now. Carefully, silently, Evie slipped out of her bedroom, down the corridor and out of the back door. It was warm; she had only her night clothes on, some shoes and a light cardigan. As she walked, her heart thudded in her chest; if she was seen, her life as she knew it would be over. But her desire was too strong; her need too compelling. She carefully lifted the hinge on the back gate, then ran down the passageway until she reached a little clearing. Then, cautiously, excitedly, she made her way to the huge, hollow tree that she'd known since she was little, which stood in the middle of the green. She eased her way inside, which was less easy now that she had grown to almost five foot five, and her eyes lit up when she saw a little candle flickering, a tall figure crouched over it.

'I thought you'd never get here,' Raffy whispered, his eyes full of longing, just as they always were at their furtive night-time meetings. He pulled himself up and wrapped his arms around her.

'I'm here now,' Evie whispered back as their lips met and her arms encircled his neck and she felt, as she always did, as though she finally belonged somewhere. A little breeze brushed her forehead as she kissed Raffy, blowing her hair back and making her feel slightly wild, like the gypsies in her mother's stories, girls and boys who lived wild and free, travelling the land in houses on wheels, never staying anywhere for too long.

No good would come of this, she knew that. The System would find out what they were doing; she didn't know how, but she knew it would because it knew everything, eventually. And when it discovered the truth, it would punish both of them for what they were doing, and bring shame on their families and the City itself. They would become D's – or worse, even; her parents too for failing in their duty of care. Her match to Lucas would be terminated immediately. Her government job would be taken away. She would be an outcast; she would be moved into manual labour, into latrine cleaning, to be pointed at by others and spat on in the street. She knew all this; this was the torment that kept her awake at night and made her hate herself, that terrified her and stopped her making friends or trusting anyone. Because she knew that her heart wasn't like theirs, that she was not good. But right now, Evie was willing to accept that fate. The System would find out, and even a D would be too good for her. She would be a candidate for a second New Baptism; she would carry that shame for the rest of her life.

But right now, right here, hidden in the darkness, with everyone else asleep, Evie brushed her fears away. The System didn't know. Not yet. Maybe it couldn't see in the darkness either. And even if it could, right this minute she didn't care. She felt free, happy, and that life was worth living. And anyway, before they were ravaged by wolves, it always seemed to Evie that the gypsies in her mother's stories always had a pretty good time of it.

3

The New Baptism was nothing to fear. It was what made the City different from all other civilisations: a peaceful, good place. The New Baptisms had been the Great Leader's big idea, back before the Horrors, before the City, when the world had been a different place and the Great Leader had been a brain specialist, a doctor, a healer.

Only he hadn't been able to heal, not in the way he'd wanted to. He'd identified a part of the brain, the amygdala, which was bigger in the brains of psychopaths and criminals. And he realised that it was the root of all evil, that it was the fundamental weakness of human beings. The amygdala wasn't dangerous in everyone, but it had to be watched carefully because it had the potential to grow, to start taking over and change people from good to bad. An enlarged amygdala stopped a person caring about others, made them want to kill and hurt people, made them want to steal and fight. It was people with large amygdalas who started every war, who lead people to hate each other, who caused others pain. It was these same people who had started the Horrors and worked everyone else up to make them want to fight, drop bombs and destroy everything. Because even good people could be weak. Everyone could, given the right circumstances.

It always struck Evie as strange that anyone would reject something that would make everything better. But that was the problem with evil – it made everyone suspicious, made them resist anything that would rid the world of evil because evil had already taken hold and it didn't want to go.

And all because of the amygdala, a bit of the human brain that evil had monopolised and made its home. It meant that people were naturally selfish, aggressive, proud, difficult and competitive and it got them into problems again and again. Wars, skirmishes, robberies, rapes and murders. Terrible things. Unimaginable things. And the most terrible of them all was the Horrors. Evie knew all about the Horrors – everyone did. It was the reason they were here. It was the reason the City existed.

The Horrors made people realise how weak and

dangerous they were. The Horrors made them realise that he'd been right all along.

Within the City this seemed so obvious. It seemed bizarre that before the City existed, only the Great Leader had seen how to cure all the ills of the world, and it seemed even more bizarre that as soon as he told everyone, they didn't jump up and down and tell him to get on with it as quickly as he could. But that was the problem with humans, the Brother always said. They were flawed; faulty. They didn't see the truth; they ran away from anything too new and revolutionary until they realised there was no alternative. Just like everyone ran from the Great Leader and refused to listen to him, refused point blank to let him try his theory out and prove what a difference it would make.

But that was before the Horrors, when humankind had looked pure evil in the face and suffered the consequences. That was before the alternatives had dried up and people realised that sometimes a revolution was what it took.

Then, a few enlightened souls started to listen to the Great Leader, and a small group of people realised that he was right. So he built the City to protect them, and no one was ever sad, or bad, or dangerous or cruel again. He made it so that evil just didn't exist any more. Not inside the City's walls, anyway.

Before the Horrors, the Great Leader had been an academic. He taught people and carried out research, because when he'd been a surgeon, when he was doing his operations, he'd come up with an idea – one which, like all good ideas, was totally rejected by everyone. They said it wouldn't work, it wasn't possible, that he was crazy. So he gave up being a brain surgeon and went into research so he could prove that his idea was a good one. He taught people, too, so his students could help him hone his idea and spread the word.

But still no one would take him seriously; every time he tried to publish a paper, everyone said he was deluded, dangerous. They struck him off the medical register. It just went to show how misguided people were back then, the Brother liked to say, shaking his head incredulously as he did so. But they were the ones who were dangerous. They were the ones who brought the entire world to its knees.

In the City, though, the Great Leader was finally able to prove that he was right. Back then, when the City had just been started, anyone who wanted to come was welcome; anyone who wanted to escape the barren desert that the Horrors had left behind, who wanted food, water, shelter and survival. They just had to have the New Baptism – to have their amygdala removed. Everyone who lived in the City had the New Baptism.

Babies had it when they were born; newcomers had it when they arrived. It was part of the deal; you couldn't live in the City if you didn't have it. Everyone had the same, small, comforting scar to the right of their fore-heads that told everyone they were safe. Because once the amygdala was gone, people were pure and free from evil. And so long as they were determined never to allow evil inside their heads again, they would stay good.

Now the City's walls kept evil out and goodness in. But goodness had to be nurtured; that's why everyone in the City was watched carefully, monitored by the System. D's were watched especially carefully, because sometimes even the New Baptism wasn't enough. Sometimes the amygdala grew back. And if it did, you needed another New Baptism. Only this time you were taken away from your friends and family, because you couldn't be trusted, because you were a potential danger both to them and to yourself.

The label you got if your amygdala came back was different from the others. It was K: a blood-red label for danger. Only you never heard that label being mentioned; never even saw K labels on people because K's were taken away as soon as they were labelled; taken to the hospital for reconditioning. They didn't come back, either; they were too dangerous to live in normal society, because if the evil came back once, it would come back again. So they had to be watched more closely, protected from themselves and kept apart from the good people of the City. No one knew where the K's went; no one was allowed to know. K's were dangerous, and those around them were treated with suspicion because the evil might have spread.

That's why no one liked Raffy.

His father had been a K, and he had been taken away when Evie was four. She still remembered seeing him being removed from his house, which was on her way home from school. She'd been with Raffy when it happened – she'd been allowed to be his friend back then, when they were little and still at school together – walking back home with his older brother, reciting the words they'd learnt that day. Lucas had seen them first, the police guard arriving at the door, his father trying to run but being stopped, his hands tied behind his back. Raffy had wanted to run after him but Lucas had held both of them back. So Evie had just watched as their father was marched away and their mother ran out of the house with books, clothes and other objects, heaping them in a pile in the front garden, then setting them alight. 'A purification,' my mother had explained later, shaking her head wearily. 'Poor woman. It goes to show, you just never know.'

Lucas had accepted the fact that his father had been taken away for reconditioning; it had appeared to act as a catalyst for his own self-improvement programme. From that day on, Lucas, who had always been fairly sensible and sober, had become a model citizen. He had worked hard, found favour with teachers by pointing out the weaker members of the class, and proved himself to be cut from a different cloth than his father. 'His mother's boy,' people would say. 'Such a shame about his brother.'

Raffy had reacted very differently to his father's disappearance. He had become disobedient and had to be disciplined again and again. He took to silence, staring angrily at teachers, and even at the Brother, when they tried to talk to him. Evie had tried to help him, had tried to stay friends with him, but her parents arranged for her to sit on the other side of the class-room; had made it clear that she was to have other friends. Good friends. Better friends.

Friends like Lucas. But when she'd finally found Raffy again, when they had started to confide in each other once more, she had learnt the devastating truth: his father had become a K because of Lucas. Because his eldest son had betrayed him. That's what Raffy had told her. That was why he was so angry.

*　　*　　*

Sunshine crept through Evie's window, telling her that it was time to get up and get ready for work. Heavily, she pulled back the blankets and swung her feet out of bed, just as she always did. But today she felt even more tired than usual, and she suspected it wasn't just because of her midnight outing. It was guilt; guilt and fear.

The thing with Raffy . . . it hadn't started out as such a terrible, terrible thing. But that was the trouble with evil; the Brother told them all the time how evil dressed itself up as something else, as something innocent and faultless. That's how it sucked you in and enslaved you. Evie had listened solemnly, all the while knowing that it was already too late, that she was already evil's servant.

But back then, when they were still young, it really had been innocent; as school children, she and Raffy were brought to the clearing to play each afternoon, to run around and burn off energy. That's when they'd discovered the tree, where they would slip in unnoticed and tell each other stories they'd heard from their parents and teachers about the past: of the Horrors, of flying machines, of a large world full of people. They told each other the things they could tell no one else, and they listened to each other and understood. Then, when they were eight and moved to the next school, when they were no longer allowed to see each other, they made a promise that they would return to the tree, that it would be their place.

It had been five years before they'd found each other again, before they had the carefully controlled independence that allowed them to visit the glade under the pretence of running practices or of meeting sanctioned friends. Raffy got to the tree first; he told Evie when she finally joined him that he'd waited there every day for a year and he'd begun to think she'd forgotten, that she didn't care, that he'd been foolish to think of her all that time.

But Evie had never forgotten. She knew, though, that what they were doing was very dangerous, so they had started to meet at night time instead – secretively, furtively, knowing what would happen if they were caught but doing it anyway because something more powerful than fear was drawing them to that place, to each other.

Every week Evie had told Raffy that they had to stop. Every week she implored him to forget about her. And every week he held her and told her that he would never forget her, that she was his only friend and she alone understood; that if that was wrong, then it meant the City was wrong. Evie knew that what he said was deviance, that what they were doing would lead somewhere terrible. But she knew Raffy was right, too. Because when she was apart from him she felt empty, and when she was with him she felt like she'd come home, somehow, even though that made no sense. No sense at all.

That's why she knew the Brother was wrong about her dream – and that he'd find out the truth eventually. No one knew how the System watched its citizens, how it monitored and measured them. All they knew was that it did, and that it knew everything. If it didn't yet know about Evie and the evil inside her, then it would know soon enough. She had already failed, already shown herself to be unworthy of the City; evil had already claimed her and made her do its bidding, and she had proved herself unable to resist.

Quickly, she got dressed, putting on the trousers and blouse that every girl wore in the City. Clothes were all made in the cloth district where her mother worked, in only three or four designs, to ensure maximum productivity and usefulness and minimum vanity and competition.

But that didn't mean that people looked the same. They might wear the same clothes, but the label sewn into their lapel differentiated them more than any piece of clothing could have done. Yellow for A's, blue for B's, pink for C's, purple for D's and . . . and the other label. The one that was never seen. The label that was the colour of blood, and inspired fear in all who saw it. The label office was at the back of the cloth district; two queues could be seen stretching out of it first thing in the morning and after work in the evening. One queue for upward changes; another for downward. Labels would be ripped off, the new one sewn on with the unique stitching only learnt by label changers.

Evie rarely went near the label office. She hated to see the stooped shoulders, the fear in the eyes of those whose labels had gone down. Even though she herself might have been the one who changed the label on the System. Maybe because of it . . .

She looked down at her own blue label and steeled herself. She was a B. For now.

Quickly she got ready, raced downstairs, ate her breakfast and cleared the table. Then she said goodbye to her parents and left the house.

Evie glanced around as she walked towards the building where she worked, looking to see if Raffy was there. He wasn't. And in many ways, she was relieved. Of course there was a little thud of disappointment, too, but she told herself it was a good thing, on balance. Today was the day she was going to stop her mind drifting into places it had no right to drift; today was the day she was going to stop dreaming, stop questioning.

She walked purposefully up the steps to her building, put her things in her locker and went up to her Unit. Smiling brightly at the supervisor, she took her reports and sat down at her desk.

'Morning,' she said to Christine, who was already there.

Christine looked at her enquiringly. 'You're very cheerful,' she said under her breath. 'What's happened?'

'Nothing,' Evie said quickly. 'Nothing's happened at all.'

Christine digested this, then leant a little closer. 'I had a visit last night from Alfie Cooper. My parents arranged it.'

Evie turned quickly. She vaguely recalled Alfie; he'd been a couple of years older than them at school. He'd been a rather round boy, prone to crying as far as she could remember. 'A visit? Did it go well?'

Christine pulled a slight face. 'Yes,' she said hesitantly. 'I mean, I think so. He talked to my parents more than me. I didn't know what to say.'

'You think you're going to be matched with him?' Evie asked.

Christine shrugged lightly. 'I don't know,' she replied, then allowed herself a little smile. 'You know he's an A? Like Lucas?'

'An A!' said Evie, trying to look enthusiastic.

Christine was a B, like her. Like most of the girls in the room. 'Well, that's great.'

'Yes, it is, isn't it?' Christine said excitedly. 'I mean, if he's an A then it means he's a really good person. Like Lucas. Kind and thoughtful, full of goodness. So he'll make me happy. That's what my mother said. And she's right, isn't she?'

She looked so convinced, so happy. Evie nodded. She was right. A's were good. Lucas *was* good. It was only because Evie wasn't that she didn't appreciate it. 'Of course she's right,' she said. 'I hope it goes well.'

'Me too,' Christine whispered, then turned back to her work. Evie did the same, head down like all the operators, their fingers clacking on their keyboards as labels were changed and protocols followed.

An hour went by, then another. And then everything stopped. Suddenly the computers went dead. Evie thought she'd done something wrong to start with, carried on pressing her keys to bring her computer back to life, but then she saw Christine was doing the same and soon everyone was exchanging glances – glances of fear, of uncertainty, excitement and anticipation. Christine put up her hand and told the supervisor, who walked over suspiciously, then stared in disbelief at the screens and told everyone to turn their computers on again, like they'd done it on purpose, like this was some kind of joke.

Then one of the managers appeared at the door. The supervisor went over and listened to him say something, then she returned, a serious look on her face.

'Okay, everyone. It's a drill,' she said. 'A security drill. Please walk silently and sensibly out of the building to the courtyard at the back. Please stay together and await further instruction.'

They walked silently; no one disobeyed orders in the City. Nonetheless, by the time Evie had got outside to the courtyard, the rumours had permeated in whispers and exchanged glances. There was something wrong with the System. It had a glitch. And apparently Raffy had found it.

Not that anyone called him Raffy – to everyone else he was Raphael, spoken with an emphasis on the 'Ra', with knowing looks and a slight pause before and after. 'Raphael' – as though that explained everything.

Lucas was the only other person Evie had ever heard shortening Raphael's name to Raffy; to her it was his only name, the only thing she'd ever called him. The name was a gypsy name, her mother had told her. Dangerous. Dirty. But it wasn't just his name that unsettled people; it was everything about him. Raffy wore his hair long – or as long as regulations would allow – not short around the ears like everyone else, and his eyes were full of questions, just as Evie knew hers would be if she let them. Her mother had been right; he never seemed to have any friends – apart from his brother, Evie never saw him with anyone. He always seemed to be alone, observing, brooding, and the other boys seemed wary of him. Evie wasn't surprised: there was something about Raffy that put people on their guard. His muscles were taut and lean; he looked constantly primed for action. She sometimes wondered what action he was primed for, what it would feel like to run with him, out in the open, and to feel the wind in her hair.

But she knew she never would. And anyway, the truth was that the gypsies from her mother's stories never wound up happy. Mostly they ended up destitute and alone.

As Evie and her Unit congregated in the courtyard, forming a neat line joining several other neat lines, she looked around anxiously. She could feel an energy in the air – expectation, excitement. Or was it fear? Never before had the government buildings been evacuated, except for the carefully orchestrated and pre-planned fire tests which happened once a year. Everyone was pretending to be silent and thoughtful, but eyes were darting around curiously, glances were being exchanged, eyebrows raised, and whispers so quiet they were almost silent, nevertheless travelled between the ranks. A glitch.

A glitch in the System. Was a glitch a fault? What did it mean? What would happen?

Evie shared the glances, felt the tension in the air like everyone else. But she had more tension of her own, more expectation, more excitement. Every time she heard footsteps behind her she felt the hairs on the back of her neck stand up. And every time the footsteps continued or stopped, telling her that it wasn't Raffy, she felt a prick of disappointment, which she inwardly chastised herself for. Had he really discovered it? Did that make him a hero? Or was he being blamed again for something he didn't do? Were people just assuming it was him because . . . well, because he was Raffy? The same reason her parents wouldn't allow her to associate with him in any way, not even to say 'hello' at the weekly Gathering. The same reason he seemed to have no friends; the same reason the teacher at their pre school had always seemed extra harsh when disciplining Raffy.

Because he was 'like his father'.

Her supervisor appeared and immediately the whispering stopped. 'The System is being rebooted,' she declared, her voice hushed, eyes staring at each of them in turn. 'Just wait outside until you're told to go in. Everything is as it should be. Everything is fine.' Evie nodded, as did Christine and the others. But she knew they were all thinking the same thing she was: it wasn't routine. Otherwise it would have happened before.

Then someone came out into the courtyard with the manager and everyone looked over, and the supervisor's sharp intake of breath told them everything they needed to know. Because the person who came out with the manager was Raffy.

Hundreds of eyes silently followed Raffy as he crossed the yard to join his Unit, the manager walking behind him. Evie's stomach was full of butterflies as he walked, his eyes darting around, and she wanted to shout, 'Over here, I'm over here,' but she couldn't, and anyway, she knew it would be dangerous if he looked in her direction, if anyone else saw.

Christine stared at Evie, allowed her head the tiniest of shakes. 'Raphael,' her eyes said. 'Told you so.'

The manager called the supervisors over and they huddled in the corner, talking in low voices and allowing everyone else the opportunity to whisper to each other again.

'Freak,' Christine said immediately. 'I bet he created the glitch. He shouldn't be allowed to work here. I can't even believe he's a B, to be honest. But he won't be for long. System glitch? He's up to something.'

'He's not a freak,' Evie replied before she could stop herself. 'You don't know anything.'

Christine looked taken aback. She wasn't used to being contradicted. Not about something like this, that everyone agreed on. 'Evie,' she whispered. 'Evie, don't defend him just because you're going to marry his brother. You don't have to, anyway; Lucas knows he's a freak, too. That's why he babysits him all the time. My brother went to school with Raphael and he says he's weird. He asks strange questions. He's got strange eyes. If you ask me, he's going to end up like his father. If you ask me, he should, too. You can see the evil in him. He's a K, Evie. A K just waiting to happen.' She shook her head sadly and let out a long sigh.

Evie felt her stomach clench with fear and anger. No one ever mentioned the K label. Ever. And Christine was wrong; Raffy didn't have strange eyes. He had mesmerising, intense, brooding eyes. Eyes full of passion, full of questions, full of longing.

'Okay, the System has been rebooted,' a voice called out suddenly from the door of the building, one of the managers. 'Please file back into the building as your Unit is called. Unit 1 first, please. As stated, this was just a routine operation. But no word of this will be repeated outside of these walls. The System will be watching you. Thank you.'

Everyone started to move; people were walking back into the building. Evie shot one last look over at Raffy, hoping against hope that he might look up, that he might . . .

'Evie. So sorry about this disruption.' Raffy had just that minute seen her, caught her eye. She looked up, startled, to see Lucas standing next to her. He smiled at her supervisor, who immediately smiled and blushed.

'We will see you inside,' she said to Evie. As Mrs Johnson ushered the other girls into the building, Evie tried to ignore their craned necks turning to stare at her and at Lucas. As well as being tall and handsome, he was a senior manager, and highly respected. He smiled at her and as she looked into his eyes she searched for something, a flicker, something that might make her feel or understand – something that might give her hope, cure her, save her. But all she saw was blue, an ocean of it; a blank ocean that said nothing to her. No longing, no passion.

'Just a reboot,' Lucas said with a little shrug. 'Inconvenient but there we are. Are you keeping well?'

'Very well,' Evie answered, forcing her eyes to stay on him and not flicker over to where she knew Raffy was standing, staring at her, willing her to look at him. 'And you? Are you well? Your family?'

'Very well,' Lucas smiled, his symmetrical face barely creasing, Evie noticed. He was perfect, just as everyone always said he was. There would be no flicker in his eye, because A's did not have flickers. Flickers were weaknesses. Lucas had no knowledge of emotions, of fears, of dreams that consumed and scared. His hair was efficiently short, his clothes never wrinkled. She had never seen his temper flare or seen him lose control. That was what it was to be good – she saw that now, suddenly.

And that's why people hated Raffy. Christine didn't see wild passion in Raffy's eyes; she saw raw, dangerous emotion.

'And your brother?' The words came out before she could stop them. There would be no saving herself. There would be no hope. 'I saw that he's—'

'Raphael is fine,' Lucas interrupted quickly, his smile freezing on his face. 'He will be fine, anyway. The System will have him under close observation.' He pulled his sleeve up and looked at the gold watch that Raffy despised. The watch had appeared on Lucas's wrist the day after their father disappeared; Raffy had told Evie that it had been Lucas's reward for betraying him. Now, as Evie looked at it, she found herself recoiling. The System was going to be watching Raffy more closely? What did that mean? How did Lucas know? 'Now, more importantly,' he continued, 'I must come over to your house one of these evenings. I shall secure an invitation from your father tomorrow. If you're happy for me to do so?'

'Of course I am,' Evie said, wishing that she *was* happy, and not full of despair.

'Wonderful. Well, look after yourself. See you soon, Evie.' He leant forward as though to kiss her; Evie, who had never kissed him before, froze, uncertain about what she should do, whether such a thing was allowed at work. She remembered just in time that Lucas was a senior manager as well as her fiancé, that of course it was allowed if he was the one doing it. But as she leant in, her face turned, just slightly, just enough to ensure that Lucas's lips didn't quite reach hers, and the kiss settled just to the side of them. An efficient kiss. So different from Raffy's. Then, as quickly as his head had moved towards her, it retracted; another smile, and he was gone, marching off towards the manager.

Evie watched him for a second, wondering what he was thinking, then remembered that he wouldn't be thinking anything. He would be focused on his work, on being productive, being a good citizen. As the Brother said, being a truly good citizen meant thinking very little. The System and the Great Leader did the thinking for them. They just had to do what was asked of them, with good grace, and with a determination to be good, honourable and true.

Slowly, Evie turned and walked back into the building. But as she approached the door, she could hear footsteps behind her; quick, urgent footsteps. She stopped, stepped aside, then froze. It was Raffy, and his supervisor was running after him. 'Raphael, do not run. Come back here. Come back . . .'

As he passed, Raffy stumbled and fell against her; Evie gasped, through the shock of touching him more than anything, the surprise and exhilaration at feeling his weight heavy on her.

'Don't kiss him again,' he whispered as his hand pressed against the wall next to her to pull himself up, making it look like the stumble had been an accident. 'Don't ever kiss him.'

'Come on,' the supervisor muttered impatiently. 'Sorry about this,' he said to Evie.

'No, I . . . it's no problem,' she replied.

'Sorry,' Raffy said loudly to her and the supervisor. 'I just lost my footing. I'm really sorry.'

The supervisor sighed wearily and marched Raffy back in; as Raffy turned, he mouthed, 'I'll be there tonight,' before disappearing. Evie watched them go, then walked quickly up to her own Unit.

'It must be love – you look awful,' Christine whispered sarcastically as Evie sat down at her desk a few minutes later. 'Can you really not bear to be without him for even a minute?'

Evie blushed hotly as she turned on her computer. She didn't know the answer to the question. She knew Christine was talking about Lucas, but all Evie could see was Raffy's lips, the anger in his eyes, the hurt. All she could hear was Lucas's voice telling her that Raffy would be under close observation. And she knew with a thud that it was time to stop, that she and Raffy were over. Because he was never going to gallop into her Unit on a horse to whisk her away to a place that she knew didn't exist. She was going to marry Lucas, and to hope that it wouldn't happen would only make it worse for everyone.

4

The Brother pushed back his chair and stood up, his large belly protruding as he made his way around his desk, past the sumptuous sofa that he liked to take a nap on every afternoon 'in order to think deeply about spiritual affairs' and towards the window, a large bay that provided the perfect view of the east of the City. His City. He felt he owned it just as much as he owned his robes or his house, his large house with a bathing pool, hidden from view by a high wall. He had been there at the start, at the very beginning of the City – one of the first to understand that the Great Leader was right and that the New Baptism was all that lay between humankind's terrible past and a wonderful future. Salvation. Hope.

That's what he had given his flock. They were safe, they were happy; they had hard work to occupy them.

And if he surrounded himself with the best the City had to offer, if he allowed himself the odd luxury, an indulgence from time to time, it was only right; it was perfectly understandable. He had a great weight on his shoulders; he needed comfort around him to give him the strength to lead.

He had been a religious man, in days gone by. He had believed that his faith would protect him, that God had a plan and that He would not forsake his people, but would only test them in order to show them the true path.

And then the Horrors had started, wreaking devastation and chaos and taking human lives in their thousands, millions, indiscriminately and horribly. And the Brother had realised in a moment of true clarity, just as the church he was worshipping in exploded around him, that there was no God, that there was no heaven or hell or greater plan or rhyme or reason. There were just people. Good people. Bad people. Kind people. Selfish people. Modest people. Proud people, violent people, nasty people, stupid evil bastards who wanted to destroy them all, who didn't care about pain, or children screaming for their dead parents, or cholera spreading amongst the survivors of the bombs, or good, honest people losing everything.

It had been a year before the Horrors juddered to a close, before the annihilation had reached a natural end point. A time in which the new world of wasteland, disease and desperation co-existed with the old world of Google, cars and coffee machines. And the Brother, who had heard of the Great Leader already (although that was not his moniker then) and had rolled his eyes at the papers he had published in independent medical journals, unable to get the established journals to take him seriously, suddenly saw that this man, unlike any other, spoke the truth. And so he turned to the world's remaining modern inventions to track him down, emailing him, driving up to Manchester, meeting him in a barely standing coffee shop that was still, miraculously, serving coffee.

Fisher had been reluctant at first. He had turned him away, told him that it was too late, that the world as they knew it was over and that they had missed their chance. But the Brother was not someone who believed in defeat. He knew it was not too late; knew it was up to him now. And so, using the skills he'd honed at the pulpit, he described a world for the Great Leader – then known as Mr Fisher, formerly Dr Fisher before he was struck off the medical register – a new world, a new start, where everyone was good, everyone was safe, order reigned and humans could live as they did in the heaven that they'd imagined for so long. A world that not only would not tolerate violence, but one where violence did not exist. A world that was in their grasp, if they worked together, if they got organised now and if they believed. A world that, later, the Great Leader described in his Sentiments using these exact same words, although the Brother would never remind him of such a thing.

It would mean, he told Fisher back then, that the evil in the world made sense. It would make sense of all the devastation, because it led somewhere, because out of the fire would fly a phoenix, a new future – a true garden of Eden.

And now here he was, he mused as he watched his citizens toiling, producing, working happily, co-existing without dispute and without competition, without hatred or fear.

There was a knock at the door. He turned and walked towards it, opening it to find Lucas there, just as he'd known he would.

'Lucas.' He smiled warmly. 'You are well, I hope?'

'Very well, Brother.'

'Good. And your brother?'

Lucas smiled tightly as he always did when Raphael's name was mentioned. The Brother reached out, touching his shoulder reassuringly. 'Would you like me to talk to him?'

Lucas shook his head heavily. 'You are kind, Brother, but Raffy is my responsibility.'

'He still tells the same story? That the glitch was a link to some other System?'

'He is a fantasist,' Lucas replied evenly. 'He always has been. I suspect this is a cry for attention, that's all. I blame myself – I should have been more of a father figure to him instead of dedicating myself to the City.'

'No, no, it is not your fault,' the Brother said quickly. 'It is because of you that he works for the government, after all.'

'Yes, Brother, it is,' Lucas replied, his face tensing slightly at the intentional reminder that he was the reason Raphael was not in a lowly position elsewhere. It was hard for Lucas, the Brother thought to himself. A K for a father. Difficult for someone to live with shame like that.

'Have a week, Lucas,' he said. 'After that, if he still insists that the glitch was planted by someone, if he still refuses to take responsibility for it himself, then we will need to leave the decision up to the System. Are you up to this, Lucas? He's your brother, after all.'

'My father was my father,' Lucas answered, his eyes as clear blue as always. 'And yet I provided you with information on him. A week, Brother. Leave it with me.'

He left the room; the Brother waited for the door to close before wandering over to his sofa. There were always problems to be dealt with. Always inconveniences that rose up from time to time. But by and large the City was the place he'd dreamt of all those years ago. And men like Lucas helped him keep it that way.

He pressed the buzzer on his secretary's intercom system. 'Sam, I'm going to have some thinking time. Please ensure that I am not disturbed.' Then he lay down on the sofa and closed his eyes.

5

There were different kinds of evil. But the worst was the evil that deviants carried around in their hearts, hiding it from others as they nurtured it and encouraged it to flourish, because they were too weak to fight it and they didn't care enough about the City. These were the people that the System protected the City from; identifying where evil lived, even if the person housing it didn't know it yet, even if they were unaware of the dangerous thoughts or feelings deep within their brain. The System knew who these people were, labelled them as D's, so that evil's influence could be minimised and these people would know that they had to fight, to strive to rid themselves of their corrupt thoughts, otherwise they would be shunned at best, and at worst . . .

Evie didn't like to think about 'at worst'. 'At worst' was when even D wasn't bad enough. When the label

65

K was given. K meant beyond redemption. K meant that evil had flourished once more.

She sometimes wondered what her label would be. Eventually. When the System caught up with her. She suspected it already had; she found herself thinking that it was just watching, waiting, to see exactly how corrupt she was before it made its decision. D? Or K? She shivered at the thought, her throat constricting. Not K. Please not K.

K's were inhabited by evil; they were evil personified. K's were taken away and never seen again. K's were like the Evils who lived outside the City walls. People who had been damaged by the Horrors, people who had been consumed by evil. These people were a constant reminder to the City's inhabitants of what it protected them from. Evie had never seen an Evil, but she knew they existed because, like every other City dweller, she had heard them. Their terrifying moans and wails carrying through the air at night made her shiver under her bedclothes and promise herself never to transgress the City laws again, to finally rid herself of evil, to be good and pure and everything she should be.

The Evils wanted to destroy the City; they feared a place where evil had no place. There was no goodness left in the Evils, no trace of the values that those within the City walls considered to be human. For as the Brother reminded them, the values of the City were not intrinsically human values; they were the values of goodness, and humans – other humans – were more predisposed to adopt the values of evil and terror. Without the City walls, without the New Baptism, without the constant vigilance, they, too, could become like the Evils – full of anger and hatred and violence, intent on destruction and devastation. Just like the humans who had started the Horrors. Just like most humans that had ever lived.

The Evils didn't come to the City very often. They knew that there was no point, that they would never get in. The City was too well guarded, its four gates too heavily armoured. But not with weapons of destruction, like the pistols and revolvers and other tools of violence that humans used to rely on, the scary, unfamiliar objects they'd been shown at school. The City was protected instead by the strength of its walls, built by its citizens and continually reinforced. By a volunteer police guard who patrolled the wall at night when intruders tried their luck. And by four key holders, men known to be valiant, brave and good, who kept the keys hidden, safe, so that no one passed in or out who wasn't sanctioned by the Brother himself. Because people still came to the City, people from far away looking for a new future. And a very small number were let in. Once a week the South Gate would open and a few lucky new citizens would enter, embracing the New Baptism and the chance of a new future full of hope. Evie never met any new people, but she saw them sometimes, filing in on a Tuesday, walking through the streets to the hospital building. They went to work on the outskirts of the City, her father told her. Newcomers had to prove themselves before they were allowed to assimilate.

But the Evils never came through the gate; they only ever stood outside, wailing, crying and threatening the citizens inside.

They came because they hated goodness and they longed to destroy the City and everyone inside. And they came to vent their anger when K's were taken away for reconditioning. Evie's father told her that evil always knew itself and tried to protect itself, too; that's why they always came whenever someone was labelled a K. Because they were angry that the K was being reconditioned, angry that evil would never win within the City walls.

The Evils always knew when to come; they could smell evil, her father said. Whenever there was a K change, word always got round; mostly people would lock their doors and try to close their ears to the screams and wails of the Evils as they arrived in huge numbers to vent their rage. And the next day there would always be a Gathering, to purify the City once more and help everyone get through the terrible knowledge that another of them had fallen, to give them the strength to renounce evil even more strongly.

Evie always knew about K's earlier than most, because her father was a key holder, one of four men who held the keys to the East, West, North and South gates of the City. He always kept vigil on the nights that the Evils came. Just in case the K escaped before they could be reconditioned, and came looking for the key to let the Evils in.

Evie knew that what lay outside the City walls was worse than anything she could imagine late at night when she tortured herself with terrible images. And she knew that if she didn't renounce evil for good, that was the fate that awaited her.

She also knew that if the System hadn't been watching Raffy before, it would be watching him now. He had found a glitch in it. Would the System be angry? Grateful? Did it even have emotions or was it more like Lucas? Evie didn't know, but it didn't matter. What mattered was that she didn't want to be a K. She'd told herself all this time that she didn't care, not enough anyway, about what happened to her. She'd told herself that her feelings for Raffy were more important than anything else, that the joy she felt in their precious moments alone were worth the punishment to come. But now, now she was afraid. Now, tonight, knowing that the System would be watching Raffy, she realised that she wasn't as strong as she'd thought.

Which was why that night, she lay down on her bed and went to sleep, ignoring the gnawing knowledge that Raffy would be waiting for her and ignoring her promise to him to meet him in the tree. She couldn't do it any more. She wouldn't do it any more.

It was time to stop. It was time to be like Lucas. To stop caring and to stop loving.

To start being good.

The next day was Saturday: the day of the Gathering. Evie woke and went straight to the bathroom to wash and to stare at her reflection. Her clothes were already laid out; since it was Saturday, she would be wearing a thick, velvet dress and lace-up boots. Girls all wore the same thing to the Gathering – different colours, slightly different styles, but ultimately the same. She could have worn a skirt suit like her mother because she was seventeen now and nearly a woman, but the suits were expensive and since she still fitted into her dress, it had been decided to delay such a purchase until it was essential.

She dressed quickly and brushed her hair before running downstairs to eat the hunk of bread and the apple that were waiting for her.

'You look nice,' she said to her mother as she walked into the kitchen looking for something.

Her mother turned and frowned uncertainly. Compliments on appearance were rare in the City; they suggested too much attention paid to the look of things or people, instead of to what lay underneath. 'Why do you say that?' she asked. 'What have you done?'

Evie shook her head. 'Nothing,' she answered. She couldn't explain that today she wanted to talk, of anything and nothing, to stop herself having to think about what she was going to do – what she had to do – to stop the dreams and to stop evil taking hold of her.

'Well, eat up. We're leaving soon,' her mother said with a little shrug, leaving the kitchen.

Evie surveyed the food in front of her, then stood up, put it into a container for later and went upstairs to brush her teeth.

At 8.45 a.m. exactly she and her parents left home, the three of them walking in a row towards the Meeting House, just like all the other families on their road.

They smiled as they overtook them, their pace quickening as they got closer. Evie tried to let the excitement infuse her, and to think of happy things.

Gatherings were the highlight of everyone's week in the City; they brought everyone together. When Evie had been younger, she could barely sleep on a Friday night because she was so excited about the Gathering the next day. Everyone looked so wonderful, and the whole occasion was so warm and loving. The Gathering made everything make sense, made everything feel worthwhile and made her feel like the luckiest girl in the whole wide world.

Today, she realised, as she walked into the Meeting House, she needed the Gathering more than ever.

The Meeting House was the largest building in the whole City, big enough to contain all 5,000 residents, and as usual it was half full by the time they got there. She happily accepted the warm Gathering drink that was always offered at the door, drank it, then found a seat at the far end of a bench towards the front, next to her parents. She watched as everyone else walked in, family after family, couple after couple, some on their own, some of the elders of the community being helped in by a carer. The A's were all at the front, then the B's, then C's at the back. Some mixed groups sat at the back also; families with different labels. It wasn't common, but it happened from time to time, usually when a young person's label was higher than that of their parents. Wives and husbands saw their seating position change when their partner's label changed; they were responsible for each other, influenced by each other. But children were different. Evie watched cautiously as Lucas (A) came in followed by Raffy (C) and his mother (B). No one knew quite how to treat mixed families, so they were kept apart from the others. An area at the side, meanwhile, was reserved for D's, who walked in with their heads bowed, shifting uncomfortably until the Gathering started.

Music was playing, uplifting music that made Evie hum and smile. Sitting there, she felt protected; knew somehow that everything would be okay. Surrounded by fellow citizens, she knew that she didn't have to worry about anything. She was safe here – they all were.

Then the Brother arrived in his long red velvet jacket. The Great Leader was too old to take Gatherings; he was too fragile to leave his house. But the Brother spread his word for him.

He walked to the front and everyone who hadn't sat down yet found a seat. Seconds later the entire place was silent.

'My friends, brothers and sisters,' began the Brother.

'It is so good to see you all here, as it always is. Let us give thanks to the Great Leader.'

'We all give thanks,' Evie said loudly, along with everyone else.

'Let us give thanks to this great City.'

'We all give thanks.' Their voices were louder, more emphatic.

'And finally, let us give thanks to the System, to ourselves, to our productivity, our love, and our ability to protect each other and ourselves.'

'We all give thanks.' Already Evie could feel the hairs on the back of her neck standing up in anticipation.

'And now that we have given thanks, let us close our eyes and allow ourselves a few moments of quiet reflection. A few moments in which to consider our fortune, to think about our community and our place within it.'

Silence fell as they all retreated into their own heads, contemplating their lives. Or, in Evie's case, trying to focus on the warm, fuzzy feeling she always got from the Gathering, and telling herself that she could still be saved, that she was not a bad person, that her dreams meant nothing. With her eyes closed, she thought as hard as she could about her parents, about her work, about the food on their table, the roof over their heads, the peace within their City walls. *I am lucky*, she mouthed silently. *I am so lucky*.

'Evie.' Evie's eyes shot open and she turned to her right, the blood draining from her face. 'You didn't come last night.' His voice was barely a whisper, but that was enough to fill Evie with terror. If anyone heard . . . If anyone saw . . .

She looked around, her eyes scanning the entire Meeting House, and when she was met by a sea of unseeing, closed eyes, the blood returned to her cheeks but it was no comfort. She shook her head violently, motioned to Raffy to return to his seat.

'Where were you? Is everything okay?'

'Yes,' she mouthed back. 'I mean, no. Raffy, I can't come. Won't come again. I'm going to marry Lucas. I can't see you again.'

Quickly she swung back round to face the front, closed her own eyes tightly; she knew that Raffy would have to go, that it would be only seconds before everyone opened their eyes again.

All those around her were still fervently engrossed in prayer. Tentatively, Evie turned, glanced behind her; sure enough, there was Raffy, a few rows back. He was staring at her; when he caught her eye, he shook his head, mouthed, 'No.' Next to him Lucas sat, eyes closed, face calm. Evie turned back quickly, her heart thudding

like mad. Raffy was crazy. If he'd been caught . . .
Evie couldn't even think about it. Her cheeks were hot
now, her palms covered in sweat.

'Now, keeping your eyes closed, breathe gently in
and out. Feel the energy as the breath enters your body
and feel the cleansing out breath, which takes with it
your aches, your pains, any unhelpful thoughts clouding
your judgement.'

Evie breathed in, and out, just as the Brother bid,
just as she always did. In and out. But it didn't calm
her mind. It made her feel sick, like her body was being
tossed around. She could feel Raffy's eyes boring into
her back, could feel his sense of betrayal, could feel her
own huge feeling of loss, of being cut adrift. And yet
she knew she was doing the right thing. She knew she
had to stay strong. For both of them.

'Now, without opening your eyes, reach out to
grasp the hand of the person sitting next to you. Clasp
their hand, brothers and sisters, and think about the
bonds that unite us, that make us strong and good and
pure.'

Evie was at the end of the row; there was no one
to her right, so she reached out her left hand, which
met her father's, and held it tight, felt its strength and
resolve and remembered how many times that hand
had meted out punishments when she'd been growing

up. That hand had taught her to follow the rules; now she was finally ready to do its bidding. She had to.

'Now hold your own hands, brothers and sisters. Hold your own hands and feel the warmth of your blood flowing in your veins, keeping your body alive. Just as the beliefs that flow through you keep this City alive. Just as the System, our wonderful System which knows us all, keeps us all productive, at peace, in our right place.'

Her father let go of her hand and she clasped her own hands together and tried, so hard, to feel the blood and the belief, just like she'd done every week for as long as she could remember. But all she could see was Raffy's face, defiant, desperate; all she could feel was the hole growing inside her.

A hole of evil, she told herself firmly. A hole that would be filled with goodness, hard work and focused dedication to the City.

'And now, brothers and sisters, open your eyes and look around at each other. At your fellow citizens. Your friends, acquaintances, those you don't know at all. And know that we are all in this together. That what each of us does affects us all, that our individual toil enriches everyone's lives, that our belief nourishes not just us, but our whole community.'

Everyone's eyes opened immediately; Evie's gaze

moved around too quickly to connect with anyone else's. She couldn't look behind her; couldn't look anywhere near Raffy even though she knew Lucas would be looking out for her. She felt short of breath, like she was falling, even though she knew she wasn't.

'And we need that belief,' the Brother said. 'Belief in our great City. Belief in the System. Belief in the New Baptisms. Belief in each other. Each of us needs your belief and your work and your commitment. Because without it, we may as well let these City walls crumble. They can protect us from what's outside, but they can't protect us from ourselves. Can they?'

Evie turned back to face the front, her heart beating rapidly, her body bathed in a light layer of sweat.

'No! They can't protect us,' she said loudly, along with everyone else; her voice was shaking.

'But our Great Leader protected us,' the Brother was saying. 'He saw, long ago, that humankind was being held back. He saw that we were slaves to a part of the brain that we didn't need, a part that was an aberration, which led people to do terrible things. Before the Horrors, humans thought they were civilised. They thought they were clever and sophisticated and that our Great Leader was wrong because they had everything they needed. But what did they have?'

'Nothing,' everyone chanted.

'Nothing! Exactly. They had murder. They had gangs roaming the streets, attacking others and robbing them of their possessions. Women were raped. People were locked up. Adults were stoned to death. But this wasn't enough to satisfy these people. They read books about murders and rape just to entertain themselves; they wrote plays on the same subjects.'

The Brother looked around the room and as he looked in Evie's direction, she felt her stomach turn – she felt sure that somehow he knew that she too had done terrible things. But his eyes continued to scan the benches and as she gripped the one in front of her to steady herself, she told herself that this was her second chance. Just as the Great Leader had given humanity a second chance.

She would forget Raffy eventually, and he would forget her. They would both be saved.

'They built religions to protect themselves, to offer moral guidance, because they were incapable of guiding themselves,' said the Brother, and her father nodded vigorously, unaware of the torment within his daughter. 'But what did they do with these religions?' the Brother continued. 'They used them to fight each other; they turned their morality into a violent war. And why did they do that, brothers and sisters?'

'Because they were enslaved by their corrupt brains,'

everyone shouted, Evie louder than ever before. 'Because they did not know any better.'

Evie thought of her own, corrupt brain; even now it was fighting with her, trying to tell her she was doing the wrong thing.

'Because they were enslaved. Because they did not know what real goodness was – they would not recognise it if they saw it. Because they did not know any better, did not know any different. But we do, brothers and sisters. We look back on them with pity, with fear. Because outside these City walls, those humans who survived the Horrors, those humans that have rejected the New Baptism and chosen to remain outside our community, they are the same as the humans who lived before. Enslaved by their desires, their pride, their anger and their hatred. They long not for peace, for happiness or for goodness; their thirst is for violence, revenge and destruction.'

A collective shiver rippled through the room. The Brother lifted his hands and everyone stood up.

'But we have been saved from these bestial instincts,' he said, and someone whooped. 'The New Baptism has cleansed our brains, removing the draw towards evil. We are no longer a danger to ourselves.'

'No longer a danger to ourselves,' everyone chanted.

The energy of the room had picked up; Evie could feel the excitement beginning to build.

'We do not long to kill, to destroy. We long to work together. To build a good future. To be pure in mind and deed.'

'Pure in mind and deed,' the congregation repeated.

'We have a System that knows us, each of us, that watches over us. We can live our lives without worry, suspicion or hardship, because the System ensures that our lives are lived as they should be. But we cannot rest on our laurels. We are free from evil, but we are not free from all that will tempt us. A conscious mind is a mind that can make choices, a mind that can make decisions. Brothers and sisters, you are good people. I know that you want only to make good decisions, good choices. Am I right?'

'You're right! Yes, sir, you're right.'

'You're right,' Evie said fervently. She would make only good choices from now on. The Evils would not claim her. She would not be left outside the City walls for the monsters who would come to find her.

'And if we're going to make those good decisions, those good choices, what do we need to quash?'

'Desire!' someone shouted out.

'Greed!' shouted another.

'Desire and greed. Oh yes,' the Brother said. 'What else?'

'Pride,' called out her father, and stood up, his hands in the air.

'Pride!' the Brother shouted back. 'Pride, desire and greed!'

More people started to stand up, their hands reaching skywards.

'We must turn away from all these things. Because desire tempts us, desire tests us, but we must turn away from these baser instincts because with desire and lust come aggression and violence. Desire is dangerous, sisters and brothers. Do not allow it to corrupt your beautiful minds. Do not allow it to find disciples within these City walls.'

'No!' people were shouting. 'We won't let it in. Not within these City walls.'

'But how do we know this? How do we know desire, pride and greed are no good? Let me tell you how.'

'Tell us! Tell us!' Nearly everyone was standing, their eyes wide, their faces full of rapture. Evie stood too: she wanted to feel what they felt, wanted to be flooded with happiness, relief, determination, with only love for the City filling her head.

'I'll tell you,' said the Brother, his voice suddenly

calm. 'I'll tell you how. Sit, brothers and sisters. Sit, please, and listen.'

Everyone sat down; the room was immediately silent, faces leaning forward in anticipation so as not to miss a single word.

'A peaceful, good society is one that is predicated on fairness, on clear rules that we all follow willingly,' the Brother said, looking around the room. Evie tilted her head, listening intently as though these words could cure her. 'We are the saved ones. We are the chosen ones. And with our pure minds, we will continue to be strong. We will allow evil no place in our hearts, no place in our brains. Evil will try to grow, but we will not give it air to breathe. We will let the System show us when we are weak, and we will show determination in becoming strong again.'

The Brother's sermon was coming to an end; everyone stood again, music started and hands shot up.

'So celebrate, brothers and sisters. Celebrate the City. Celebrate our communion. Celebrate this day of rest, and tomorrow go out to work with a strong heart and the desire to start that wonderful future right here, right now.'

'Yes! Yes!' people called out. 'Hail the Great Leader!'

Evie's father turned to her, his eyes shining, and he

wrapped his arm around her, then wrapped the other arm around her mother, who reached out across his back and squeezed Evie's shoulder, a rare display of emotion that caught Evie by surprise. She felt tears fill her eyes as she reached out herself to squeeze hands, arms; to show her parents how much she valued their guidance, how much she wanted to make them proud of her.

As the Gathering finished, Evie followed her parents as they shuffled out of the Meeting Room; there were people everywhere, cheeks rosy, mouths upturned, friendly smiles exchanged between acquaintances as they passed each other.

Evie stayed close to her parents, kept her gaze straight ahead to make sure that she didn't see Raffy, didn't catch his eye. But at the door, her parents saw some friends – a man her father worked with and his wife – and they moved to the side to talk. Evie tried to follow them but was swept up by the throng of people moving forward, and before she knew it she was a few metres from the door, on the path, on her own. She tried to walk towards her parents but there were too many people moving in the other direction; she was trapped. Instead, she waved at them, but they didn't notice; they were laughing, talking.

And then Evie felt someone behind her, standing still, not moving like everyone else, and she knew it was Raffy. Every instinct in her told her to reach out her hand, to touch him, to forget everything she had told herself she would do.

But she knew she had to fight her instincts. She knew it was their only hope.

'You have to come. I can't live without you.'

His voice was low, urgent; she felt it in the base of her stomach.

She shook her head, desperately seeking out her parents, whose strength she needed before it was too late. Raffy's body was pressing against hers. 'I have to go,' she managed to say. She could hardly breathe, barely think. 'Don't do this again. Never look for me again. It's over, Raffy. It has to be over.'

'No,' he said, a note of desperation in his voice that made her want to turn, hold him, put her lips to his as she had so many times before. But instead she pushed her nails into her palms.

'Raffy? Come and look after Mother. Evie, what are you doing here on your own?'

Evie looked up with a start to see Lucas approaching, his expression unreadable as always. Had he seen anything? Did he know? Evie shook herself. He couldn't have seen anything.

'I . . . I got separated from my parents,' she managed to reply. 'I was just looking for them.'

'And here they are,' Lucas said with a tight little smile. 'Your mother, anyway.' He turned back to Raffy, the smile disappearing. 'Go. Now,' he ordered. Raffy slipped away.

'Evie, there you are,' her mother called, appearing through the crowd, her cheeks flushed, a rare smile on her face. 'We're with Philip and Margorie over there. I was just telling them how well you're doing at work. Come over.'

'Yes, of course,' Evie replied, allowing her mother to take her hand and lead her back through the crowd.

As she approached Philip and Margorie, she turned, in desperation, to get one last look at Raffy and to somehow let him know that she was doing this for both of them, that there was no alternative; but the only eyes she met were Lucas's, staring at her quizzically before he turned and walked in the other direction.

6

Evie couldn't sleep that night; she tossed and turned as the evil within her fought with her desperation to be good, to be pure and strong just as the Brother had called for her to be at the Gathering. She wanted to renounce evil, wanted to have only good thoughts in her head, and yet all she could think about was Raffy, the devastation in his eyes and his refusal to accept what she'd told him. All she could feel was a longing deep inside her to see him again, just one more time; to think of a new way – a good way – they could still be friends, even though she knew it was impossible and that she could never see him.

Her thoughts were so feverish, her mind so full, that she didn't hear the tap at the window the first time. And when the second tap came, it shocked her so much that she sat bolt upright in bed, pulled the bedclothes to her and stared at the window as though fearing that the Evils themselves were coming for her, that they could read her thoughts and that they knew she was one of them after all.

'Evie. Evie.' And then her heart stopped because it wasn't the Evils. It was Raffy. He was here – he had come to her house. And her fear at what would happen if he was discovered was mixed with a desperate need to see him – to comfort him, to explain and to have him understand and absolve her.

Shaking, Evie approached the window and hesitantly drew back the curtain. Even though she knew it was Raffy, she still jumped when she saw him looking at her, balancing precariously on the window ledge, his face so full of sadness she almost wanted to cry.

Immediately she opened the window and pulled him in, putting her finger to her lips to tell him to be quiet, to not make a sound because if they were caught now, there would be no going back, there would be no forgiveness.

He sat on her bed; she looked at him, unable to speak, unable to think of the right words. And so it was Raffy who spoke first, his voice low, taut and tired.

'You're making a mistake,' he said. 'You can't do this.'

'Yes, I can,' Evie replied, looking down. 'And you have to, too. The System will be watching you. It probably knows everything already. I don't know why it hasn't punished us yet, but it will, if we don't stop. I am going to marry Lucas. And we can't meet again.'

'Because the System will punish us? I don't care. So I'll be a D. Everyone treats me like one anyway.'

'What if you're not made a D?' Evie whispered fiercely. 'What if we're made K's? We'll be thrown out of the City. We'll be left for the Evils to claim.' Tears of fear and unhappiness filled her eyes. 'Raffy, there is no alternative. We have to stop seeing each other. You have to understand that.'

'No. What I understand is that you can't marry Lucas,' Raffy said, his jaw clenching. 'You just can't. He isn't a person, he's a machine. He won't take care of you. He won't listen to you. He won't love you. Not like I do. He doesn't deserve you. He . . .'

Raffy's arms reached out to touch Evie, but she shrank back.

'He's not a machine,' she said, falteringly.

'Yes, he is,' Raffy said, his eyes seeking hers out, uncompromising.

'Then maybe we need to become machines, too,' Evie replied, wiping at her eyes. 'Maybe that's the key to being good. Maybe evil lives in emotions, in our hidden thoughts.'

'If that's being good then I don't want to be good.' Raffy stared at her angrily, challengingly, but Evie refused to rise to the bait.

'You don't mean that,' she whispered.

'Don't I?' He folded his arms. 'When Dad was taken away, Lucas didn't say a thing. He just threw all his stuff out, said he'd brought shame on our family and we were never to mention his name again. His own father. Is that good?'

Evie tried to swallow, but a huge lump had appeared in her throat. She remembered it so well – Raffy's misery at losing his father being compounded by Lucas's response, and the cold flash in Lucas's eyes whenever Raffy tried to mention the man who had raised them both. 'Your father was made a K,' Evie said, hesitantly.

Raffy's eyes narrowed. 'So you're turning into a machine too,' he responded bitterly. 'My father was a good man. Not evil. Not evil.'

He turned away, burying his head in his knees. Evie tentatively reached over.

'He didn't mean to be evil,' she said. 'I'm sure he didn't. But the System . . .'

'The System's always right. Of course it is.' There

was a note of something dangerous in Raffy's voice. Evie's eyes widened as she looked at him. Could the System hear him?

'The System *is* right,' she said, looking around fearfully. 'It knows us all, and it can see deep into our hearts, and—'

'And my father went straight from an A to a K? The System can't have been on the ball, can it?' Raffy stood up. 'Don't you see, Evie? I thought you'd see. I thought you understood. It's all rubbish. It has to be. I'm not evil. You're not evil. The feelings I have for you aren't evil. The feelings you have for me. Or had, I should say.'

He stared at her again; Evie felt herself getting warm.

'Have,' she whispered. 'Have.'

A smile crossed Raffy's face. He sat down on the bed again, grabbed her hands, pulled her towards him.

'The other day,' he said, his voice so quiet she could barely hear him, 'when I found the glitch. It wasn't a glitch. It was a communication device. There were messages there to people outside the City. People who must have a System too. The Brother says there's no one outside except Evils and savages. But I saw the messages. I saw the device. Don't you see? If they're lying about that, they're lying about other things, too.'

Evie's eyes were like saucers now as her heart began to thud anxiously in her chest. She shook her head.

'No,' she whispered. 'No, Raffy. That's impossible.'

He rolled his eyes. 'Yeah, that's what Lucas said. Said I imagined it, that I was hallucinating. But I know what I saw.'

'But . . . but . . .' Evie stammered, her mind racing, compounding her confusion, making her feel like she'd lost her balance.

'But nothing,' Raffy said. He squeezed her hands and his eyes suddenly lit up. 'If another place exists, then let's go to it. Together.'

'Go to it? You mean leave the City?' Evie recoiled.

'I mean, find somewhere better. With no rules. Where we can just live.'

'You mean like the Evils live?' Evie said, shaking her head violently. 'No, Raffy. No. We're not going anywhere. You're going to go home and not come here again and I'm going to marry Lucas.'

'No!' Raffy cried angrily. 'Evie, listen to me. We always talked about this, about finding faraway places where we could live happily. We always talked about escaping. Well now we can. Now we have to.'

Evie pulled her hands away. 'That was make-believe, Raffy,' she said angrily. 'That was children's talk. We're grown up now. You have to stop living in a fantasy land. You live here, in the City. You are lucky to be here; we both are. You have to stop, Raffy. You have to . . .' She dried her eyes, stood up on the bed and opened the window again. 'You have to go, Raffy,' she said. 'Now. Please.'

'You really want me to?'

Evie nodded; she could barely bring herself to look at him, to see the confusion and pain in his eyes which she knew would weaken her resolve.

'Fine. I'll go,' he muttered, his voice angry. 'But I'm telling you, this place exists. It's not a fantasy. It's real. Just like this is real.' He grabbed her, pulled her towards him and kissed her, and she tried to pull away but she couldn't. She wouldn't. Instead she held on to him, his shoulders, his hair, pressing him into her, breathing in the scent of his skin so that she might never forget it.

'Bye, Evie,' Raffy said, his voice hoarse and quiet. 'Look after yourself.'

And then he let go of her, and she had never felt quite so alone, quite so cold, quite so adrift. But she steeled herself; took a deep breath. She was doing the right thing. For once, finally, she was doing the right thing. Raffy moved towards the window; Evie pulled the curtain back further so that he could open it fully. And then they both heard something, a rustling from the garden below. They froze, staring at each other, brows furrowed. 'What was that?' Raffy whispered.

'Get down behind the curtain,' Evie mouthed, then tentatively inched up to look below and identify the source of the noise. A fox, she told herself. Another animal. A . . .

But it wasn't an animal. She saw him immediately; he was looking right at her and now she really was falling into the abyss. Because standing in the middle of the garden, his blond hair shining under the moonlight, was Lucas. And she knew immediately that he had seen everything; they had embraced in front of the window, in front of the open curtain. He must have followed Raffy. And now he knew. And now . . . She started to sweat. She had to warn Raffy, but by turning to him, by signalling, Lucas would know beyond doubt. She had to at least pretend. Just in case he hadn't seen. Just in case.

Evie leant out of the window. 'Lucas,' she whispered. 'What are you—?'

'Send Raffy down to me,' he whispered back, his voice emotionless.

'Raffy?' she asked.

'Evie, don't make this worse than it is. Send Raffy

down immediately. I need to take him home. Don't make me wake your parents.'

Raffy heard the voice; his face went white. Evie turned and looked at him in despair. There were no words, nothing to say.

Raffy went to the window. 'Look, I'll make sure he knows this is my fault,' he said. ' I'll tell him I forced my way in. I'll tell him you tried to get me to leave . . .'

Evie shook her head. 'He knows,' she said again. 'He saw us.'

Raffy held out his hand, took hers in it and squeezed it so hard she yelped in pain. 'I'm sorry, Evie,' he said, his voice choking up. 'I love you. I'm so sorry.'

'Don't be sorry. I love you too,' she replied through the lump in her throat as Raffy climbed out of the window, down the side of the house and back into the garden where Lucas was waiting for him. They didn't exchange a word; Lucas put a commanding hand on Raffy's shoulder and steered him out towards the back gate.

He didn't look back at Evie, who lay down on her bed, pulled the bedclothes over her and waited for the morning, for everything to change. Through her fear she felt something almost approaching relief that the truth was out, that she would be known for what she really was, that the pretence would be over. And with that thought, she fell asleep.

The next morning, Evie felt a strange sense of calm as she came downstairs. Lucas would have told someone. Her parents would know. But her mother was busy getting ready and seemed to barely notice Evie as she attempted to eat some breakfast.

Apprehensively, she got washed and dressed, then left the house, waiting for someone to point at her, shout at her or take her away. And yet nothing happened; it was almost as if what had taken place last night was another dream, as though it hadn't occurred at all. And when she arrived at work and her supervisor barely looked up, and Christine gave her usual little smile of greeting, Evie began to think that maybe it had been a dream, that maybe none of it had happened at all.

She didn't see Raffy anywhere, but that wasn't unusual. He was probably at work already; could even be on the early shift. And when she didn't see him at lunch, either, at the government canteen where they all exchanged tokens for plates of vegetables, bread and cheese, she told herself that it had all indeed been a dream. Raffy had not come to her house; he had accepted what she'd told him. He was staying out of the way to make things easier. Everything was going to be okay.

But try as she might, she couldn't suppress what she knew was the truth. Raffy had come to her room and Lucas had seen. If Lucas hadn't told anyone yet, there would be a reason. She had seen the anger in his eyes. She had betrayed him; she had violated the laws of the City, and she had fraternised with his brother. Whatever was going to happen, it would not be good, and waiting for it was only going to make it worse.

'Deviant! Going home to plot, are we? To wallow in dangerous thoughts?'

Evie jumped – there were men behind her, running towards her with violence in their eyes. Immediately she froze, knowing that they were coming for her – that somehow, in the time between leaving work and now, the truth had come out and everyone knew her for what she was.

But as she stood stock-still, the men ran past her. Dazed, she watched as they moved in on their real target, surrounding him, baying for blood and shouting loudly. Before they closed in on him, she saw his face, saw the terror in his eyes. It was Mr Bridges, the man demoted to a D the week before, the man the Brother had warned them about.

She wanted to run, but she couldn't; something in her had to witness the attack, told her she should know what lay ahead for her.

'No,' Mr Bridges was calling out. 'I'm sorry. I . . .'

'You what?' heckled one of the men. 'You're not sorry. You're a D. You're a deviant.'

'You've brought evil into the City,' another man shouted, as Mr Bridges was thrown to the ground.

'Corrupting our families,' yelled someone else.

One of the men shouting caught Evie's eye. It was Mr Adams, who lived a few doors down from her. He had been a D just the year before. He knew what this was like. He knew . . .

Evie crossed the road; she couldn't watch after all. She felt sick to her stomach. She had to go, to get far away.

Mr Adams was still looking at her. 'See?' he crowed. 'See how young Evie is crossing the road to avoid you? No one even wants to look at you.'

Evie hesitated. If she were brave, if she were reckless like Raffy, she'd tell Mr Bridges that it was not he who made her want to cross the road, but his attackers. But she was not brave; she was afraid. Attacks like this were accepted in the City, encouraged even. Not sanctioned, but the police guard and the

Brothers would generally look the other way when a D was under siege. 'Violence is wrong,' the Brother would say, shaking his head sadly when he heard of such an attack. 'But sometimes we must meet evil on its own terms in order to destroy it.'

So instead Evie ran into the bakery on the corner, pretended that she was studying the bread so that she wouldn't have to see what was happening, wouldn't have to be a part of it.

'You want something?' asked the woman behind the counter. 'We've got some lovely flat loaves today. Just three coupons each. Or a wholemeal, if you like that sort of thing. Four coupons, I'm afraid, because the flour's more expensive. But it's big. Look.' She held up a large loaf and Evie stared at it blankly. She could not think about bread, about food; she could think about nothing but what was happening to Mr Bridges, what would inevitably happen to her.

'I . . . I'm not sure,' she said to the woman. 'I'll have to talk to my mother.'

'Right you are.' The woman shrugged, looking a little disappointed. She peered out of the window at the attack on Mr Bridges. 'Horrible business,' she muttered. 'Just shows you can't tell, can you? Think you know someone and all the time they're a deviant waiting to corrupt you. He was in here every day buying bread. I never thought he was . . . well, you know. One of them.'

Evie nodded uncomfortably, then turned to look back out over the road where the men were still taunting Mr Bridges. One had picked up a stick and started to hit him with it. Another followed suit. How long would she be trapped here? How long would she have to watch this torture?

And then, suddenly, she heard another voice cut through the men's braying, which made them halt their beating. 'You have been authorised by the Great Leader himself to mete out this punishment, I assume?'

It was a harsh voice, one so distinctive it could be no one else. She poked her head out of the door to see Lucas approaching the group, his gaze steely with anger.

The men stared at him furiously then, seeing his yellow label, appeared more hesitant. 'What's it to you?' one of them growled, approaching Lucas warily. 'He's a D. He's dangerous. He lives on our road. And we don't want him here.'

'What's it to me? I'm a citizen of this City and my understanding is that the System is there to ensure our safety and order,' Lucas answered icily. 'This kind of behaviour is, as far as I'm aware, driven by anger and a need to assert yourselves, which are corrupt values that have no place within the City's walls.' He was

smiling, but even from across the road Evie could see
the ice in his eyes. She felt a wave of fear wash over
her; they were the same eyes she had seen the night
before in the moonlight.

'How dare you?' shouted the leader of the group,
a heavy-built man with a shock of dark hair and
insolent eyes. 'How dare you suggest that we're in
the wrong? He's the wrong'un. He's the one who's
waiting to attack our families.'

He moved towards Lucas and lunged at him, but
Lucas was too quick; he grabbed the man's wrists, spun
him around as if he were half the size, and held his
arms behind his back. Evie gasped as she watched him;
it made no sense. Why would Lucas protect a D? Why?

'And you think that attacking him is what our
Great Leader has in mind when he tells us in Sentiment
78 to "accept our label and that of others, for the
System knows its business and we must know ours
and strive only to improve, strive only to better
ourselves and in so doing, better our community, our
City and our civilisation"?' he quoted through gritted
teeth. He threw the man to the ground. 'Get out of
here. Go home,' he ordered them, staring at each in
turn as though daring them to defy him.

No one did. Their eyes cast down, they left, one
or two turning every so often to shoot a remorseful

look at Lucas. Then Lucas held his hand out to Mr Bridges, who was cowering on the ground. Evie watched wide-eyed, trying to make sense of it, of why Lucas would do such a thing.

'Can you walk?' he asked.

Mr Bridges nodded. 'I don't know how to thank you,' he croaked. 'I don't know how to—'

'Don't thank me,' Lucas barked. 'I want no thanks from a D. I was simply protecting those men from themselves, from being corrupted by you.' He looked around and Evie ducked back behind the door. The next time she looked, Lucas was giving something to Mr Bridges – a card, his card – then he turned and started to walk. Right towards the bakery. Right towards Evie. She looked around frantically but there was no time to escape, and nowhere to hide in the small shop.

He opened the door heavily and she braced herself. Perhaps he would be kind to her just as he had been with Mr Bridges, she found herself thinking. Perhaps Lucas was not a machine after all. Perhaps . . . As he walked in, he saw her immediately. 'Evie,' he said, his eyes narrowing, the emotion disappearing from his face. 'What are you doing here?'

'She's not sure which bread she wants,' the woman behind the counter said with a sigh.

'I am sure,' Evie said quickly, trying to see some

indication in Lucas's face of what he was going to do, of what her future might hold. 'I just . . . I need to check with my mother. It's three coupons a loaf.'

'Then you should not waste Mrs Arnold's time,' Lucas said impassively.

'No, no, of course not . . .' Evie replied, flushing guiltily.

She caught Lucas's eye and he held her gaze for a few seconds until she could stand it no more and had to look away again.

'I spoke to your father this afternoon,' he said then, and Evie felt the blood drain from her face.

'My . . . father?'

Lucas nodded. 'I said I would pay you a visit this evening. If that is agreeable.'

Evie stared at him uncertainly. 'Pay me a visit?' she asked.

'It has been too long,' said Lucas evenly, his expression betraying no emotion at all.

'Then I'll see you later,' Evie managed to answer as she backed out of the shop. She hesitated for a moment before letting the door close; opened her mouth to say something to Lucas. But she realised there was nothing to say. He had decided that he would tell her parents tonight, and there was nothing she could do. So she left, and went home, and waited.

7

'Lucas, how nice to see you.'

Evie and her parents had finished supper and had been waiting, artificially, around the table for twenty minutes, not wanting to move because Lucas had specifically been invited for post-supper coffee. A tradition in the City for evening guests, coffee was always served at the kitchen table, and to move into another room would only highlight to Lucas the fact that he was later than agreed.

Evie looked up as her father ushered Lucas into the kitchen. She had barely managed to eat more than a few mouthfuls, had hoped against hope that he wouldn't come, that something would crop up to prevent him, that he would find a reason to stay away. But he was here; she forced a smile, and reluctantly scraped her chair to the left as her mother ushered her to do, as Lucas took his seat next to her.

'And how are we all?' he asked, looking around the table.

'We are very well, thank you for asking,' Evie's mother said quickly. 'Will you have some coffee? It's freshly brewed.'

Without waiting for an answer she jumped up and started to fuss over Lucas's coffee, finding him a biscuit to go with it, asking him if he would like some of the apple bake they'd had for pudding. Evie had never forgotten the look in her mother's eye when news of her match to Lucas had been announced, when the Brother had come to her and Evie's father and suggested that Lucas would be interested in marrying their daughter. Not that Evie had been in the room; she had been looking through a crack in the door, listening intently as her fate was set out for her. Her mother's eyes had lit up. But not with excitement, or pleasure, but with surprise. Then with relief. Evie would not be her responsibility any more; at least that was how Evie read it. Her father had been more sober; he had asked more questions, nodding thoughtfully as he considered the answers. It had been he, too, who had suggested asking Evie. It was only a courtesy; Evie knew she would say yes, knew there was no choice but to agree, but it was still nice to be asked. Nice to be given the impression that she was in some way involved in the decision and not simply an object being passed around.

Lucas turned down the apple bake and the biscuit; he took his coffee black. No sugar. Evie watched him as he drank it, his lips appearing not to feel the heat of the drink that still had steam rising from it. Was he entirely unfeeling? she wondered. Did emotions simply not register with him? Perhaps he was made of wood. Perhaps he *was* a machine underneath his human veneer. That afternoon she thought that she had seen something else in Lucas. Something that didn't quite add up, that she didn't quite understand. But she knew now that she'd been mistaken. Lucas had broken up the fight because he was following the Sentiments precisely. Logically. It was not because he felt for Mr Bridges, not because the hatred of those men had upset him. It was because he could not understand their anger and fear; he did not know what it was to feel such things.

'And how are you, Lucas?' asked Evie's mother, leaning forward expectantly as though the answer Lucas would give was more interesting to her than any other piece of news in the world.

Lucas smiled. 'I'm very well. Very well.'

'And your mother? Is she well?'

'She is,' Lucas confirmed. Then he hesitated for just a second before continuing. 'Unfortunately, however, my brother is ill. He is quarantined. But I myself am in good health.'

Evie's eyes widened and her cheeks started to burn. Raffy was ill? What was wrong with him? She stared at her parents, willed them to ask the question that she couldn't. Instead her mother picked up the coffee pot.

'More coffee, Lucas?' Lucas assented and held out his cup. 'It's nice to have such good company,' her mother continued ingratiatingly. 'Particularly these days. I suppose you heard about Mr Bridges? Just a stone's throw from here. Such a terrible business. Makes you worried about talking to people, really. There are so many corrupting influences around.'

Evie turned sharply to see Lucas nodding slowly. 'It is a terrible business,' he agreed. 'But that is the nature of evil. That is why we must be on our guard and fight evil at every turn. Wouldn't you agree, Evie?' He caught her eye and her flush deepened. Was he playing with her? Threatening her? Evie stared back, her anger emboldening her. 'I heard that Mr Bridges was attacked,' she said levelly. 'What do you think about that?'

'Attacked by right-meaning people who want evil

off our streets,' her mother said immediately. 'Deviants must know that we won't tolerate them. That they have no place here.'

'You're right, Delphine,' Lucas said. 'You don't mind if I call you Delphine?'

Now it was Evie's mother's turn to flush. 'Not at all, Lucas. Please,' she said, smiling gauchely, reaching out to squeeze his hand.

Evie looked away in disgust; this was the woman who had instilled fear in her as a child, the woman who took no prisoners, who laid down the law with Evie every time she did something that she disagreed with. And yet here she was with Lucas, behaving like a young girl. Evie caught her father's eye; his expression told her that he was thinking the same thing.

'You think that violence has a place, then?' Evie asked carefully.

Lucas turned and smiled at her, a smile that didn't reach his eyes – but then again, none of his expressions reached his eyes. It was as though they were incapable of being anything but cold, steely blue.

'I think that we must be understanding and forgiving of our fellow citizens who are working hard to provide for their families and doing what they can to keep them safe. The City is a place for goodness. It can be hard when evil rears its head.'

'But . . .' Evie started to say, then stopped when she saw her father look at her meaningfully. It wasn't her place to argue, wasn't her place to even have this conversation. She could not ask Lucas how he could say one thing and do another; she could not challenge him and ask what Mr Bridges had done that was so terrible anyway.

Lucas cleared his throat. 'Might I . . . use the bathroom?' he asked. Evie's mother nodded immediately. 'Of course. Up the stairs, first on the left. But you know that.' She shot him another simpering smile, which disappeared the moment he had left the room and she rounded on her daughter.

'Evie,' she snapped angrily. 'What is wrong with you today? Are you completely incapable of polite conversation?'

Evie shook her head. 'No. I'm sorry. I just wondered, that's all . . .'

'Don't wonder,' her mother said, her voice low and threatening. 'Don't ask difficult questions. You have made a very good match here, young lady. A match that some might say you don't deserve. Lucas is a good man. If you are to marry him, you are going to have to buck up your ideas.'

'Go easy on her, Delphine,' said Evie's father gently. 'Evie has always had an active mind. Perhaps that is what Lucas likes in her.'

Her mother opened her mouth to disagree; Evie could see the derision in her eyes. But then she apparently thought better of it. 'Perhaps,' she said instead, her lips pursing. 'Perhaps.'

'Evie.' Her father turned to her with a half smile. 'Why don't you go to the stairs and wait for Lucas to come down? Perhaps you could show him the sitting room. You could play some cards, if you'd like.'

Again her mother's mouth opened, again a look of protest crossed her face, and again her self-control appeared to step in at the last minute, forcing her to smile and give a tight little nod.

Uncertainly, Evie slipped down from her chair and out of the door, loitering at the bottom of the stairs for a minute or so, wondering what to say to Lucas when he reappeared. But then she heard a sound coming from her father's study; surprised, she padded towards the closed door and inched it open to see Lucas standing there.

'Lucas,' she said, staring at him. 'What are you doing in here?'

He looked up, evidently startled by her appearance.

'Evie,' he replied. 'I'm sorry. I was just . . . admiring your father's artefacts.'

He was standing just to the side of her father's desk, in front of the cabinet in which his various medals and trophies were displayed. There were no competitions in the City; there was no winning or losing because both these things smacked of subjugation, and both resulted in emotions that could be dangerous, be it the self-satisfaction of winning or the devastation of losing. Instead, trophies and medals were given to citizens who made notable contributions to the City in excess of any expectation. Evie's father, Ralph, had made many of these, he'd told her when she was little – beginning with fetching stones to build the City walls over forty years before. It took two years to build the wall, and many more to build all the houses, roads and farms that stood today. Back then he'd been just a boy, and a grateful smile from the Great Leader had given him all the energy he needed to work tireless twelve-hour days, just as everyone else did. He'd known even then that what he was doing was important. All that lay behind him was suffering and all that lay ahead of him was hope. And when the City wall had been built and the structures – both physical and logistical – had been established, Ralph had been offered a government post for his hard work: an office job, a desk, a secretary. But he had preferred to join the woodworkers, to continue to build with his hands – much to the disappointment and irritation of Evie's mother, who still rolled her eyes at the decision and berated her husband for thinking so little of their future and their position.

Evie slipped into the room, closing the door behind her. 'You wanted to see his medals? But surely you've already seen them?'

She knew very well that Lucas had been in her father's study before. It had been where they had talked once the match had been made; when her father had given his permission.

'I have.' Lucas smiled easily. 'But in your father's company it did not seem appropriate to look at them in too much detail. Your father is a modest man.' He spoke calmly, but something told Evie that he wasn't calm. Not at all. And it encouraged her. For the first time in her life she felt she could speak her mind. Lucas was somewhere he shouldn't be and he knew it; she was determined to use that to her advantage.

'What is wrong with Raffy?' she asked, folding her arms and looking him right in the eye.

'He's ill,' Lucas said levelly. 'An infectious disease.'

'It must have sprung up very suddenly,' replied Evie, realising as she spoke how unafraid she sounded, how inappropriate were her tone of voice, her questions. But she realised, too, that she was beyond appropriateness with Lucas. He knew her for what she was; she could finally be herself.

'It did,' Lucas said, returning her stare, as though challenging her to question him; to accuse him of lying, of doing anything it took to keep Raffy away from her.

Evie was just formulating the right sentence to do just that when the sound of footsteps startled them both. She was surprised to see a glimmer of fear in Lucas's eyes as they both turned towards the door to see her father appear. He looked taken aback to find them in his study, momentarily lost for words. The study was his domain and his domain only; Evie and her mother only entered when he was at home and only with his permission.

'Lucas wanted to ask me something. Something very private. Important,' Evie said quickly, feeling a sudden wash of shame because the lie tripped so easily from her tongue. 'I thought that we might be disturbed in the sitting room. That Mother might—'

Their eyes met, and there was a flicker of understanding as her father registered her meaningful look. 'Of course,' her father cut in, smiling, his eyes moving from her to Lucas and back again. He had inferred what Evie had hoped he would infer. 'Forgive me. I will be in the kitchen if you need me.'

He shot her a little smile, then left. Lucas looked at her quizzically, then he closed his eyes for a second before opening them again. 'Thank you for that, Evie. You were right to suggest that we were talking about private matters. Otherwise your father might have got the wrong idea.'

'Yes, he might have,' Evie replied. 'But he has still left with the wrong idea, hasn't he? He thinks that you're setting a formal date for our marriage.'

'I believe he does, yes,' Lucas said cautiously.

Evie wanted to shake him, to scream at him, elicit some kind of reaction. But she knew Lucas was incapable of such a thing. Like Raffy said, he was a machine. A strange, unfeeling machine of a man. Instead, she would just concentrate on what mattered; on the reason she'd lied to her father.

'Tell me the truth about Raffy,' she demanded. 'What have you done with him? He's not ill. I know he isn't. Tell me, or I'll tell my father that you were in here snooping. Were you snooping on him? Because you're wasting your time. He's a good man. My father is a key holder.'

Lucas walked towards her; they were just inches apart. And Evie could see no fear in his eyes any more; she could see nothing but blue. 'I know that your father is a good man. That's why he has medals. And that, let us remember, is why I am in here. Not snooping, but simply admiring his medals,' he said smoothly. 'I can't imagine he would be too upset. I might have forgotten my manners, perhaps gone against usual protocol, but I believe your father would understand. Whether he would be as understanding of you receiving midnight visits from my brother, however, is another thing entirely.'

Evie stepped back. She was shaking. She had felt so strong, so clever, and now she saw that she was neither of those things. And as she looked up at Lucas she knew that she hated him more than she ever thought it possible to hate someone, even if he was an A. Especially because he was an A. A's were meant to be good – the best – and Lucas . . . She breathed out slowly. Raffy was right – the City was twisted. Or, more likely, she was. She'd rather spend her time with D's any day of the week.

'You'll have to tell my father something,' she said, turning, defeated but determined not to let Lucas see. 'He'll be expecting it.'

'I will explain that these things take time,' Lucas agreed, already walking towards the door. 'Thank you, Evie. We must do this again.'

And with that he left the room. She heard him talking briefly with her parents, and then he was gone.

'You had a good conversation?' her father asked, making her jump as he came back into his study.

Evie nodded, not trusting herself to speak.

'Good,' he replied. 'But next time, not in my study. Lucas is not family yet, Evie.'

'No, father. I'm sorry,' she said, her eyes cast downwards. Then slowly, heavily, she made her way upstairs to bed.

8

The Brother was standing when Lucas knocked at the door. He always like to stand when he had important news to communicate. It gave him gravitas, he felt. Made him look, and feel, as though he was taking the news seriously.

It also meant, usually, that without the comfort of a chair to cling to, the person he was conveying the news to left quickly.

'Lucas.' Lucas's expression was unreadable as he walked into the room, just as it always was. Or perhaps it *was* readable; perhaps there really was no emotion there to be read.

'Brother.' Lucas didn't scan the room for a chair as others often did. He squared up to the Brother, his posture as straight as always, his eyes reminiscent of a brilliant summer sky, only without the sun to lend it warmth. The Brother found them almost unnerving, but he would have them no other way. Lucas was loyal, committed, unquestioning. A model citizen. The best man he had.

'I read your report,' the Brother told him. 'I understand your reasons for believing that Raphael was not capable of planting a communication device in the System. That he only found the strange code and reported it. That his interpretation of the code is itself of dubious merit and a result of his rather fantastical imagination. I see that you yourself have analysed the code and found it to be no more than a system error.'

'That is correct, Brother.'

'And you're absolutely sure?'

A little frown settled onto Lucas's face. 'Brother, with respect, if there were a device of any sort embedded in the System, I would know. Raphael found some erroneous code, a mistake from many years ago that had gone unnoticed because it did nothing, because it is nothing. It has now been deleted. What Raphael found and what he said he found are two different things. My brother has always been a fantasist. He escapes into a dream world. Here, he got confused between that dream world and reality. That is all. You have my word, Brother.'

He was like a soldier, the Brother found himself

thinking. Perhaps the technology Unit was not the place for him after all. Perhaps he would be better placed running the police guard, instilling some of his sense of purpose and duty into them. But no. Lucas knew more about the System than anyone; his understanding of technology and computer programmes knew no bounds. Anyone could run the police guard; only Lucas could run the System.

'I see.' He breathed out heavily, walked over to his desk and picked up Lucas's report. 'The problem is, Lucas, all this raises more general questions about your brother's fitness.' He saw a flicker of something on Lucas's face, but it disappeared too quickly for him to be able to analyse or interpret it. 'I think that Raphael is a troubled boy,' the Brother continued, lowering his eyeline so that he was looking vaguely at the level of Lucas's chin. 'More than troubled. I think that we have done what we can for him, contained him for as long as it is safe to do so.'

'And your evidence for this?' Lucas asked abruptly. The Brother started slightly; was there a mutinous tone in Lucas's voice or was it really just a question, a clarification? He shook himself. He was projecting his own fears onto Lucas, seeing anger where there was none. Lucas did not know what it was to feel anger. He was the closest thing the Brother had ever had to a son, and yet he felt he knew him less than anyone else he spent time with.

'I know,' he said sadly, wearily. 'Or rather, the System knows. I had hoped . . .' He looked over at Lucas, felt himself almost recoil at the lack of emotion on the younger man's face. 'A report has been generated. It means that Raffy will be leaving us.'

'He's to be made a K?'

'That is what the System has decided,' said the Brother gravely, putting his hands together as if in prayer, a habit that he had found impossible to break.

'He will have a second New Baptism tonight?'

'He will be taken tonight, yes, for the safety of everyone,' the Brother replied, searching Lucas's face for a sign of sadness, of anger – something that he could connect with. But of course there was nothing.

'Very well. If the System has decided,' Lucas said. 'Is that all?'

'That's all,' answered the Brother, not sure why he felt a stab of disappointment at Lucas's lack of reaction.

Lucas went to the door and opened it, then he hesitated. 'Brother?' he asked, his voice tentative, something that rather took the Brother aback.

'Yes, Lucas?'

'Might I have one more night with Raphael? Might my mother?'

The Brother stared at him. So he did care, after all. 'You're asking me to delay the implementation of the System's decision?' he asked.

Lucas nodded slowly. 'It is a great deal to ask, I know,' he said, his voice catching slightly. 'But it would mean a lot. To my mother.' The Brother looked at him carefully. It *was* a lot to ask. It was unheard of. But one day would make no difference. And the Brother could finally see clouds in the brilliant sky; for some reason he felt cheered by this. Lucas was human. He was real, after all.

'Tomorrow, then,' he said.

'Thank you.' A smile. The first smile, perhaps, that had ever reached Lucas's eyes. And then he was gone.

Slowly the Brother walked over to his desk, pulled out Raphael's System change file and placed it in his drawer.

Evie knew Raffy wasn't at work. Partly because she got there early and skulked around outside until she saw Lucas arrive on his own, and partly because she just knew. And she also knew he wasn't ill. She'd heard whispers that he was under surveillance, that his brother had been charged with finding out what he knew.

The rest, she filled in with imagination, fear, loathing of Lucas, and with the anger and frustration she felt at him, at everyone.

Because really, it was her fault. She should have stopped earlier. She should have been stronger. And now Raffy was . . . what? Locked away somewhere? Being tortured by Lucas, not because of some glitch in the System but because he had visited her, because Lucas had followed him, because Lucas didn't care about feelings or family bonds or anything like that. Because he was cruel and angry and jealous.

On her way home, she passed Raffy's house and was tempted to bang on the door, to demand to see him, but she knew it was pointless. She could no more bang on his door than she could choose not to marry Lucas, not to go to work, not to obey the City's rules. She had to do what was expected of her, because that's what everyone did. Unquestioningly. She wondered if everyone else who lived in the City found its rules as frustrating, whether everyone longed to break them and allow the temptations of desire and anger take them over. Were A's A's because they were naturally good or just because they had more self-control than everyone else? Did Lucas have urges that he had to control sometimes? Evie let out a hollow laugh. Lucas had never had urges or feelings, of that she was sure.

She got home to find her mother waiting for her in the kitchen, a pile of half-made clothes on the table, her sewing machine all set up next to it.

'Evie,' she said with a sigh. 'Here you are at last. Belle was off today with the flu. I need your help to make up her quota.'

Evie stared at the pile. Before she'd started working for the government she had regularly helped her mother with her work, making clothes and bedlinen. She would come home from school and sew for an hour or two before helping her to prepare supper. Now that she was working ten-hour days, her mother never asked for her help. She never even seemed to bring work home any more.

'Okay,' she said, putting down her bag. After all, the only activity she had planned for that evening was to rage against Lucas and worry about Raffy.

'Good. I'll cook, you can sew. It will be like the old days.'

Evie washed her hands before sitting down at the table and reacquainting herself with the long-forgotten workings of her mother's sewing machine. She did a few test runs to start with and was pleased she had; the first few times she pressed the pedal, she went too fast and her stitching went off track, but she quickly got back into the rhythm, and soon she was enjoying the gentle hum which seemed to soothe her as she concentrated on keeping a straight line.

'Your father tells me that Lucas talked to you last night,' her mother said after a few minutes of silence.

Evie didn't reply. She had enjoyed not thinking about Lucas for a minute or two.

'You are very lucky to be courted by such a good man,' her mother continued, regardless. 'I do hope you appreciate that, and that you make him feel he has made the right choice. That you are good enough for him.'

Evie stopped sewing, looked up at her mother. 'You're not concerned about whether he is good enough for me?' she asked.

Her mother rolled her eyes. 'Evie, don't say such things, even in jest. You have done very well with Lucas. Very well.'

'So you keep saying,' Evie replied, pushing her chair back. She suddenly felt claustrophobic, like the warm kitchen that had felt so comforting seconds before was now slowly suffocating her.

'I keep saying it because I'm not sure you appreciate it,' her mother answered tightly. 'I'm not sure you appreciate anything. You are lucky to even be here, Evie. Very lucky indeed.' She was whisking something in a bowl; her hand started to move even more quickly and

Evie found herself wondering what would happen if the bowl and all its contents went flying across the room. Then she realised she wasn't wondering what would happen; she was hoping that it would.

Because she was evil. She acknowledged this with no emotion; it didn't even upset her any more. It was just a fact. A fact she had accepted.

'You think I should appreciate Lucas because he's good. Because he's an A,' she said flatly.

Her mother put the bowl on the counter, moved to the other side of the table from Evie and sat down. 'I think you should appreciate that you have a good marriage ahead of you. A good husband with good prospects. Not like . . .'

She didn't finish the sentence, but Evie knew what she had been going to say.

'Not like you?' she asked, then stood up, anger flooding through her veins. She was tired of controlling her urges. She couldn't do it any more. 'Father loves you. He is a good man. A truly good man. His study is full of medals and trophies and he is well liked and respected. He is a holder of the key. But that's not enough for you. I wish *you* would marry Lucas. I think you deserve each other.' Leaving the sewing half done, she fled from the kitchen up to her room, ignoring her mother's calls, then threats, then ultimatums that there would be no supper, no food until she apologised.

She wasn't hungry anyway.

And there was no way she was going to apologise.

It was late, but Evie couldn't sleep. Instead, she sat on her bed, trying to ignore the hunger pangs in her stomach, trying to rise above such mundane, unimportant things when there was so much else to make sense of and to worry about. Raffy, Lucas, her own future.

And yet it was something else that was at the forefront of her mind, that kept niggling, that wouldn't leave her alone. Something her mother had said: 'You are lucky to even be here.'

But where else would she be?

Evie looked out of her window. It was dark, silent; she could see houses, hundreds of houses just like hers, their lights glowing. She knew that inside, families just like hers would be sitting around tables, playing card games, reading the Sentiments. Good people. Productive people. She closed the curtains. How thick was the line between good and evil? she wondered. How close did the good people come to crossing it? Was it like a thin line on the ground that could be tripped over easily if you weren't looking, or was it like a river that had to be actively crossed? If so, she would willingly cross the river, she realised, guided by Raffy. In fact, she already had.

The door opened and Evie looked up anxiously. It was her father. The moonlight danced on his face, revealing that his eyes were surrounded by dark shadows. He sat down at the end of her bed. 'Evie,' he said quietly. 'I am sorry to disturb you so late.'

'It's okay,' she said uncertainly, looking at the clock on her bedside table and feeling her stomach clench when she saw that it was nearly midnight. Her parents were usually asleep by 10 p.m. at the latest. 'I'm sorry,' she said then. 'I'm sorry about what I said to Mother. I didn't mean it.'

'You argued with your mother?' her father asked sadly.

'Yes. I . . . I thought that's why you wanted to talk to me,' Evie said, frowning.

'No,' her father replied. 'No, I have just come from a meeting with the key holders. Evil has been detected in the City, Evie. There is to be a second New Baptism.'

Evie felt a film of sweat cover her instantly. Was he talking about her? Had he come to tell her that she had been made a K? No, please no. She would change. She would . . . She realised her father was looking at her expectantly and she recovered herself.

'Yes, father,' she whispered.

'Evie, there is something else.'

Evie felt a cloud of foreboding gather over her. It was the look on her father's face. His hesitation. His unwillingness to look her in the eye. It *was* her. They were coming for her. She was the K. She started to shake.

'Evie, I'm afraid that the evil one is . . . Raphael.'

Evie looked up in shock. 'Raffy? No!' She was shaking more violently now.

'The System has decided,' her father said gently. 'It is not for us to judge. But I know that you and he . . .' He took a deep breath. 'You were friends once. You are marrying his brother. I want you to know that I am sure this won't reflect badly on Lucas. He is a good man. I don't want you to worry.'

'You don't want me to worry?' Evie gasped. 'Raffy isn't evil. He isn't. He—'

'The Brother himself has told me that Lucas has been pivotal in collecting information for the System,' her father said, putting his hand on her shoulder. 'And I will not view him any differently just because he has been so close to evil. So go to sleep, Evie. Tomorrow will be a challenging day.'

Evie couldn't speak; instead, she watched in silence as her father left the room, waited to hear his footsteps reach the bedroom he shared with her mother, and waited for the door to open then close again.

Then, her mind racing, she stood up, looked around her room frantically and started to pull on some clothes. She had to get to Raffy, had to warn him. She didn't know how, but she'd do it somehow. If he had a second New Baptism she'd never see him again and she couldn't bear that. They would run to the place Raffy told her about, away from this terrible City that purported to be full of good, but didn't know what goodness was – how could it, when its idea of true goodness was Lucas, a man who would betray his own brother? Lucas was the one who was evil. He was beyond evil. He was . . .

She heard a sound, a tapping at the window, and she felt her body flood with relief. It was Raffy. He had escaped. He was here. He was safe. She pulled open her curtains, tugged at the window to open it. But when she did, her mouth fell open and the hairs stood up on the back of her neck. Because it was not Raffy she saw. It was two blue eyes, two vile emotionless eyes that met hers and her first instinct was to close the window again, to shut Lucas out, to push him from the wall he had climbed. But he was too quick for her; he grabbed her wrists, pushed her back, swung his legs though the window and landed in front of her.

'Evie,' he said, one eyebrow raised as he took in her half-dressed state. 'Are you going somewhere?'

9

Evie opened her mouth to scream but nothing came out; Lucas immediately put his hand around her mouth, pulling her against him so that her back was against his chest. Then he leant down so that his mouth was next to her ear.

'I want you to listen,' he said, his voice low. 'I want you to listen very carefully, Evie, do you understand? And I don't want you to make a sound. Not a single sound.'

Evie nodded, her eyes wide, her body shaking. His hands were pressing into her; she felt unable to breathe. Was he going to take her to the Brother? Have her labelled a K, too? She told herself she didn't care; that she wouldn't let herself care. But she did care. She was terrified.

'I need you to get me your father's key,' Lucas said.

Evie felt her whole body tense. Her father's key? She didn't understand.

He released his hand slightly, allowing her to speak. 'I won't give you anything,' she whispered angrily. 'You betrayed Raffy. He isn't a K. He can't be.'

'I know he isn't,' Lucas replied evenly. 'That's why I need the key. Raffy needs to get out of the City. And you're going to help me.'

Evie started; she couldn't have heard correctly. 'I don't understand,' she managed to say. 'I'm not sure I—'

'You will understand. I'm going to let you go. If you make a noise, you will regret it.'

Evie nodded and Lucas released her, removing the hand from her mouth, turning her around so that she was facing him. And what she saw shocked her; it was Lucas, but not the Lucas she knew. His blue eyes were clouded, heavy; there was an urgency in them; pain. He reminded her of something . . . of someone. And immediately she realised who: Raffy. For the first time she understood that they were brothers; for the first time Lucas actually bore some resemblance to his sibling. But she still didn't trust him. He was still Lucas. He was still the man who had betrayed Raffy.

'You know what K stands for?' Lucas asked her.

'Raffy is not a K,' she said, her voice shaking. 'He isn't. What we did . . . It wasn't evil. We didn't mean to—'

'It stands for Killable,' Lucas spoke as though he hadn't noticed that she was talking. He was looking at her unflinchingly but she noticed that above his left eye a tiny muscle was throbbing. 'Killable. They're not reconditioned. They're left outside for the Evils to kill them. Tomorrow, Raffy will be a K. Tomorrow night the Evils will come. So tonight we are going to get him out of the City.'

Evie stared at him in disbelief. The Evils always come when someone was made a K; everyone heard them wailing and the key holders were on high alert. But they didn't kill anyone. They couldn't. They couldn't get in. 'No,' she gasped. 'You're wrong.'

'You think the Evils come because they're angry? They come because they're brought here. Because they're hungry,' Lucas said bitterly. 'They come to do the City's dirty work for it.'

'No!' Evie shook her head. 'No,' she said again, her eyes narrowing. 'You're lying. I don't know why you're here, Lucas, but I'm not falling into your trap. You want me to be a K, too. You want to get rid of both of us because you're full of hate.'

Lucas shook his head angrily. 'I'm here because I need your help,' he said, his voice wavering slightly. 'Because Raffy needs your help. Otherwise he's dead. If you want to help Raffy, you have to get me your father's key.'

Evie gaped at him. Was this some kind of trick, some kind of test? 'The other day,' she said suddenly. 'When you were here. You were looking for the key. That's what you were doing in my father's study.' Her mouth hung open even when she'd stopped speaking; the flicker in Lucas's eye told her she was right.

'You knew even then he was going to be a K,' Evie said, anger filling her veins. 'Because it was you who told the Brother. And now you want my help? You're a liar, Lucas. You're a liar and I'm not helping you. I don't know what you want the key for but I'm not helping you.'

'You're right about one thing,' Lucas agreed. 'It's my fault Raffy's been labelled a K.'

'Because you told them about us?' Evie asked, a tear pricking at her eye, a tear that she managed to hold in because she didn't want to cry. She was too angry to cry. 'Because you had to follow him? Couldn't let your brother break one of your City's precious rules?'

Lucas raised an eyebrow then looked away. 'Because of you?' he asked bitterly. 'You think I'd . . .' He stopped, swallowed; the muscle above his eye was throbbing more quickly. 'No, Evie. Not because of that.'

Evie felt her stomach clench. 'Then why?' she demanded. 'Why is Raffy a K? And why are you telling me you want to help him now when you've never wanted to before, when you've treated him like a second-class citizen all his life, when you've behaved like a machine?'

She didn't know until she said the word whether she'd be brave enough to do it. And when she had said it, and she saw Lucas's face darken, she wondered whether she'd gone too far. But then Lucas slowly nodded. He sat down on the bed, allowing his head to drop into his hands.

'I'm sorry, Evie,' he said then, looking up at her. His blond hair was dishevelled and for a moment he looked not just human, but vulnerable. Evie almost wanted to reach out, but she didn't. It was Lucas. He wasn't really vulnerable. He was just up to something and she didn't trust him. She would never trust him.

He breathed out deeply. 'I have been hard on Raffy. But I've been trying to protect him. He couldn't see . . . couldn't understand that what he was doing, the way he was, the way he looked at people . . . He couldn't see that it was going to get him into trouble. He couldn't see that Dad was the same. I was trying to protect him . . .' Lucas's voice cracked slightly and Evie moved towards him warily. 'Your father?' she asked. Raffy had been young when his dad had been labelled a K, too young to understand that he was evil, that he was dangerous. But he'd learnt soon enough what his father's legacy meant: that people were wary of him, didn't trust him, just because he *looked* like his father.

'Our father believed in this place. He thought that by learning more he could help. But he wouldn't follow the rules. He wouldn't follow protocol, didn't see that the rules existed to . . . to . . .' Lucas trailed off again, his eyes gazing into the middle distance.

'To what?' Evie asked breathlessly.

He met her eyes, then shook his head. 'There's no time,' he said. 'Not now. We have to get Raffy out while it's dark. While everyone is asleep.'

Evie looked at him warily. Then she sat down next to Lucas on the bed. 'You haven't told me why Raffy was made a K. Why it's your fault, if you didn't tell anyone about me. About us.'

Lucas looked around the room furtively as though there might be people in it, waiting to hear what he had to say. 'It was the glitch,' he said eventually, his eyes darkening further as he spoke. 'I taught him how to use and manipulate technology. I thought it would give him a future. But he got too good. He found . . . something. Something that he shouldn't have found.'

Evie gasped. She immediately remembered what Raffy had told her about the glitch; remembered telling him he must be wrong. 'You mean the communication device?' she asked, the hairs on the back of her neck standing up.

Lucas stared at her in alarm. 'He told you? He told you about it?'

'I thought he'd just made it up. He was always making things up,' Evie said, her voice breaking as she spoke.

'Did you tell anyone?' Lucas was looking at her intently; Evie shook her head.

He appeared to digest this. Then his eyes were back on her, uncompromising; they seemed to look right inside her. 'So will you help? Will you get the key?'

He was looking at her intently – his whole face seemed completely different to the Lucas she'd known all her life. He looked like a real person. Like a person who needed her. Like a person who really cared about Raffy.

'You've known all this time? You've been pretending all this time?' she asked Lucas.

He nodded. 'I had to,' he whispered. 'I'm sorry.'

'And me? What was that? Why match with me?'

'Because I knew Raffy loved you and would never have you. I thought I could at least make sure you were safe.'

A lump appeared in her throat. And emotions she couldn't make sense of flooded her.

'I'll help you,' she whispered.

A shadow of a smile brushed over Lucas's face, then it was gone again. 'Okay.' He stood up. Evie did, too. 'We need the key. You go and get it. Meet me outside. If one of your parents wakes up, pretend you were sleepwalking. Pretend you couldn't sleep. Anything, okay? But do not mention my name. They mustn't know that I am here. Do you understand? A great deal depends on this, Evie.'

Evie nodded. She still wasn't used to this new Lucas; she kept expecting him to suddenly round on her, his clear blue eyes cold as ice again as his lip curled triumphantly at her stupidity. But instead he just shot her a look of gratitude and climbed back out of the window, leaving her alone, her mind racing but fixed on one thing: she would help to save Raffy. She would do whatever it took.

She crept towards the door and opened it a fraction; the corridor was quiet. Hesitating outside her parents' bedroom, just as she had done many times before as she left the house to meet Raffy, she waited until she could hear her father's rhythmic breathing before continuing on her way towards the stairs. The stairs themselves creaked; they always had, but Evie knew which steps could take her weight without groaning too loudly. Delicately she moved down them, as though on stepping stones, until she was at the bottom. Then, seconds later, she was in her father's study, looking up at the portrait of her mother, behind which she knew was the safe that held the key, the safe that her father opened only on the nights that the Evils came. He did it alone, unwatched, according to protocol. But Evie had learnt as a small girl how to slip into a room unnoticed, to watch, to observe.

Nervously she climbed up onto the desk and removed the picture. Then, her hands moistening with sweat, she started to turn the dial of the safe just as she'd watched her father do. 4-5-24. Her birth date. The door slid open and for a moment she stared at it, before reaching in to take the key.

And then she stopped. What was she doing? She was playing into Lucas's hands. All his life he had been cold, heartless, cruel. And now, suddenly he was telling her that it had been a pretence? Now she was expected to believe that he wanted only to help her and Raffy? Lucas didn't have feelings. He was ruthless. He was clever. And whatever his plan was, she wasn't falling for it.

She edged backwards, climbed off the table, then went out of the study and out of the house. Lucas was waiting for her. 'You have it?' he asked, holding out his hand.

She shook her head. 'I'm not doing it,' she said, looking him right in the eye. 'I don't trust you.'

Lucas grabbed her by the shoulders. 'Evie, you have to trust me. Don't you get it? There is no other way. You get me the key or Raffy . . . Raffy . . .' His voice broke; Evie stared in disbelief as tears appeared in his eyes. He brushed them away roughly.

'But how can I trust you?' she asked miserably. 'How, after everything you've done?'

'Everything I've done? Like covering up your little midnight meetings with Raffy? Making sure the System never picked up on them? That kind of thing?' Lucas asked, his eyes shining angrily.

Evie stared at him, her eyes wide. 'You knew?'

'Of course I knew,' Lucas sighed. 'How else do you think you've been getting away with it?'

Evie digested this slowly. The System hadn't known; hadn't been waiting to judge her. Lucas had been protecting her all this time. Protecting both of them. Or, she thought suddenly, the System had primed him with this information to get her trust. Would he really have stood by if he'd known about her meetings with Raffy?

'I don't see how you could stop the System from knowing,' she said, doubt filling her head. 'You can't control the System.'

Lucas closed his eyes. Then he looked at her strangely, uncertainly. 'Okay. There's something else.'

'What?' she asked him, her eyes narrowing. 'What is it?'

'I'm going to tell you something, Evie. Something important. So that you'll trust me. Okay?'

'Okay,' she replied dubiously.

He looked skywards, then back at the floor, as though searching for the right words.

'What is it?' Evie repeated, frowning. 'Tell me.'

He took a piece of paper out of his pocket and handed it to her. Evie looked at it uncomprehendingly; it was a certificate of some kind. Her name was on it, along with her parents' names. 'Your parents,' Lucas said then, his voice barely a whisper. 'Your parents are not your parents.'

Evie raised an eyebrow. 'Of course they're my parents,' she said.

'No, Evie.' He exhaled, stepped back, looked at her apprehensively. 'They're not. They adopted you when you were three.

Evie's eyes narrowed as they scanned the document

again until she saw the word she was looking for. Tucked away at the bottom. 'Adoption'. She felt sick, crumpled the paper into a ball.

'What are you talking about?' she said angrily. 'Is this another lie? What are you talking about, Lucas?' She prodded him in the chest with her finger, then the prod became a thump, and before she knew it she was hitting him. Hissing at him. All decorum had gone, she realised, all pretence had vanished. 'What are you talking about, Lucas?' she demanded again. 'Tell me.'

Lucas crouched down, pulling her down next to him. 'It was part of the growth programme,' he whispered, his voice taut with emotion. 'There weren't enough people, not young people. After the Horrors not everyone could have children. Not everyone . . .' He took a deep breath. 'So they let people in. People who were desperate. There were people who'd travelled long distances. They were hungry, starving. They'd been surviving, but only just. They thought the City would save them. They came here and . . .' He trailed off; his eyes were glistening with tears.

'And what?' Evie asked. She was getting a strange feeling at the bottom of her spine. 'What happened to them?'

'They took their children. Gave them to good couples. Couples who couldn't have children of their own.'

Evie felt a lump appear in her throat. 'That's not what I mean. What happened to them? What happened to my real parents?' Her voice was low, guttural.

Lucas shook his head in response.

Evie stepped back. She couldn't speak. She turned, stumbled towards her house, the house she'd grown up in, the house she'd thought of as her own. A house that now represented only a lie.

She felt sick.

She wanted to shout. Scream. She wanted to shout at Lucas, tell him to stop lying, to stop telling her these things.

But she didn't, because she knew, somewhere in her heart, that he wasn't lying. She knew because she remembered. The man from her dream, carrying her against his chest. The woman, stroking her head, telling her about the wonderful place they were going to, telling her to be strong. Her parents. They had been her real parents.

She turned back to look at Lucas and realised that her eyes were swimming with tears. 'I dreamt about them,' she heard herself say, her voice nothing to do with her for she was lost again, a little girl being carried by a man who loved her. 'The Brother told me I was dreaming about the City. They knew. They . . .'

She met Lucas's gaze, saw the pain in his eyes,

knew that he understood. And as he walked towards her she fell against him and felt his arms wrap tightly around her, and it was almost as though she was in her dream again. 'You see?' he whispered desperately. 'There are so many lies here, Evie. We have to get Raffy out. We have to.'

And Evie nodded, because she knew he was right. But she knew something else, too. 'I'm going too,' she said, and as she spoke her body filled with fear because beyond the City walls lay only danger, the Evils, a brutal world filled with brutal souls. But she would take her chances.

'No,' said Lucas immediately. 'No, you stay here. You're safe. I've planned it. It will look as though Raffy stole the key. You must stay.'

'Never,' Evie said, shaking her head vehemently. 'I'm going with Raffy. I don't belong here. I don't want to live here. I don't want any part of this place any more.'

Lucas didn't say anything for a few seconds. Then he pulled back, held her shoulders again but more gently this time. 'It's dangerous out there,' he said, then. 'Are you sure?'

Evie nodded. 'I can't stay. Not now. And anyway, they'll know it was me. Raffy would have to have broken a window or something. And if we do that my father will wake up and raise the alarm and no one will escape.'

Lucas met her eyes; he looked miserable. 'I shouldn't have come here,' he said.

'You had to come,' she replied. 'And anyway, if what you've just told me is true, about my parents, I mean, I can't stay here. Not now. They took them away from me. They lied to me. My whole life here has been a lie.'

'They lied to everyone,' Lucas said quietly.

'So then we'll all go.' Evie swallowed, trying to pretend the huge lump in her throat wasn't there. She wanted to be cold like Lucas used to be, wanted to be a machine so it didn't hurt so badly. And suddenly she understood why he was like he was. Because machines didn't feel pain. Because if you were made of ice, you didn't get hurt.

Lucas caught her eye and for a moment she saw something in it. It was something she half recognised, something that reminded her of Raffy again but in a way that unnerved her, because she suspected her eye had the same desperation in it. She had hated Lucas. She had despised him. And now, now . . .

'I can't come,' Lucas announced suddenly, turning and breaking the connection that had existed between them for those few, strange seconds, and leaving Evie feeling as though she was stumbling backwards, but into what she didn't know. 'I must stay here. There are things I must do. I . . .'

His eyes were darting around the front garden; Evie knew that it was his head talking, not his heart. And suddenly she understood him – not everything, but enough. She saw that he had survived, that he had done what he'd had to do. She saw that he was real, that he had suffered and that he was still suffering. 'There are things to do. Things to . . .' Lucas muttered, then looked up at her again, and this time Evie felt the full power of his stare: the desperate need in his eyes, the hunger for solace and for understanding. Without meaning to, without thinking too much about what she was doing, she moved towards him again and allowed her hands to touch him, his chest, his shoulders, his neck. He wrapped his arms around her once more and his lips found hers. She could feel his tears mingling with hers, his pain mingling with her pain until it felt almost as though they were one and the same person, full of the same anger, the same desperation, the same fear. And then, as soon as it had begun, it was over; they pulled away, their hands holding on to each other for just a few seconds longer before they, too, dropped away. And Evie knew it was the same thought that had made them stop, had broken the connection once more. The same thought of the same person. Raffy.

'I'll be back,' Evie whispered, and headed to the front door. 'I'll be back with the key. But I am leaving the City, Lucas. I can't stay here. Not now.'

'I know,' Lucas said, looking away, his blond hair glinting in the moonlight, his clouded eyes now surveying some arbitrary object on the path below. 'I'm so sorry, Evie. For everything.'

10

Evie took one last look at the house she thought she'd live in until she got married, before closing the door. Lucas squeezed her hand.

'You ready?' he asked. Evie nodded. 'Okay. Let's go and get Raffy.'

He didn't let go of her hand, or perhaps it was she who was holding on, she wasn't sure. She just knew that she couldn't do this on her own, that she needed to feel Lucas's skin, his warmth, needed to know that she wasn't alone. She had thought that in the City you were never alone; the entire civilisation had been built on community, citizenship and togetherness. But now she knew that she'd never been part of it, that her life had been a lie. That she was on her own; that she always had been.

It only took a few minutes to get to the house that

Lucas shared with his mother and brother. But as he walked towards the door, Evie pulled him back, looked up at him; there was so much she wanted to know, so much she couldn't comprehend beyond a vague feeling of trust and respect.

'All this time?' she asked. 'You've really been pretending? All this time?'

Lucas met her eyes, then looked away. 'Surviving,' he said quietly. 'We all have to survive in our own way.'

'And . . .' She frowned as she tried to piece together the jigsaw in her mind, but there were too many parts, too many questions. 'The communication device? Does it mean . . . Do you know what it is? Did you . . . ?'

Lucas nodded. 'My father put it there,' he whispered.

'Your father?' Evie stared at him incredulously.

Lucas nodded. 'Evie, there is a world outside these walls. Not a pretty world, not a world full of resources, but a world nonetheless. There are people who can help you. People my father made contact with . . .'

'Another City?'

Lucas nodded. 'You need to find it. You'll be safe with them.'

Evie opened her mouth to speak but Lucas shook his head. 'No more questions. There's no time,' he whispered. 'Once we're in the house, there will be too much to do. Raffy won't listen to me, it will take him too long to understand. But you need to listen to me now. You have to lead the way. Leave by the East Gate, then head north. Can you do that?'

Evie nodded.

'Keep moving until it's light, then find somewhere to hide. There are caves to the north that you should reach. If not, find any cover you can. You need to understand that the world was almost destroyed by the Horrors. You'll need to take water and food. And you'll need to be careful, Evie. Look after Raffy. He can be too rash, too quick to get angry.'

Their eyes met and something flickered between them, but before Evie could interpret it, Lucas had looked away again.

'Go east through side roads until you reach the edge of the City.'

'The swamplands?' Evie asked, trying to stop her voice from wavering. Everyone knew about the swamplands that surrounded the City, the swamplands that divided good and evil. Evie had only seen them properly once, many years before, when her father had taken her. He had told her that the swamps were there because of a clever irrigation system that kept the water flowing in the City's rivers, and as a further defence of the City's boundaries. He told her that contrary to schoolchild mythology, there were no monsters in the swamps – they were nothing to fear and they protected and nourished all the City's citizens. And Evie had listened seriously and nodded her head, but she'd still been relieved to leave, to get back through the small fields just inside the swamplands where farmers grew food, to the safety of the roads and houses that made up the inhabited part of the City, the part she knew. The part she thought back then she'd never leave again.

'There's a path through the swamps,' Lucas said, nodding. If you keep due east, look out for a cottage. It looks derelict but it isn't. There's a watchman in there and he's got dogs.'

'Dogs?' Evie gulped.

'You'll be okay. You'll have waterproofs. They'll mask your smell a bit. Go directly behind the house and you'll find the path there. It will lead you to the East Gate. Go through, start to run, heading north, and don't look back.'

'And you?' Evie asked. 'What about you?'

Lucas shrugged, managed a little smile. 'I'll be fine,' he said. 'Don't worry about me. So – ready?'

Evie took one last look at him – at those eyes, once so cold, that now radiated sunshine – and she nodded.

'Ready,' she said, and Lucas quietly opened the front door.

The house was pitch black; Evie held onto Lucas as he guided her up the stairs and into Raffy's room. He turned on a small light and Evie gasped; Raffy was tied to the bed, his eyes closed, his breathing laboured. Every so often he tugged at the ropes in his sleep and for a moment Evie's stomach clenched in fear, because Lucas had tied his brother up, because this was not what she'd expected. And for the briefest of seconds she looked over at Lucas and half expected to see his cool eyes laughing at her for having believed him, for having fallen for his trick. But all she saw in Lucas's eyes was pain; his expression was one of tenderness as he leant over his brother and untied him. 'I'm sorry, Raffy,' he whispered as he did it. 'I'm so sorry, but it was the only way.'

Suddenly Raffy opened one eye, then two, and they looked glassy as they surveyed the scene. Then, seeing that his hands were untied, seeing Lucas looming over him, he hurled himself at his brother, pushing Lucas to the floor, then jumped up and ran towards Evie. 'Quick,' he said urgently. 'We have to get out of here. We have to get away from him.'

But Evie shook her head. 'Raffy,' she said. 'We're leaving. Lucas is helping us leave the City.'

Raffy looked at her in surprise and shock. 'Lucas? The machine? Don't trust him, Evie. He tied me up. He's been keeping me prisoner here.' He grabbed Evie and tried to run but he fell, pulling her to the ground. Immediately Lucas jumped on him.

'Quiet,' he hissed. 'If Mother wakes up . . .' He looked at the door apprehensively and motioned for Evie to hide. 'Just in case,' he whispered. Evie scurried behind the thick curtains that lined Raffy's windows, but no sound could be heard except for the juddering of Raffy's body as he tried to escape his brother's clutches. Eventually Evie came out again.

'Raffy,' pleaded Lucas, but it was no use – his brother was thrashing against him, refusing to listen. Evie crouched down next to him.

'Raffy,' she said, taking his hand. 'Do you trust me?'

Raffy's eyes travelled from her face, to Lucas's, then back again. He nodded.

'You're going to be made a K tomorrow,' she whispered. Raffy's eyes widened in alarm and he started to thrash more violently, but Evie tightened her grip on his hand and he stopped. 'We're leaving the City. You and me, together. Lucas is helping us. I've got my father's City key. Lucas isn't who you think he is, Raffy. He's not a machine. He's been protecting you.'

Raffy looked at her in disgust. 'Protecting me?' he seethed. 'He's the reason I'm being made a K. He tied me up. He told me I was a danger to myself.'

'You were,' Lucas said, his voice low but measured. 'You were talking about things that could only bring you harm. I had to pretend you were ranting, that you were disturbed. Otherwise—'

'Otherwise what?' Raffy asked angrily. 'Otherwise it would reflect badly on you? Affect your glorious career?'

'Raffy, don't,' Evie said, understanding his anger but unable to bear the look of hurt on Lucas's face, however hard he was trying to disguise it. 'You just have to believe me.'

'You have to leave now,' Lucas said. 'Tie me up so it looks like you overpowered me.' He let go of Raffy and reached under Raffy's bed, pulling out two water-proof overalls and some waterproof boots. 'You'll need these for the swamp,' he said, matter-of-factly, putting them into a rucksack that was sitting at the foot of the bed. 'There's food and water in here too, enough for a few days.'

Evie stared at them, then at Lucas. 'You knew I was going to go?' she asked quietly. 'You had this all planned?'

Lucas looked at her intently. 'I thought I'd be going,' he said.

'You did?' Evie asked, trying to disguise the wobble in her voice.

Lucas turned his eyes away. 'But this way is better. If I'm here I can protect you until you're safe.'

'Safely out of the City, you mean?' asked Evie.

'Safely out of Lucas's way and starving to death pretty quickly. Right, Lucas?' Raffy asked sarcastically.

'And then you need to find your own food and water,' Lucas continued, ignoring their questions. 'If you take more than this it will weigh you down too much. There are water sources from the City river. It's been dammed to the west but it flows in from the east.' He finished packing the rucksack and handed it to Raffy. 'Can you carry this?'

Raffy snatched it from him. 'So we're seriously going to run away? And you're just going to let us?' He rolled his eyes. 'No way. I know what's going to happen. You're going to send the police guard after me. Just like you sent them after Father.'

'Raffy.' Evie shot a warning look at him. 'Don't say that. It isn't true. Lucas is helping us.'

'It is true,' Raffy replied angrily. 'I heard him do it. I heard him talking to them. He's not helping us. He wouldn't know what it means to help someone.'

Evie turned to Lucas uncertainly. He didn't meet her eye.

'Tell me you didn't call the police guard on your father,' she said, her voice catching slightly. 'You didn't. You couldn't have done.'

'I did what I had to do,' he told her, his voice low.

'No!' Evie gasped; she couldn't stop herself. 'No, that's impossible.' She blinked away a stray tear, stared at Lucas, willing him to explain, to tell her it wasn't true. She had believed that he was good, that he was her friend, that he was angry with the City because of his father. He'd made her believe that he had suffered and that he understood. But Lucas didn't say anything,

'Not impossible,' Raffy said, his eyes narrowing. 'Anything's possible, right, Lucas?'

Lucas stayed silent; his face was flooded with guilt as he pulled Raffy's ropes towards him and started to tie them around his own ankles, then his own wrists. Evie saw his gold watch glint in the moonlight and felt herself shudder.

'You . . .' Evie stared at Lucas in dismay, her head shaking in disbelief as Raffy tied the knots for him, tightly; Lucas winced but didn't say anything. 'You really called the police guard on your father?'

'Of course he did. This is Lucas we're talking about. He may have tricked you, but not me,' Raffy said, picking up the rucksack and shooting his brother a look of disgust. 'Come on, Evie. Let's see how far we get before Lucas sends them after us. Let's see how long it takes him to betray his family this time.'

Evie nodded hesitantly; she didn't understand, wouldn't understand. But Lucas was looking away; she spoke his name, but he only glanced at her long enough to motion that they had to leave.

'Goodbye,' she mouthed as she followed Raffy out of the room. But Lucas didn't see her; he was staring fixedly at the wall ahead of him, and Evie couldn't be sure, but she thought she saw his eyes lose their warmth once more and slowly return to steel.

They left by the back door and slipped through the garden to the path that lay beyond. They didn't speak; at every corner they stopped, surveying the path or road ahead before continuing again, their heads down. The rucksack on Raffy's back seemed huge; several times Evie asked if it was too heavy, if she could help, but Raffy just grunted in reply. Then they started to leave the City behind, the densely populated roads made way to the farming districts; fields of corn and wheat, and grass for the few herds of cows that were allowed to graze. With each step, Evie felt herself get colder, as though she were leaving the comfort of a fire. But the fire wasn't there to keep her warm, she kept reminding herself. The fire was going to consume

Raffy if they stayed. Her, too. And so she kept her head down and half ran after Raffy, suppressing the worries and fears that circled in her head, telling herself that she had no choice, that the Evil-inhabited land outside the City was still safer for them than the world within the City's walls.

Then Raffy stopped, and Evie did too, and they gazed around in surprise. They were at the swampland, the land so soaked in water that their shoes felt like they might sink into it, the land that her father had shown her, warning her never to set foot in it because it would swallow her up, just as it swallowed up any Evil who tried to invade the City.

Evie took a deep breath and pulled Raffy's rucksack off his back; in silence, they put on the waterproofs.

'Where now?' Raffy asked, his voice tinged with sarcasm. He still hadn't forgiven her for being part of Lucas's plan, Evie realised. She wasn't sure she had forgiven herself, either. She'd kissed Lucas. He'd looked into her eyes and she'd felt something, something she shouldn't have felt.

'There's a cottage. A shack,' she said suddenly under her breath. She scanned the horizon, then felt her stomach tighten when she saw it – with relief, but also with anxiety, because it was real and they were so close now. 'Over there.' She signalled to the ramshackle cottage in the distance, which was exactly as Lucas had described it. 'There's a watchman in there with a guard dog. Behind it is a path which leads to the East Gate.'

'A path. Through swampland?' Raffy raised his eyebrows.

Evie shrugged in response. 'That's what Lucas said.'

'Oh, well, if Lucas said it then it must be true,' Raffy retorted angrily. 'And how long have you and Lucas been planning this anyway? Since when have the two of you been such good friends? Oh, but I forget. You're matched. What a huge shame you're leaving with me. Or is that another bit of the plan you haven't told me yet? The bit where you ditch me outside the gate and come back in so you can live happily with Lucas, just like you've always wanted to?'

Evie stared at him, her lip beginning to quiver. 'That's not true,' she whispered desperately. 'Raffy, don't do this. Not now. We have to get out before anyone realises you've gone.'

Raffy glared at her, then shrugged. 'Fine. So, we head for the house?' he asked, starting to walk.

Evie followed him. 'We have to be careful of the dog,' she said, but Raffy wasn't listening; he was striding ahead and Evie had to break into a jog just to keep up.

When they reached the house, Raffy circled it then

rounded on Evie. 'Path? There's no path. There's just bog. We're trapped. Now do you trust Lucas?'

Evie swallowed uncomfortably. Raffy was right – there was no sign of a path, just swampland. Already their boots were sinking into the ground; if they went any further they would be swallowed up. Was that really what Lucas had wanted? No. No, she knew it wasn't. Lucas was good. Lucas had to be . . .

There was a bark and they both froze. 'So now the dog gets us,' Raffy said bitterly. 'I told you. I told you.'

But Evie wasn't listening. She was running up and down frantically looking for the path. It was here; she knew it was. She tried to remember what Lucas had said. Directly behind. Directly . . . And then she looked back at the house and realised their error. They were to the side of it. They had run to the back from where they had seen the house, but it was slanted to the side; they were in the wrong place.

'This way,' she hissed, tugging Raffy's arm. She tried to run but the ground was too heavy underneath her feet; it took for ever to go just a few steps. The barking was getting louder; she saw a light go on in the shack.

They got to the back and Evie stared, willing herself to find the path, thinking she could see paths every-where that were just shadows on the ground. And then, suddenly, she saw it in the moonlight. A slightly raised section leading out from the back of the shack; made from stone, or something similar. It was stopping the shack from disappearing into the swamp; it would lead them out of it.

'Here,' she whispered, pointing it out to Raffy and striding towards it as quickly as she could. When she reached it, she stood on it, shot a hopeful smile at Raffy and started to walk. The path was a few feet wide, wide enough to run down. But as she upped her pace and called to Raffy to be quick, the back door of the shack opened and a dog charged out, large fangs emerging from its mouth as it emitted a deadly growl and ran towards them. Evie froze: she was beyond the flatter swampland. If she lost her footing, if she left the path, she would drown. But the dog was on the path already; it was running towards her. There was no escape. Evie braced herself, gritted her teeth and felt her hands curl into fists as everything seemed suddenly to slow down in front of her. As she watched, she saw Raffy run towards her then lunge at the dog, forcing it off the path into the marshlands. The dog opened its mouth and tried to jump at him, but its back legs were sinking – just as Raffy's were. He caught Evie staring at him and started to scramble. 'I'll be fine,' he shouted. 'You go. Run for it!'

But Evie wouldn't go. Instead she ran back down the path towards him, took off her waterproof and threw it out across the marsh, holding on to one arm so Raffy could grab the other. It was still a few feet away from him; resolutely he moved towards it, each step seeming to drag him lower. 'Raffy,' Evie screamed. 'Raffy!'

He grabbed at the arm, once, twice, and finally captured it in his hands. Evie lay down on the path, holding the waterproof in both hands, pulling with all the strength she could muster. Twice Raffy's head disappeared beneath the swamp, twice she cried out his name, and twice she saw him reappear, his eyes full of fear, his teeth gritted with determination. And then, finally, he was there at the path, pulling himself up, a vile stench covering him from top to toe.

The back door of the shack opened again; this time a man appeared, grey and grizzled, something in his hand. A rifle. Evie recognised it from books she'd seen, pictures that had been handed around at school to show them the extent of human evil before the City. They'd been told that no guns existed within the City walls. And yet . . .

'Come on,' Raffy said, seeing the rifle too, and pulling Evie towards him. 'Quick.'

They started to run; then fell as a sound louder

than anything Evie had heard before, louder than thunder or lightning, rang out.

'You okay?' Raffy whispered.

'I'm okay,' she replied.

'Stay down. We'll crawl until we're out of sight.'

Evie nodded and followed Raffy, crawling on her belly as shots rang out behind her; eventually the man appeared to give up and they stood again, running for their lives.

'The gate,' Raffy said, after what felt like an hour but had probably been mere minutes. 'It's here. Lucas was right.'

Evie saw it appear before her like an angel, like all her wishes coming true at once. A huge, metal gate with spikes at the top and bottom and sticking out horizontally all over. On the left hand side there was a lock. Tentatively she took out her key and handed it to Raffy,

'You do it,' she said, not trusting herself.

Raffy took the key, put it in the lock and turned it. Evie didn't know what she expected – another shot, perhaps, or an army to appear. Something. But instead, the gate quietly opened; on the other side was a grey, flat barren land.

'You're really sure you want to leave the City?' Raffy asked her then. She looked at him – at his matted hair, his swamp-covered face, his shivering body, his soulful eyes. And suddenly she wasn't afraid any more, because what was there to fear? They were leaving behind the place that would have Raffy dead, that had lied to her about everything.

'I'm sure,' she whispered.

Raffy smiled, his eyes crinkling, and he took her hand; they walked through the gate together, then closed it again behind them.

'Now what?' Raffy asked, leaning back against it, surveying the landscape ahead.

'Now we run,' replied Evie. 'Now we run and we don't stop.'

11

Raffy stirred and opened his eyes. Then he stretched, stood up. 'Did you sleep?'

Evie shrugged her shoulders half-heartedly. She hadn't slept a wink, but didn't want to say so. It had been light – too light even in the cave that they'd found. And strange noises had whistled around them, sounds that made Evie tense up with fear and she'd longed to wriggle nearer to Raffy, to feel his body close to hers, for comfort, protection. But there was no comfort to be found with Raffy, just anger and sarcasm.

'So what now?' he asked, looking down at her insolently. 'Run some more? Stay here and wait to be ravaged by wild animals? What did Lucas say? Or did he not plan this far ahead?'

Evie closed her eyes and forced the tears pricking at them to recede. She'd hoped that sleep might help, that Raffy might be calmer. But if anything he seemed more angry. She was sick of fighting. They'd fought ever since leaving the City – over whether they were heading north or not, whether Lucas had told them to escape just to get rid of them, over how much water they should drink. And then, slowly, the sun had started to rise and they'd argued over whether they should run some more or find somewhere to hide. Eventually Evie had won and they started to look for somewhere they could rest, somewhere they would be safe until night fell again. But they had chosen this cave in silence, had eaten and drunk in silence; Raffy had barely looked at her before announcing that they should sleep and curling up with his back to her.

The land they had travelled through had been strange and horrible, like a fevered dream; buildings that had been taken over by trees, roads that had crumbled, huge areas of grey, lifeless land that seemed to stretch out indefinitely, and then more fallen buildings. Had people lived here? Had they raised children, gone to work, lived, unaware that annihilation lay around the corner? Had they fled before the Horrors started or did the bombs take them by surprise? These were the questions that Evie had asked her teachers at school; these were the questions that had plagued her. But she'd never been given answers; the teachers were unable or unwilling to respond. The people had brought the Horrors on themselves, they'd told her. The people had been corrupted by their amygdalas; violence, selfishness and pride held sway over everyone. Evil was a way of life for them.

'He just said to keep going north,' Evie answered quietly. She opened her eyes and saw Raffy staring down at her; as she looked at him she saw his eyes soften slightly.

'Hungry?'

She nodded.

'Me too. Let's eat. Then I think we should get going.'

She was tempted to caution Raffy, to remind him that they had so little food they needed to ration themselves, but she stopped herself. She was tired of conflict. This new world was harsh and empty enough as it was; she could not contemplate more loneliness than she felt already.

Raffy opened his bag and threw her some bread and cheese which she started to eat half-heartedly, then found herself wolfing down as hunger got the better of her. But she eyed Raffy cautiously as she ate. All their lives they had longed to be together; now they were and they could barely talk to each other. Was this what the world outside the City would always be like?

'Should we head for the other City?' she asked eventually. 'The place that was communicating with the System?'

Raffy finished eating, got a bottle of water out of his bag and took a swig. Then he stood up. 'So you believe me now?' he asked. 'Well, don't. Lucas made it clear that I was wrong. It was a glitch, that's all.'

Evie shook her head. 'He told me he said that to protect you. So you wouldn't tell people. He told me it was a communication device. He said it was his fault you found it.' She met Raffy's eyes and stopped talking; he had heard the warmth in her voice and his expression was hostile. 'That's what he told me, anyway,' she said abruptly. 'When he asked me to help you escape.'

'Then it must be true,' he said again, looking away. He took another swig of water from the bottle, then stood up. 'Look,' he said, packing the bag. 'We can't think about the other place. Not now. We've got to get as far away from the City as we can. They're going to be looking for us. And we need to avoid the Evils. And find food, water, shelter. I think that's probably enough to be getting along with, don't you?'

He was barely looking at her; it was as though she was the last thing he wanted to see.

'But . . .' Evie's face twisted involuntarily. She knew he was right. But she didn't want to hear it. She wanted to run towards something, not away. She wanted answers; she wanted to vent her rage at the City and to find the other place. The place that she had come from.

'But what?' Raffy sighed impatiently.

'But we'll look for the other City when we're sure we're safe? Lucas said to head north, and I'm sure that's because—'

'Lucas says a lot of things,' Raffy interrupted angrily. 'But Lucas isn't here now. I'm going this way. Are you coming?'

He started to walk towards the mouth of the cave and for a few moments, Evie watched him go. She was on her own. She was on her own in the middle of a desolate nowhere. She was tired, she was hungry, and Raffy was angry with her for saving his life.

'You know that K stands for Killable?' she shouted suddenly. 'You know that they were going to let the Evils kill you? If I hadn't helped you to escape. If Lucas hadn't helped you.'

Raffy stopped and turned around. 'Killable?'

'Yes, Killable,' Evie said, running to catch up with him. 'K's aren't reconditioned,' she said breathlessly. 'They're left outside the City walls for the Evils to kill. They eat them. Like savages.'

'And my brother told you that, did he?' Raffy asked, his voice still defiant but a look of something close to fear crossing his face.

'He told me that he kept you locked up so no one could talk to you. He tried to tell them that you were delusional, that you'd made up all that stuff about the communication device. He said he was trying to protect you.'

'Like he tried to protect my father?' Raffy asked. 'Evie, he called the police guard. He called them on our own father. Our father was a K. So you're saying he was stuck outside the City walls? That Lucas knew?' He bit his lip and looked away, wiping his nose with his sleeve.

Evie looked down. Could Lucas have done such a thing? Was Raffy right about him after all? No. She steeled herself. No, she couldn't believe that. 'Maybe he did, Raffy. I don't know. But he still helped us escape. He stopped the Evils from killing you. And he . . . he . . .'

'He what?' Raffy asked sarcastically.

'He told me that my parents aren't my parents,' Evie said, her voice cracking as a lump appeared in the back of her throat. 'He said that I was brought to the City. He said they killed my real parents.'

'What?' Raffy froze.

'He said they let people in who had children, then took them away and . . . and . . .'

Raffy shook his head; his eyes were flickering as though he was processing information. Then he grabbed her shoulders. 'Your dream. Your dream!'

Evie nodded, tears cascading down her cheeks. Tears of grief, exhaustion, fear and betrayal. 'They kept telling me I had to fight my dreams. And then they said I was dreaming about the City. The Brother knew – he knew all along. And Lucas told me. Why would he tell me the truth if he wasn't trying to help somehow? Maybe my parents came from this other City. Can't you see we have to go there?'

Raffy stared at her for a few seconds and then pulled her towards him, wrapping his arms around her, his sobs merging with hers as they clung to each other.

When he released her, she looked up to see that his eyes were full of fire, and the hopelessness that had taken up residency had finally been evicted. 'We'll find the other place,' he promised her. 'We'll find it. I promise you. I'm sorry, Evie. I'm so sorry.'

Evie smiled through her tears. 'I'm sorry too,' she managed to say. 'I'm sorry too.'

Raffy kissed her tenderly. 'We've got each other, and that's all that matters. Right?'

Evie looked at him, at the boy she had loved for

so long, her best friend, her confidant, and she nodded. And even though as Raffy pulled her towards him once more her mind filled with images of Lucas, of the pain in his eyes and the desperation in his face, she forced them out again, burying the guilt in her heart.

'Come on, then,' Raffy said, shooting her a smile. 'It's getting dark. Time to get moving.'

They made their way out of the cave, back out to the eerie, forgotten landscape. They ran, then walked to catch their breath, then ran again, across cracked, dry earth, through ceilingless warehouses, down dirt paths that they realised had once been pavements.

'Wait,' Evie said suddenly as she saw something in front of her. She stopped, bent down and pulled it out of the earth.

'What is it?' Raffy asked.

'It's a toy,' Evie replied, turning it over in her hands. A perfect form of a baby girl, made from plastic, a substance rarely found within the City walls. Only old things were made of plastic and old things were frowned on because they were the things of the evil people, because plastic was not manufactured in the City, and because only new, City-made things were truly good as they encouraged industry and productivity and all the good things that made the City so wonderful. As Evie inspected the doll she could hear the scorn of the

Brother, of her mother, ridiculing it, calling it a toy of evil, telling her that it would corrupt her. Toys weren't allowed in the City; the only ones she'd seen were from the Old World, found occasionally and played with before being confiscated by teachers or anxious parents. But she wasn't in the City now.

'I'm going to keep it,' she said.

'Seriously?' Raffy screwed up his face into an incredulous frown. 'It's dirty. And it's a child's toy.'

'I was a child once,' Evie said quietly. 'It shouldn't be left here on its own.'

'Well, if you really want to keep it, I'll put it in my bag,' Raffy said, then stopped as they heard something. A rustle.

They looked at each other in alarm. There was no sign of anyone, but that didn't mean they weren't in danger.

'Let's go,' whispered Raffy and they started to move, as quietly as they could, Evie hardly daring to breathe as she willed her feet to land lightly in front of her.

As they ran, a wooded area appeared in front of them and Raffy grabbed her hand, pulling her towards it. 'This way. Through the trees,' he panted, and as they ran between them, Evie was taken aback by the majesty of these trees, bigger than she had ever imagined they could be, so high it was as though they could touch the moon itself. Their huge trunks emerged from a ground knotted with weeds and brambles that clawed at her ankles and stung her flesh. But she barely noticed the pain, such was her wonder at this overgrown place, this place of secrets, of something stronger than anything the City could achieve. They ran until they could run no further, and could hear nothing but a gentle breeze shaking the branches.

'Okay,' Raffy said, leaning over to catch his breath. 'We should stay here.'

'Do you think it was the police guard?' Evie asked anxiously.

Raffy shook his head but she could see the fear in his eyes. 'It was probably nothing,' he said, obviously doing his best to sound relaxed and confident. 'But if it was the police guard then this is the best place to hide from them. We can climb up the trees if we have to.'

Evie nodded cautiously. 'And if it wasn't the police guard?'

Raffy met her eyes; they both knew that the alternative was just as horrifying. The Evils.

'I don't think it was anyone,' Raffy said with a shrug that belied the tension in the air. 'But no one will find us here. Look, there's a tiny stream so we know there's water. We can find shelter and food.'

'Food?' Evie looked around doubtfully; all she could see were trees and brambles.

'Berries.' Raffy declared confidently. 'And there will probably be rabbits. Birds. I can catch some.'

Evie digested this, her brow furrowing. 'How will we . . . eat them?' she asked eventually.

Raffy laughed. 'You'll have to kill them,' he said, his eyes glinting. 'Then you'll cook them. It's only fair, if I catch them.'

Evie stared at him in alarm. 'I can't kill a rabbit,' she said, edging backwards. 'I can't. I wouldn't know how to. I . . .'

He laughed again and grabbed her playfully. 'You've never skinned a rabbit?'

Evie shook her head. They had rabbit in the City, but that rabbit was killed in the farming district; by the time Evie saw it, it was always diced and sold in a bag. Not covered in fur with a head and eyes and . . .

'Nor me,' Raffy grinned. 'No idea how to catch one, either. To be honest, I'm not sure they even live in places like this. I was just, you know, trying to impress you. Let's focus on berries for the time being, shall we?'

'Idiot,' Evie laughed. Although as she watched Raffy crawl around looking for berries, it occurred to her that whilst it was a relief she wouldn't be killing a wild animal later, their chances of survival out here were looking pretty slim.

She walked towards him, trying not to wince every time brambles stung her ankles or scratched her arms. 'Have you found something?'

'Blackberries,' Raffy said, holding one up. 'Not quite ripe yet, but I think they're edible.'

Evie reached out to take it from him, but as she did so she felt something grab her around the ankle, hurling her up in the air, tangled into a net, ten feet from the ground. Raffy ran towards her but he too was immediately swept up into a net, hanging from the tree above where they had stood.

Seconds later, men appeared beneath them and the nets were cut down. Paralysed with fear, Evie watched in agonising silence as she and Raffy were grabbed, their mouths covered with the men's hands, and dragged away.

12

She is with Raffy; they are holding each other, clinging to each other, because they know that people are trying to pull them apart. 'You love me,' he whispers. 'Only me.' And she nods fervently because she knows that it is the truth, she knows that they are bound together, that there is something between them that cannot be broken, that it has always been Raffy and her, and it always will be. And then it becomes cold and the hairs on her arms stand upright. She knows that Raffy feels it too because he stiffens and looks around, and suddenly they are there, surrounding them; they are like ghosts, ominous floating creatures, but she knows immediately who they are. She knows that they are Evils, that they have come for them and they have to run . . . And they are running, but they can't run fast enough, and as her heels hit the ground she is leaping into the air, up into the clouds, but it is not enough, it will never be enough. Evie stumbles; she is on the ground. Raffy turns and she can see the fear in his face, and even as he runs towards her she knows it is too late. He is shouting that there has been a mistake, that it is all a mistake, and then he is gone, he has been replaced by Lucas, who is looking deep into her eyes and telling her that she has to be strong, that she has to be brave, that he is depending on her. He puts his arms behind her head and lifts it gently, then he leans down and she sees the pain and anguish in his eyes, sees that he needs her. Her match. Lucas. And she can't help herself as his lips find hers, and he is kissing her, and she feels safe, complete, everything suddenly makes sense. But she closes her eyes and when she opens them again he is gone and she is alone and it is very cold . . .

Evie woke to find herself shivering, a man staring at her, just a few inches away. Her head hurt in a way it had never hurt before. She tried to move, but her ankles and wrists were tied together. Her stomach clenched as she remembered the trap and the strong hands pinning her down, Raffy fighting and losing, being thrown down on the floor face first. She remembered their bags being ransacked, questions shouted at them, demands for information. She remembered being made to walk for hours until she could walk no further; remembered being offered a drink of water, accepting it and collapsing on the ground. She could remember nothing else; she had no idea how she'd arrived in this cold, dark place. She could smell the man's breath, sweet and acrid at the same time, like the Gathering welcome drink, like bonfires, like . . .

'So you're awake. Well, that's good,' he said. 'Sorry about the pain. Had to remove your chips. Just a precautionary measure.'

Evie stared at the man apprehensively. She didn't know what he was talking about. She just knew that he was one of the men who had cut her and Raffy down. He had no hair on his crown; the rest of his hair was closely cropped and silver-grey. His face was lined with creases and dirt; it was nut brown from the sun. He wore a vest; no shirt. In his hand was a gun. Its metal glinted at her menacingly.

He wasn't civilised, she realised with a thud. He was an Evil. He was an Evil and he was going to murder them.

She knew this deep in her gut. She also knew this meant that in all likeliness she would be dead within hours.

The man studied her for a few seconds, then

laughed, putting the gun in his back pocket. 'Don't worry, I'm not going to kill you. If I was, I'd have done it by now. I do want to know who you are, though, and what you were doing on City land.'

'City land?' Evie asked uncertainly. 'We weren't . . .'

'Oh, yes, you were.' The man smiled. 'Thought the land outside the City belonged to no one? They patrol it. Don't like anyone coming too close. And you were close.'

Evie's eyes darted around, searching for Raffy, but he was nowhere to be seen. Had he escaped? Were they torturing him? Had they killed him already? She studied the man, looking at his face, searching for signs of an amygdala that was directing his every move and corrupting his every thought.

'Looking for your boyfriend? He's behind me.'

The man shifted slightly and Evie could see what looked like a pile of clothes on the floor on the other side of the room. It wasn't moving. Her mouth fell open.

'He's alive,' the man said, 'if that's what you're worried about.'

Evie said nothing. The man seemed to be reading her mind and she didn't like it.

'So,' the man continued conversationally, as though this were normal, as though she hadn't been captured, brought to this strange place, then tied up like an animal. 'Who are you? Why are you here?'

Evie looked at him angrily. The ropes were digging into her wrists and ankles; she willed them to loosen, willed this evil man to leave her so that she might wake Raffy and they could work out some way of escaping. Then, suddenly, out of the corner of her eye, she saw something move; the pile of blankets that was Raffy jumped up and hurled itself at the man, pulling him backwards. Evie jumped up to help him but immediately fell down again as the ropes cut at her skin.

The man cried out; seconds later, another man appeared, an ugly squat man with arms that bulged with muscle; he dragged Raffy away, punching him in the stomach and throwing him back to the floor.

'So that's how it's going to be,' the first man said through gritted teeth, spitting some blood onto the floor. He stood up and looked at Raffy in disgust.

'Talk some sense into him,' he said to Evie, then he and the other man walked out, closing the door behind them.

Immediately Evie shuffled along the floor towards Raffy, who was lying on his back, his face covered in blood. She couldn't touch him, couldn't clean him up; she could only look down at him, her eyes suddenly filling with tears because this wasn't supposed to happen, because they had come so close to escaping, to finally being free.

'Raffy. Raffy, are you okay?' she asked, blinking furiously because she was unable to wipe her tears away.

'I'm fine.' Raffy sat up and pressed his forehead to Evie's, then pulled away and looked around. His eyes were flashing, his jaw set in an angry grimace. 'I nearly had him.'

'I know,' Evie said, nodding violently to prove to him that she knew, that she understood. 'But they're Evils, Raffy. They're not human. Not like us.'

Raffy pulled a face. 'My head,' he muttered. 'It hurts. What is this place, anyway?'

They looked around properly; Evie could see that they were in a large, high-ceilinged room with grey walls, a concrete floor and not much else. It was bigger than any room Evie had ever been in, even the Meeting House. Light had begun to filter in through grimy windows, revealing half-crumbling walls, large patches of damp and plants growing through cracks and several broken windows. At either end was a heavy door, which she was fairly sure would both be locked. There was no furniture in the room, just the thin mattresses that they'd slept on and their musty-smelling blankets.

'I don't know,' she said. 'It looks old.'

Raffy shifted slightly, wincing at the pain. 'Pre-City,' he concluded. 'Those men didn't build this.' He looked around in awe. 'Not bad for a bunch of evil people, huh?' he said.

Evie didn't know what to say. She knew that humans with amygdalas were capable of great things as well as terrible ones; that humanity had made huge achievements with their amygdalas intact. But it still scared her, still made her uncomfortable that the people who built this hall, the people waiting outside, had evil in their brains which continually looked for ways to corrupt them.

'What do you think they're going to do to us?' she asked, then immediately regretted it when she saw Raffy's expression darken.

'I should have seen the trap,' he said. 'I should have—'

'It was my fault we got caught,' Evie said quickly. 'It doesn't matter anyway. What matters is what happens next.'

'What happens next is that we wait for them to kill us,' Raffy said bitterly. He looked around the room again. Then his expression brightened slightly. 'We could climb out of those windows,' he said. 'Untie ourselves and I'll help you up, then—'

'They're ten feet up the wall,' Evie retorted. 'We'd

need a ladder. And they'd probably be waiting for us anyway.'

'You got any better ideas?' Raffy asked irritably. 'Is waiting to die any better?'

Evie didn't get a chance to respond; as Raffy finished his sentence, the door swung open again. 'Had some time to come to your senses?' It was the same man as before; he strode in purposefully and grabbed Raffy by the shoulders. The other, squat man came into the room carrying a wooden chair, onto which he thrust Raffy roughly. Then the squat man grabbed Evie and pulled her upright, then dragged her along the floor until she was standing facing Raffy, just a few feet away.

'So,' the original man, the one with the close-cut hair and the balding crown, said, a little smile playing on his lips. 'You' – he pointed at Evie – 'are going to talk, otherwise he' – he pointed at Raffy – 'is going to be in quite a lot of pain. My friend here has a good right hook. If you don't want him making contact with your friend's face, you'll tell me who you are and what you're doing here. Okay?'

Evie started to shake. She didn't know what a right hook was but she knew that they were going to hurt Raffy and she couldn't bear it. But worse than that was the realisation that the Brother was right, that the world outside the City was a brutal, disgusting place where humans were savages, where everyone was led by their baser instincts. And this new world was now her world. 'Tell them nothing,' Raffy said defiantly; moments later the man next to him delivered a blow to his head so hard that Raffy appeared to lose consciousness for a few seconds. Evie cried out in alarm.

'Stop. Please stop,' she begged, trembling.

'We'll stop when you talk,' the man said with a little shrug. 'So, again?' he said to his companion, who pulled his fist back.

'No,' Evie screamed, and the first man raised his hand to halt the punch. 'No. You can't. I know you're Evils but can't you see that this is wrong? You have to stop. You have to . . .' She tried to hobble forward to Raffy but the man stopped her.

'Evils?' he asked, his eyebrow arching. 'You think that we're Evils?' He laughed.

'I know you are,' Evie said quietly. 'Only Evils live outside the City. Only Evils would do this.'

The man laughed again. 'Trust me, Evils couldn't do this. All right, Angel. Hit the boy again.'

The second man hit Raffy again and blood started to pour from his nose.

'You . . . evil man,' Evie shrieked, wishing her

184

vocabulary had more insults in it, more ways to express her hatred.

The man sighed. 'Evil. Sure. Just tell me what you're doing here. Is it really that hard? Your friend here won't thank you for staying silent, I can promise you that.'

Evie looked over at Raffy who spat something onto the floor – it looked like a tooth. His eyes were unfocused but he managed to shake his head. Evie saw the man draw his fist back again; she knew she had to do something, that Raffy couldn't take any more even if he would never admit it. And she knew that she couldn't reason with evil; couldn't appeal to their better natures.

'Wait,' she said. 'Please wait.'

'You tell me who sent you, and what you're here to find out,' the man said. 'Then we stop. That's the deal.'

'No one sent us,' Evie said angrily. Raffy's face was covered in blood; she knew that the man would kill him if he carried on hitting him. 'We escaped from the City.'

'You escaped.' The first man sighed. 'Yeah, I'm sorry, but that's not good enough.' He moved towards Raffy and this time it was he who swung at him.

'No!' Evie screamed. 'You said you'd stop if I told you why we're here.'

'You lied,' the man said. 'No one escapes from the City. Tell us the truth and then we'll stop.'

Evie said nothing. The man clicked his fingers and the other man left Raffy's side, grabbing her instead. 'Let's see if your friend will talk to save you,' he said as the second pulled his fist back yet again. Evie braced herself; she had never been hit before, had never known such acute, physical fear, but she was determined not to show it.

'No!' Raffy roared. 'You get your hands off her. We did escape,' he thundered. The man's fist stopped just short of her face; she could smell the dirt on his hands. 'Out of the East Gate. Her father was a key holder. She took his key.'

'She took his key, did she?' the first man asked; the other man's fist stayed where it was, so close to Evie she had to close her eyes. 'Okay then. Let's say you're telling the truth. Tell me this – why would two nice young people like you want to escape from the City? I mean, it's not exactly a holiday camp out here, is it now?'

'Because otherwise they were going to kill me,' Raffy seethed. Evie was suddenly released from the second man's grip; disoriented, she sank to the floor before she could find her balance. 'Because they made me a K.'

'You? You're a Killable? Really?' The man was looking at Raffy incredulously.

Raffy glanced over at Evie, then back at the man. She knew he was thinking the same thing she was, that this man knew that K stood for Killable.

'Oh, yeah. I know all about Killables,' said the man, catching their expressions. 'But what I'd like to know is why a boy like you was made a K. What *could* you have done?' He peered at Raffy as though inspecting a calf; prodding his shoulder, examining his face.

'Because I found something on the System and they seemed to think I put it there.'

The man started; his brow furrowed as he turned around and took a few steps, apparently deep in thought. Then he walked back over to Raffy and leant down, his face just centimetres from his. 'You found something in the System? What? What did you find?'

'I dunno,' Raffy said through gritted teeth. 'Something just wasn't working properly.'

The man started to pace up and down. 'You know the System?'

Raffy nodded. 'Kind of. I was an operator.'

The man breathed out. 'Trouble is, this still isn't making sense to me. You say you were made a K. So how come you weren't taken away and imprisoned? How could you leave?'

'Because I wasn't a K when I left. I escaped the night before,' Raffy said heavily.

The man shook his head. 'No,' he said. 'No. And here is how I know you're lying. This is why my friend Angel here is going to have to hurt that girlfriend of yours unless you start telling me the truth. Because, my friend, what you're telling me is impossible. No one knows a System change in advance. No one.'

The squat man began to approach Evie threateningly and she shrank back. Raffy noticed the movement. 'Wait,' he said immediately, his voice urgent. 'Wait. My brother told me about the change. He told me I had to escape.'

'Your brother,' the man said. 'And your brother knew because . . . ?'

'I don't know,' Raffy said helplessly. 'Because he's high up in the government.'

The squat man stopped moving. 'So let me get this straight,' the first man said. 'You're made a K because you find something on the System, your brother is high up in the government and he risks his career to help you and your girlfriend escape? Doesn't sound very City to me. The System can't be challenged, can it?'

Raffy didn't say anything; the man shrugged, then swung round to face Evie. 'And you just left with him? You were happy to leave the City just like that?'

Evie nodded anxiously. 'I had to leave,' she said. 'I'd have been made a K next.'

'And you know that because?'

'Because I took the key from my father's safe.'

'Because you took the key from your father's safe,' the man said, smiling. 'Of course you did. See, Angel? It all makes sense.'

The squat man grunted and the first man turned back to Raffy. 'Makes perfect sense for a cock and bull story created by the City. You're here to spy on us, aren't you? Aren't you?'

'No,' Raffy scowled. 'I hate the City. I'd never spy for them. Just let us go.'

'Go where?' the man asked. 'Nowhere to go, son. Not now you're outside the City.'

'There is, as it happens,' Raffy said under his breath.

'Oh there is, is there?' The man swooped down so that his face was just inches from Raffy's. 'And what is this place?'

'Another City,' Evie said suddenly. 'There's another City.'

'Another City, you say?' The man walked over to her and chuckled. 'And you're sure about that, little lady?'

'Yes,' Evie said defiantly. 'Because Raffy's father discovered it. He was communicating with it. Raffy found the communication device. That's why he was made a K. That's why we're here. So please, just let us go. We're not spies. We're not anything.'

The man stared at her for a few seconds. Then he stared at Raffy. 'Let you go?' he said eventually. 'We let you go and you're dead in a day. No, my friends, we won't let you go. But don't worry. We'll look after you. Won't we, Angel?'

The man who had hit Raffy nodded silently. Evie could not imagine a more inappropriate name for someone. Angels were beautiful mythical creatures from the Old World; people turned to angels to save them when they were in trouble. Although, as she'd learnt at school, that was the folly of humans; they turned to non-existent creatures to save them instead of real-ising that they could save themselves. But even so, she couldn't imagine anyone turning to this angry, violent man to save them.

'My name's Linus.' The first man held out his hand to Raffy, who stared at it dubiously. 'I'm sorry, I forgot,' Linus said with a little smile. He reached under his shirt and pulled out a knife. Raffy eyed it cautiously and held his hands out behind him for Linus to cut away the rope. Angel, meanwhile, cut the ropes that tied Evie. Slowly, painfully, she pulled herself up off the floor. Her legs ached. Her whole body was stiff and bruised. Raffy stood too; Angel left briefly then returned with a wet cloth which Raffy used to clean his face. Then Angel nodded at Linus and disappeared again.

'Welcome to our temporary home,' announced Linus, holding out his hand to Evie. 'So temporary we're leaving today. You'll need some better clothes. And some food. We've got a long way to walk today. You're going to need your energy.'

'Why?' Raffy asked sullenly. 'Where are you taking us now?'

'Wait and see,' Linus answered. 'You'll find out soon enough.'

13

They were led out of the room and through a second, ceilingless room, to what had probably at one time been a road. From the outside Evie could see that the place they'd been in must have been quite wonderful once, with ornate pillars reaching skywards and honey-coloured stonework. She gazed back at it in wonderment; she had never seen anything like it, could not comprehend how a world full of evil could produce something so beautiful. Beyond it lay nothing; a road that stretched into nothingness, scrambled plants weaving through rubble.

'You like it? Used to be the law courts once,' Linus said, looking around, his clear blue eyes glistening. 'Then again you probably don't know much about the law, do you?'

He was looking at Evie and she reddened awkwardly. 'No,' she said eventually. 'What is it?'

'Law?' He chuckled; as his smile broadened lines appeared from his eyes right down to his mouth, deep lines that gave his face such warmth and depth that Evie realised she wasn't afraid of him any more. 'Law is what enables civilisation. Law is what stops society descending into a scrum of vengeance and crime.'

Evie frowned. 'It's like the New Baptism?' she asked.

'The New Baptism?' Linus froze, the warmth disappearing from his face. 'You think that protects you?' He sighed, stopped walking and put his hands on her shoulders. 'Law is nothing to do with the New Baptism. Law is a system of rules and principles whereby no one can be accused and punished for something without having the opportunity to defend themselves. Its overarching principles are to make society fair and just for all. The law is . . . is . . .' He seemed to think for a moment. 'Is something that should never be used in the same sentence as the New Baptism, unless the word 'against' is included. Do I make myself clear?'

'Yes,' Evie said anxiously, even though it wasn't clear at all, even though she had no idea what he was talking about. All she knew was that her fear had returned, that she had angered Linus, upset him. And she didn't want to upset him. She wanted him to like her. She knew that Raffy didn't trust him – she could see that from the way he didn't take his eyes off him

– but she wanted Linus on side, wanted to see his laughter lines again. Because if Linus knew about the City, he might know more. He might know about the people who came to the City all those years ago. He might know about her real parents.

'Good,' he said gruffly. 'Okay, come on. This way.' He herded them around the corner and into another building; but once inside they were outside again – the building was only a façade. Camped on the grass within were three tents, and sitting between them was a group of five people, one of whom Evie immediately recognised as Angel. He gave her a little wave as they approached; Evie looked away quickly and tried to stop her shoulders from tensing with fear.

Linus noticed. 'Angel's a good man,' he said, putting his hand on Evie's shoulder as they stepped past one of the tents. 'He's one of my best. Don't worry about him, he'll never hurt you so long as you don't become our enemy.'

Raffy tugged Evie away from him so that Linus's hand fell back down to his side. 'And how are we supposed to know if we're your enemy or not?' he asked, his jaw set angrily. 'We don't know who you are. You say you're not Evils, but why else did you capture us and torture us?'

'All in good time.' Linus smiled. 'Sit down. Have some food.'

He sat down cross-legged next to an auburn-haired woman who immediately started to open various containers in front of her and spoon what Evie could only imagine was food onto three paper plates. Then she handed them to Linus one at a time; he handed one to Raffy, one to Evie and the other he kept for himself. 'Eat,' he said, motioning with his head. 'Eat and then we'll talk.'

Tentatively, Evie looked down at the food. A roll. Something green. Something white. Nothing was iden-tifiable, nothing was recognisable from the food they ate in the City. In the City, food was simple and unadorned. Boiled, grilled, cooked with a little oil if absolutely necessary. Bread and oats formed the bulk of the diet, with milk and potatoes propping them up. The plate in front of her, on the other hand, was full of colour; she thought she could see carrots, but they were cut small, mingled with something else, maybe onion, with a red liquid covering them. It could be poison, she knew that, but it smelt delicious and she was so hungry that her stomach felt like it might touch the back of her spine.

'Eat,' Linus said again, more gently this time. 'You'll enjoy it – Martha here is an incredible cook.' He smiled at the woman to his left, who flushed in response to the praise. 'Swap plates with me if you're worried we're planning to poison you,' he went on, offering her his dish, his eyes twinkling. Evie started slightly; she was unnerved by the way Linus always seemed to know exactly what she was thinking.

'That won't be necessary,' Raffy interjected. He reached his hand out and squeezed Evie's wrist. 'We'll both eat together.' He shot her a little smile, a smile that said they wouldn't just eat together; they were in this together, they'd get through it together, it was the two of them, just like it was in their tree: laughing, talking, sharing secrets and fears. Evie immediately picked up the bread roll and stuffed it into her mouth, and she had to stop herself from squealing in delight because it was the most delicious thing she'd ever tasted.

'Try the avocado,' Linus said, pointing at a green substance smeared over her plate. 'Dip the bread.'

She did as he suggested; she had never eaten avocado before. And it was heavenly, the texture more decadent than anything she had ever tasted.

'It's good,' she breathed as she ate and Linus smiled, and winked at Martha. They watched as Evie devoured the bread and avocado and allowed Martha to heap more onto her plate. She smiled at Raffy; she needed to share her pleasure with him. But he was looking to his side and she noticed something that she hadn't seen before. An angry red line, new blood, just next to his left temple. She hadn't noticed it before because his whole face had been spattered with blood, but his scar, his amygdala scar, looked as though it had been re-opened. And it was in the same place that she had felt such excruciating pain – pain that now seemed to have gone. What had they done to her and Raffy? She touched her own temple, felt the slightly soft indent, something scratchy that felt like stitches. And she put her plate down, because her heart was thudding in her chest and she had suddenly lost her appetite.

'What did you mean about a chip?' she asked, her voice catching slightly. 'Before, when we woke up?'

Linus smiled; his mouth was full of food. 'I thought we were eating,' he said.

Evie tried to swallow, but there was no saliva in her mouth now. She couldn't have eaten if she'd wanted to. She turned to Linus again. 'Can't we eat and talk at the same time?' she asked quietly.

This time Linus laughed. 'I can see why you left the City,' he said. 'I can't imagine you got on too well there if you were this demanding all the time.'

Evie shook her head. 'I don't want to talk about the City.'

'Well in that case, I'll talk,' replied Linus with a

little shrug. He put his plate down in front of him. 'Probably not a bad idea anyway; we're going to have to get going soon.'

'Get going where?' Raffy asked.

'Ah,' Linus said. 'Well, that's the question, isn't it? Not one I'm going to answer, if you'll forgive me. Let's just say we're going back to Base Camp.'

'Base Camp?' Evie exchanged a glance with Raffy. 'What's that?'

'That,' Linus said, 'is where we come from. Where our people live.'

'The other City?' Evie asked cautiously, the hairs on the back of her neck pricking up.

Linus looked at her, held her gaze for a few seconds, then turned his head slightly. 'Not exactly a City, no,' he said.

'So then what is it like?' Raffy asked, leaning forward, watching Linus carefully.

'It's . . .' Linus looked thoughtful for a few moments, then he pulled a face. 'It's a work in progress,' he declared.

Raffy put his plate down too. 'You said we were going to talk,' he said.

'We are talking,' replied Linus, looking enquiringly at Raffy.

'No, we're not. You're not telling us anything. How

do you know about the City? What did you mean when you said you removed our chips? What chips? Who are you? Where do you come from? Why did you trap us and why are you keeping us now? Why aren't you killing us, or letting us go? Tell us.' Raffy's voice was low, his eyes intense. Evie could see every muscle in his neck, along his arms, flexed ready to spring.

Linus saw too; Evie thought she could glimpse something approaching respect in his eyes. Or maybe she'd imagined it; maybe she'd looked for it, created it. Either way, she stared at Linus with all the determination she could muster because she needed him to answer, because they deserved an answer – because each question that she formulated only led to others, and her brain was hurting with all the uncertainties that were crowding it.

Linus sat back. His eyes were bright with amusement, as though this were a game, as though he was planning his next move. And then he leant forward.

'The chip I told you about,' he said, looking from Evie to Raffy and back again, 'is an implant that you both had in your heads. It's a tracking device. I took it out so that the City police guard couldn't follow you. Couldn't follow us.'

'An implant?' Evie's hand moved to her temple

again. She glanced at Raffy; he was doing the same, thinking the same thing – about the blood, the pain when they'd first been captured.

'Sorry, but I had to do it,' Linus said quietly. 'The water I gave you had painkillers in it. You should be feeling okay now.'

Evie moved closer to Raffy; she could feel herself getting hot. A chip? In her head? In Raffy's? Keeping track of them? But then the System would have known – about their meetings, about the tree. It would have known everything.

Raffy reached out his hand, took hers and squeezed it. Then he turned back to Linus. Evie could see from the way his jaw muscles were tightening that he was thinking the same as she was. 'You're lying,' he said, his voice tense. 'There are no implants in the City. No chips. There can't be. Otherwise how did we escape? Tell me what you were doing. Studying our brains? Why? What did you do?'

Linus exhaled loudly and leant back on his elbows. 'Studying your brains? Well, that might have been an interesting exercise, but I prefer not to study the brains of people who are alive. For some reason the brains don't seem to like it.'

He smiled at them for a moment, then sat forward, his expression suddenly serious. 'Listen to me,' he said, his voice soft but insistent. 'Everything you were told in the City, you have to forget.'

'Why should we?' Raffy asked crossly. 'When you're telling us nothing?'

'I'll tell you when it's time,' Linus said, standing up. 'I'll tell you everything when I think you're ready to hear it.'

'We're ready now,' seethed Raffy, standing up and blocking Linus's path. 'You said we were going to talk. So talk. Tell me something. Anything.'

'I told you about the chip,' Linus said in measured tones. 'And you don't believe me.'

'Because I know you're lying,' Raffy said, standing firm. 'Tell me something else. Tell me something true.'

Linus appeared to consider this. Then he shrugged. 'You asked me why we haven't killed the two of you.'

'So?' Raffy demanded. 'Tell us.'

'Because there's no need to,' Linus said, walking past him. 'Because if you carry on like this, you're going to kill yourselves.' He stopped, then turned and walked back towards Raffy until he was just centimetres away. 'You're not in the City now,' he said then, his voice low but forceful. 'The rules are different, but they still exist. And out here, they're our rules. For our protection. So think about that, will you?

'You'll find out what you need to know when you

need to know it and when I want to tell you. Until then, enjoy our hospitality, eat well and have a rest. In an hour, we're leaving. Your head pain will come back. Martha there has the painkillers you need. Keeping hydrated will aid your recovery. You'll get those things if you do as you're told. Your friend will get those things if she does as she's told – and she'll follow your lead, my friend, so think about that too. Think about all of this. I'll see you later.'

And with that, he left, back out through the building façade, leaving silence behind him.

Raffy picked up his plate again and started to eat, motioning for Evie to do likewise. Hesitantly, she followed suit.

'I'm glad you're eating,' Martha said, an enigmatic smile on her face, her voice soft and lyrical after Linus's gravelly tone. 'It must be difficult, being here. We all find it unsettling at first. But Linus is a good man. He has our best interests at heart.' Then she stood up and retreated into one of the tents; one by one the others retreated also until it was just Evie and Raffy alone on the grass.

'Best interests,' Raffy whispered sarcastically. 'I don't believe a word of it. There's something weird about this place. About Linus. We're not hanging around to find out what.'

Evie's eyes widened. 'We're not?' she whispered back.

'We're getting out tonight,' Raffy said, his eyes glinting. 'Linus is a liar. They all are. There's something they want from us, but they're not getting it. Pretend everything's okay. Then, when I give the signal, we run. Okay? But eat now. We may not eat again for a while.'

Evie nodded. Then they ate and when they couldn't eat any more, Raffy lay back and Evie nestled into his shoulder. And slowly, fearfully, but comforted by the sound of Raffy's breathing, she fell asleep.

'I see,' the Brother said, looking at his chief police guard, a squat and honest man who wore his baton proudly. No guns for his police guards, no weapons of evil. Sometimes the Brother found his own rules frustrating and restrictive; he longed for people who could see the world as it really was, who saw what had to be done but also saw the truth. The old man at the lodge with his gun and his dog knew what the world was really like, but he was also an alcoholic, a waster, a man who would do what was asked of him in return for a weekly supply of Gathering drink, a sweet fermented wine that helped everyone to be moved, spiritually. He was no companion. 'And there was no sign of them?'

'No sign, Brother,' the man said, his head hung low. 'We searched. We didn't stop searching until nightfall.'

'Very well,' replied the Brother. 'Thank you.'

He waited for the man to leave before allowing his head to fall backwards. Today had been a terrible day. First the discovery that the boy had escaped. Then that the girl had helped him. Her father had been ashen-faced at the news, her mother angry, screaming that she'd always known the girl had been wicked. And now the police guard had failed to find them, failed to track down two teenagers.

Had it been an accident or design? How could they have designed such a thing? Impossible. They couldn't have known what was in store for the boy. Not unless Lucas had told them. And that was impossible. It was . . .

He sighed loudly, then buzzed his assistant. 'Send Lucas to see me,' he barked, his tone shorter than he would have liked. 'Please,' he added, just in time.

'Yes, Brother. Of course.'

His hand fell off the buzzer and moved to his fore-head where it joined his right hand, the position they always took in moments of difficulty, of challenge.

'It is times such as this that make us,' he whispered to himself. 'It is in challenging times that we are able to rise to become our better selves. Our strongest selves.' He had said those words so many times to so many people, offered such solace, such hope. And yet all he felt was a seething resentment, an anger that seemed to consume him but in a lifeless, heavy way that left him gasping for air.

How had they known? How had they planned such an escape? How? How?

A knock at the door; the knock of his assistant. Gentle, unthreatening – a knock that he always appreciated.

'Send him in,' he called out; moments later Lucas appeared.

'Brother,' he said, his face level, unmoved.

'What have you learnt?' the Brother asked, trying and failing to keep the weariness out of his voice.

'I think they were planning this for a long time,' Lucas said gravely. 'The timing appears to have been a coincidence, a result of my brother's incarceration rather than the imminent label change. We know now that the girl and he used to meet. He knew the System better than we realised, had worked out a way of covering up their movements. I should have known that the girl was evil too – she was my match, Brother. I should have seen it. But I didn't. I believed her. I . . .'

He stopped briefly, composed himself. 'She must have come to the house in the night. I blame myself. I should have known, I should have kept watch.'

'You were not to know the lengths to which they would resort,' the Brother said, shaking his head. 'You were not to know that the evil within them ran so deep.'

'No,' Lucas said. 'But I should have anticipated the worst.'

The Brother nodded. 'Perhaps. What else. She took the key? How?'

'Her father insists that he did not show her the combination.'

'Then how?'

'Her mother says that she is devious, that she must have watched him.'

'Watched him when? The key has not been needed for many months.'

Lucas didn't say anything; he simply raised his eyebrows and his eyes said the rest.

'I see,' the Brother answered.

'Are we likely to find them?' Lucas asked.

The Brother shook his head. 'No. The police guard have exhausted their search. The likelihood is that they have been savaged by wild animals or killed by the Evils by now. I try to protect my flock, Lucas, but I cannot protect those who choose to leave.'

'No, Brother,' said Lucas. Not a hint of sadness, the Brother found himself thinking and a little shiver ran down his spine. Not a single tear for his own flesh and blood.

'Thank you, Lucas. That will be all.'

'Yes, Brother.' Lucas walked towards the door. Then he turned, briefly. 'The file on Raphael. On the glitch. Shall I close it now?'

The Brother nodded. It was no use now. Lucas opened the door. And then the Brother noticed something. Lucas's jaw was clenched. Not relaxed as it always was, not firm and strong, but clenched. Tightly.

'But send it to me,' pronounced the Brother thoughtfully. 'I would like to have it in this office, you understand.'

Lucas hesitated for a fraction of a second, enough to tell the Brother he had made the right decision. 'Very good, Brother.'

'Thank you, Lucas. Thank you, as always,' the Brother said, leaning back against his chair and realising that his heaviness had lifted. That something else had taken its place, something that brought with it energy and meaning and all the things he had lost in the past few days. An inkling. Of what, he didn't know, but he would, eventually. And in the meantime, he would stay alert, on his toes. That was why he was the Brother.

That was why he was in charge.

14

Evie didn't sleep for long. It felt as though no sooner had her eyelids closed heavily over her eyes than Raffy was gently shaking her. 'They're packing up,' he said. 'Wake up, Evie.'

She didn't want to wake up, didn't want to return to this strange world, to the pain in her head, to the questions circling. But as she opened her eyes she saw Raffy looking down at her, his haunted eyes somehow softer than they'd been since they left the City. Gently, his fingers traced the line of her jaw, then his thumb moved over her eyebrow and she closed her eyes again, just for a moment, because they were out in the open, because for the first time they weren't hiding, not in a tree, not in a cave; they weren't looking over their shoulder or fearing what might lie around the corner. They just *were*. They were here, together, in the warm sun, together, and it was the closest to happy she could remember feeling. She wanted to preserve the moment, to remember what it felt like. Because though it was happening, although she could feel Raffy, his touch, the rise and fall of his chest against her cheek, she knew that it wasn't real and that it couldn't last. Because moments like this never lasted; she knew that in her bones. They existed just briefly to give you strength, to have something to remember, to cling to when darker days came.

'I love you, Evie,' he whispered, and she felt a tug at her heart, a need for him, but it was something more. 'You're the only person in this whole world that matters. You and me, Evie. It's always going to be you and me.'

And she nodded, grasped his neck, felt his kisses on her, moved herself against him. But all the time, there was just one thought in her head. Lucas. She closed her eyes and saw his face, looking up at her, his eyes full of pain full of . . .

'Raffy,' she whispered. 'Raffy, there's something . . .'

But even as she spoke, she heard footsteps marching towards them, a voice calling out to Raffy. It was Linus. 'Hey,' he shouted. 'Over here. Help us.' Evie quickly roused herself and stood up so that Raffy could, too. Linus looked around vaguely then turned to Evie. 'You, help Martha.' He didn't know her name, she found herself thinking. He'd been so keen for answers and yet he'd never asked their names.

Quickly, Evie ran over to Martha, who was dismantling a tent. Like the gypsies in her mother's stories, Evie thought to herself as she pulled pegs out of the ground. Never in one place for long, always running away. Would this be her life now? Had she joined the gypsies just as her fake mother had warned that she would?

She took out the pegs, rolled up the groundsheet and did her best to fold the tent, then watched in awe as Martha expertly packed it up into a bag that appeared far too small to contain it. And as she watched, Evie's hand moved inadvertently to her temple, to her new scar that throbbed – not only with pain but with something else, something she couldn't identify.

And then she realised what it was. It was fear. Because for all his smiles, all his talk of answers and explanations, Evie didn't trust Linus. She didn't trust any of them.

The truth was, she barely trusted herself.

'Is your head hurting?' Martha asked, her expression kind and warm.

Evie shook her head. 'No. I mean, a little. But I'm fine.' She didn't want their medicine. Martha seemed okay but she would rather feel her pain, would rather know the truth of it than disguise it with drugs. In the City medicine was rare, illness brought on by individuals through weakness or pride. Men and women had to suffer their illnesses, the Brother always said, otherwise they would not learn from them, they would not grow stronger.

Then again, she wasn't in the City any more, Evie thought with a thud.

'Ready?' Linus appeared in front of her, Raffy at his side; it was clear from the sweat on his forehead that he had been helping the men to pack up. 'We need to leave soon. Once it's dark we're too vulnerable. Can you carry these?' He proffered two rucksacks; Raffy felt them both then handed one to Evie.

'Vulnerable?' Raffy asked him as he swung the rucksack onto his back and helped Evie with hers.

'Wild animals. Worse,' Linus said with a little shrug. 'So come on. Let's get moving.'

Raffy held out his hand and Evie took it gratefully.

'How long have you been here?' she asked Linus.

'Here at this camp? Oh, a week, or thereabouts,' he said, rounding everyone up.

She digested this. But she still didn't understand. 'And why were you here? Why didn't you stay at . . .'

She tried to remember the name of their City, their home.

'At Base Camp?' Linus asked. He gently bobbed his head up and down as he checked off people and baggage until he was satisfied that everyone and every-thing was ready. 'Good question,' he said, turning to bestow a smile on her. 'One that I'll answer later, if that's okay. When I know you better.' He winked, then walked to the front. 'Right, people. Let's get moving.'

He started to walk and everyone followed, carrying bags on their backs; two men at the rear held a large canvas bag over a stick. In their spare hands they both carried binoculars; Evie recognised them because her father had some. Her fake father. He had shown her how to use them, watching her amazement as she looked through the lenses to see that the sky, so far away, was suddenly close at hand, the birds flying through it now almost touchable.

Although not actually touchable, she'd been disap-pointed to learn.

She pointed the binoculars out to Raffy, who raised his eyebrows. 'They're the look-out,' he whispered.

The look-out. To protect them from wild animals. Or worse. She shivered, even though the sun was beating down on her. She longed to talk to Raffy, alone, to make sense of things together just as they always had. But it was impossible; they would be heard. They were allowed to be together, which was something, an improvement on the City. But without sharing their thoughts, without revealing their fears to each other, it was as though there was a huge, invisible wedge between them. Evie wondered if Raffy felt it as keenly as she did; the resolute expression on his face suggested otherwise. Then again, she found herself thinking, it had always been she who had shared the most in their conversations, she who had talked for so long her throat became sore. What she missed was Raffy listening, his silent nods, his dark soulful eyes which told her that he understood, that he didn't judge, that he accepted her for all she was.

They walked quickly, soon leaving the ramshackle group of buildings and half-buildings behind to wander through a landscape far more barren than even the land around the City.

Evie felt Raffy tug at her hand; when she turned, he pulled her towards him. 'Okay,' he whispered, so softly she could barely hear him. 'I've got a plan.'

Her heart quickened. With excitement, with fear.

Raffy started to walk more quickly, pulling Evie with him, overtaking Martha and Angel so that they were right behind Linus. Linus heard them approach and turned, flashing them a warm grin. 'Yes?' he asked, anticipating a question.

'Will we reach Base Camp tonight?' Raffy asked.

'Will we reach Base Camp tonight,' Linus said thoughtfully. 'And why would you want to know that?'

'Because Evie isn't feeling well,' Raffy said, squeezing her hand as he spoke. 'I just want to know how much longer we're going to be travelling.'

'What's wrong with you?' Linus said, stopping suddenly and turning his attentions on Evie.

Evie felt herself flush bright red. 'I'm . . . I don't know,' she said uncomfortably.

'It's her stomach,' Raffy piped up quickly.

'Ah,' said Linus. 'Maybe the water. Okay. We'll stop whenever you need to, Evie. Just let me know, okay?'

'Okay,' she said, her cheeks burning.

'And Base Camp?' Raffy insisted. 'Will we get there tonight?'

Linus considered this, appeared to consider Raffy. Then he shrugged. 'No,' he said. 'We'll get to Base Camp tomorrow. Tonight we'll pitch one tent for all of us. Safety in numbers.'

His face crinkled into his infuriating grin again, then he turned and started to march. Evie met Raffy's eyes and they dropped back so that they were behind

Angel and Martha once more. 'Tonight,' Raffy mouthed. 'In the night, when it's dark. When we get to Base Camp it'll be too late to escape.'

'Tonight,' Evie mouthed back, but her throat was suddenly dry and her heart was thudding loudly in her chest. And she marched, side by side with Raffy, settling into a rhythm and trying not to think about the weight of the rucksack on her back, the fear of what lay ahead.

They arrived at sundown, or at least they stopped – Evie couldn't be sure whether Linus had been heading for the spot where they set up a temporary camp, had arrived just in time, or whether he had simply waited for the sun to start setting and stopped. Either way, Evie told herself, it didn't really matter. What mattered was that soon she and Raffy would be on the run again, fending for themselves. The same thought must have been at the forefront of Raffy's mind because he, like Evie, had devoured all the food and drink on offer that lunchtime. And again, as though they had discussed the evening in detail, they both avoided each other's eyes when they arrived at the clearing where the tent was being pitched, both refrained from asking questions or from causing any bad feeling. Instead, they watched, listened and helped set up camp for the night.

No one seemed to be paying much attention to

them; they were called in to help from time to time –
Evie to help Martha prepare some food, Raffy to
help Angel and Linus find firewood. But other than
that it was as though they'd been accepted, as though
this strange little community had become *their* community. Evie still hadn't forgotten the way Angel had hit
Raffy, or the way Linus had sneered at him as he
tortured him for answers. But somehow those memories
were receding, somehow they felt less real than the
camaraderie that she felt between them now,
the protection.

'We eat. Then when everyone goes to bed, we wait.
Once they're asleep, we make our move.'

Raffy had appeared next to her; his voice was low
and urgent, his eyes looking straight ahead as though
he wasn't talking to her at all.

Evie swallowed; her throat had dried up again.
'You're sure we should leave?' she whispered.

'What?' Raffy forgot himself and swung round to
face her, a frown on his face. 'What are you talking
about?'

'I just think there might be safety in numbers,' Evie
said anxiously; she could feel that her palms were damp
with worry. 'And where will we go?'

'We'll go where we want,' Raffy said, his eyes
narrowing. 'On our own terms.'

'But they've got food and shelter,' Evie said. She could see that Raffy was getting angry with her but she couldn't stop herself.

Raffy turned away and folded his arms. 'If you want to stay with Linus, with his lies and his rules and his threats, then you do that,' he seethed. 'But I'm not. I'm getting out of here.'

Evie took a deep breath. Then she wrapped her hand around Raffy's arm. 'Then I'm coming with you,' she said quietly.

'You're sure?' Raffy asked, looking at her intently. 'It's you and me? You don't want to stay here because Lucas told you to?'

Evie ignored the sarcasm in his voice. She deserved it, even if Raffy didn't know why. 'It's you and me,' she said. 'Only you and me. If you go, I go.'

The words gave her courage, made her feel less apprehensive about what lay ahead. She could see Raffy respond to them too, his eyes softening, his whole face warming.

'Okay then,' he said. 'Just wait for my lead.'

'You two hungry? We're eating now,' Linus called, appearing out of nowhere. An hour before, the sun had been setting; now, already, they were covered in a blanket of darkness that Evie had barely noticed falling.

'Sure,' Raffy said immediately. 'Thanks.'

He walked towards the campfire; Evie followed, but hesitantly. Linus walked next to her. 'He's an impetuous young man, your friend,' he said. 'Courageous, but impetuous. That isn't always a good combination.'

Evie bit her lip and stayed silent.

'You, on the other hand . . . Well, you're different,' Linus continued thoughtfully. 'It's not because of you that you're on this side of the City wall, is it?' Evie didn't say anything, but it was as though Linus wasn't expecting her to reply; he carried on regardless. 'You're here to protect him. Which is ironic, because he thinks that he's the great protector. But protection isn't about strength. It's about intelligence, understanding. Knowing when to run and when to stay. Don't you think?'

Evie stared at him and was grateful for the darkness because it hid her burning cheeks. Could Linus really see inside her? How did he always seem to know what she was thinking, the feelings she was hiding deep down in her heart?

Linus chuckled. 'He's a good boy. I can see that. But he's going to get himself into trouble unless you stop him. You know what you have to do. And I think I can count on you to do it. Just like Raffy's brother counted on you.'

Evie felt dizzy. He knew. He knew about Raffy's plan.

Linus squeezed her hand gently, then moments later she saw that he was no longer next to her but was striding ahead, joining Angel and Martha around the campfire, proferring a plate to Raffy as he took his seat on the ground. Evie went to sit next to Raffy, her cheeks still hot, her eyes unable to meet his. Because she didn't know if anyone could count on her any more. Especially Raffy.

15

Evie tried to eat; she half-heartedly spooned the porridgey gloop that Martha had made into her mouth, but her stomach wasn't interested in food. It was too busy churning, too busy flip-flopping every time Raffy looked at her, every time Linus caught her eye.

But although she couldn't eat, in spite of Raffy's attempts to encourage her, she wanted only for the meal never to end, for Linus and Angel and Martha and the two other taciturn men whose names she had learnt were George and Al, never to go to bed, or to sleep, never to force her into the position of having to make a decision. To leave with Raffy or to stop him from going. To betray him, or to allow him to run to his death – to their deaths.

Linus was the first to stand up. 'Right, well, I'm off to bed,' he announced. 'I suggest we all get a good night's sleep tonight.' Was he looking directly at Evie when he said that? She wasn't sure. She felt like he was, like his eyes were boring into her soul.

Angel followed shortly after Linus; Martha cleared up first, helped by Evie who was desperate to occupy herself, then George and Al grunted goodnight and followed her into the tent. Raffy stood up.

'Time for bed,' he said loudly, yawning. 'I'm exhausted.'

Evie nodded. She knew that Raffy intended her to join in the charade but she couldn't. Instead, she followed him silently, stepping over the sleeping bags of Al and George, who had positioned themselves at the mouth of the tent, and over to the area reserved for her and Raffy.

And then they waited.

They waited for an hour, until all around them was heavy breathing and gentle snoring. Then Raffy reached over to give Evie a little shake; Evie, who had barely dared blink, immediately sat up, her heart pounding.

Carefully Raffy got to his feet, still crouched down, and started to edge towards the tent opening. Evie followed, trying not to breathe, trying not to think about what they were doing or about what lay ahead. Carefully, delicately, they inched their way forward over sleeping bodies, through the warm, sleepy air of the tent. Raffy stepped over Al and started unlocking the opening; there were three layers with various zips and padlocks, just as there were on all the tents. To keep out the wild animals, Martha had explained to Evie as she'd helped dismantle them. They would have no protection from the wild animals on their own.

But she would have Raffy, she told herself. They would be together, and free, just as they had always dreamt.

She had taken a slightly different route from Raffy; she had wanted to keep as far away from Linus as possible, so had tiptoed behind Martha instead. Now she stepped towards George anxiously; he was broad and tall and his form took up a huge section of the tent. She couldn't cross him. She couldn't hope to; her legs weren't long enough. She would have to jump. Raffy looked up and saw her dilemma; he turned, tried like her to find an alternative, but the only other route would mean retracing her footsteps to where they'd been lying, to follow the path Raffy had taken. Evie took a deep breath and leapt; Raffy's eyes widened and they both held their breath. Then she landed, colliding with the tent wall slightly, but not enough to wake anyone. She smiled. It was a good omen. They were going to be fine.

Raffy finished unlocking the tent. 'Are you going

to lock it again afterwards?' Evie whispered. He shook his head.

'No time.'

'But they'll be vulnerable to attack,' Evie said, guilt flooding her veins once more. 'We have to.'

'They'll be fine,' Raffy replied, his eyes clouding slightly. 'They're in the tent, aren't they? And it's their fault for capturing us in the first place. They weren't worried about us when Angel was beating me, were they?'

Evie shook her head. She supposed he was right. She reached out, took his hand and felt a reassuring squeeze. Then, cautiously, she followed him out of the tent into the crisp night air. The ground was moist beneath their feet – it must have rained whilst everyone was sleeping, but any water had been greedily absorbed by the land; all that remained was a vague dampness.

'This way,' Raffy said authoritatively, pointing to the way they had come. 'We want to get as far from Base Camp as we can.'

'But that's back towards the City,' Evie said. 'Let's go north. That's the way Lucas said we should go.'

'And that led us into Linus's hands,' Raffy snapped, his mouth tightening.

Evie stared at him. 'Lucas didn't know that,' she replied.

'What if he did? What if he wanted Linus to do his dirty work for him,' Raffy said, his tone cutting.

'And what work would that be?'

They froze as a voice they recognised all too well rang out clearly. 'You think your brother sold you out?'

In the moonlight Evie could see the anger and desperation on Raffy's face. And she knew it was her fault. She shouldn't have argued; they'd have been away by now. Had she done it on purpose? Did Raffy suspect as much? If he did, he didn't show it; he wasn't even looking at her. He was looking at Linus, all his energies directed towards him. Raffy looked ready to pounce, to run; all his muscles looked taut and ready to spring into action.

'Let us go,' Raffy said hoarsely. 'You don't need us. We don't need your protection. We can look after ourselves. Let us go.'

Linus looked thoughtful for a few seconds. 'You really want to go?' he asked. 'You really want to fend for yourselves? Evie, is that what you want too?'

Evie hesitated, long enough for Raffy to turn and glare at her. 'Yes,' she said then. 'Yes, I do.'

Linus nodded slowly. 'I see.' Then he shrugged.

'So we can go?' Raffy asked, a measure of hope in his voice. 'You'll let us leave?'

Linus's eyes gleamed in the moonlight. He looked

wise, Evie found herself thinking. But whilst his eyes were twinkling, it wasn't with joy. It was with something else. She recognised it. It was pain. Then he shook his head slowly.

'Angel?' he called softly; his henchman immediately appeared. Raffy tried to run and cried out to Evie to run with him, but it was no use; Angel grabbed Raffy first, handing him to Linus before capturing Evie. She watched as Linus pressed Raffy's face into the earth as he tied some rope around his wrists. Angel then tied her wrists together.

'You're not going anywhere unless it's with us,' Linus said quietly. 'You try to leave this camp again and you're dead.'

'Why?' Raffy fumed. Angel was holding him tightly and he was resisting, straining. Evie stayed still; she knew when a fight wasn't winnable. 'Why won't you let us go?'

Linus shrugged. 'Because I made a promise to your father a long time ago,' he said quietly, 'And I don't break promises. Promises are the last bastion of civilisation; if we can't keep them, we're doomed.'

'My . . . father?' Raffy asked, the words barely audible. 'What do you mean? You don't know my father. You don't—'

'You don't know what I know,' Linus said evenly.

'Now, I'm going back to bed and you are too. Get some sleep. We've got a lot further to go in the morning. Please don't disturb us again.'

Before Raffy could press him for more answers, Linus disappeared back into the tent. Angel motioned that they should go back in too. Stumbling, they made their way to their sleeping bags and fell in a heap on the floor. They didn't say a word, but Evie wriggled forward so that her forehead was pressing against Raffy's back, so that he could feel her and know that she was there, that she understood – or wanted to. And Raffy wriggled backwards so that his back was pressed against her stomach, so that his warmth felt like a blanket. And like that, their bodies pressed together, they lay still until it was morning again.

'Come on. Quickly.' Evie woke abruptly to see George poking them through their sleeping bags with his foot. He saw her eyes open and stepped back. 'Linus says we leave in five,' he announced with a shrug and walked away. Immediately Raffy pulled himself up. He looked as though he hadn't slept, even though Evie had been comforted by his heavy sleepy breathing through the night. His eyes had dark shadows around them; they seemed darker than usual, more tortured.

He didn't mention Linus or what he'd said the night

before; he just got up and packed away the sleeping bags. By the time they were ready to leave the tent it had been dismantled around them. Angel untied their hands; Martha gave them a hunk of bread each and some water, and then it was time to go. Raffy and Evie hadn't exchanged a word; she watched him carefully but she wasn't sure what to say. She couldn't speak before he did. And Raffy showed no sign of wanting to say anything. His eyes followed Linus like a hawk, furtively sometimes, more openly at others as they marched across the barren landscape towards the place that he'd feared, that he'd been so determined to run from.

They stopped briefly for lunch when the sun was at its hottest, taking some shelter under a patch of trees for an hour or so. But then it was straight back to marching, Martha at the front with Linus, Angel to the rear, George and Al just in front of Evie and Raffy.

And then just before sundown, Evie saw something in the distance. A hill, a tall hill that wasn't covered in trees but in . . . She squinted, tugging at Raffy's sleeve. In tents. Structures. Raffy's eyes followed hers and he stopped briefly, causing Angel to bump into him. The man swore, then saw what Raffy was staring at and grinned. 'Home,' he breathed. 'Home at last.'

He motioned for Raffy to start walking again and after a brief pause, he did. Evie kept shooting worried looks his way but the closer they got, the less agitated Raffy seemed.

'There's no wall,' he said, frowning, as they approached Base Camp. It was an appropriate name, Evie found herself thinking – it wasn't a City, the structures were all temporary. And it was nestled a little way up the hill.

'Don't need a wall,' Linus said, turning, and for the first time that day, looking at Raffy and Evie, his face crinkled into its now-familiar grin. 'Got the natural landscape and watchtowers for protection, but we don't imprison our people. That's not our way.'

Silently they walked past the first watchtower and into the camp. People in overalls bustled around, serious looks on their faces which broke into grins when they saw Linus. There were strange greetings that Evie had never come across before; clapping of hands, slapping of backs. She braced herself, but no one clapped her hand or her back, just Linus and Angel, George and Al. Martha, they hugged, spun around, kissed on the head. And Evie and Raffy they just looked at, cautiously.

'What is this place?' Raffy breathed.

'This place?' Linus asked, suddenly appearing behind them. 'Son, this is army headquarters. We're preparing for battle and pretty soon we're going to be ready. I have a feeling it might be sooner rather than later.'

There were about a hundred people in the camp in total, each of them gainfully employed. But where the City was divided into different working quarters for the different trades, which were divided by gender – male stonemasons, female breadmakers – Base Camp seemed to throw everyone in together. Everywhere Evie looked she could hear talking, arguing, laughing. People sang as they worked, men and women joshed together, sharing jokes and teasing one another.

And there were no labels.

She found herself staring as she walked around; Linus noticed and looked at her. 'Not what you were expecting?' he asked.

Evie reddened. 'They made us think that everyone outside the City were savages,' she said quietly. 'That people were evil. But they're not. Are they?'

'No, Evie, they're not,' Linus said. Then he put his arm around her and Raffy. 'Come with me. I want to show you something.'

He walked them down between two large tents and along a passageway to another tent with reinforced walls and a guard outside, carrying a rifle.

'The City lied to you about a lot of things. Most things, probably,' Linus said.

'The whole place is a lie as far as I can tell,' Raffy answered gruffly.

Linus smiled. 'You're right. Of course you're right. But . . .' He looked at them carefully. 'But this is the worst of all. At least I think so. These people. In this tent.'

'There are people in this tent?' Evie asked uncertainly. 'Prisoners?'

'Not prisoners,' Linus said, shaking his head. 'Absolutely not prisoners. At least not of our making. Take a look for yourselves.'

Evie approached the tent. Through narrow plastic windows she could see faces, strange mournful faces. One of them saw her and rushed towards the window, pressing her face against it, distorting it horribly. Evie stifled a scream as more faces joined the first, their eyes rolling, saliva coming out of their mouths. Then they started to shout, to moan, and Evie cried out and tried to run but Linus wouldn't let her.

'You know who these people are?' he asked her.

Evie nodded. She knew that sound. It was the sound that told her everything was over. The sound she had heard many times before, hiding under her bedclothes as her father left the house to protect the City, to protect her. Raffy recognised the sound too. He stared at Linus uncomprehendingly.

'These are the sacrificial lambs of the City,' Linus said, guiding them away from the tent, then stopping, his face serious. 'They are irreparably brain-damaged. The victims of everything your great City set out to achieve.'

'Brain-damaged? But . . .' Evie said, her brow furrowing. 'But they're not. They're . . . they're . . .'

Linus smiled, but it didn't reach his eyes. 'Of course,' he said, 'you will know these people as the Evils.'

16

No one spoke for a minute; it was Evie who eventually broke the silence.

'You . . . you keep the Evils here? They're your prisoners?'

Linus shook his head and guided them away, down a covered corridor, out into a courtyard then into a large warren of tents. 'In here,' he said; they followed him and found themselves in a cosy room full of rugs and cushions. There was a large dark wood desk covered in green leather towards the back of the room. Evie couldn't take her eyes off it.

'Nice, isn't it?' Linus said, catching her eye. 'One of my saved treasures. Sit, please, both of you.'

He positioned himself on a large cushion; they sat down too. Linus looked at them; he appeared to be trying to read them, to see deep inside their souls. Then he breathed out. 'Tea?' he asked.

Evie nodded; Linus jumped up and stuck his head out of the room, called to someone, then sat back down again. Moments later a man arrived with a tray; on it was a pot of tea, some milk and some biscuits. Linus served them; Evie took her cup gratefully.

'The Evils are not our prisoners,' Linus declared, after taking a sip of his tea and putting the cup down carefully in front of him.

'But . . .' Evie interjected before she could stop herself.

'We have some prisoners, yes,' Linus said, 'but it's not what you think.'

'Then what is it?' Raffy asked, looking directly at Linus, unafraid, undaunted.

Linus smiled. 'Would you indulge me a little?' he asked. 'Would you let me tell you a story?'

'A story?' Raffy asked suspiciously. 'Why?'

'Because then you'll understand,' Linus said gently. 'Because then you might see the world the same way I do.'

'And what if I don't want to see the world like you?' Raffy asked, his tone abrupt. 'You're a liar. You lie about everything and now you're lying about my father. I'm sick of people lying to me, sick of it.'

'Raphael, I'm not lying to you,' Linus said, looking up at him, his eyes suddenly mournful. 'And I'm sorry if you think I am. I might not have told you everything, but that was for our protection. I needed to know you were really . . . I had to be careful, that's all. But I'm not going to lie to you any more.'

'Then tell me what you meant about my father,' Raffy said, his gaze steady.

'Let me tell you the story. And if you have any questions afterwards, I'll answer them,' Linus promised.

Raffy digested this for a few seconds; he looked suspicious, uncertain.

'Tell us,' Evie said, reaching out and clasping Raffy's hand. 'Tell us the story.'

'Thank you.' Linus smiled. 'Once upon a time there was a man. Some thought a great man, some thought otherwise. He was a man of science, a doctor. He had an idea which he believed could save mankind, could rid the world of the violence and terror that constantly threatened to destroy all the beautiful, incredible things that humans had built. He saw a nirvana where peace reigned, where people lived in harmony with each other, where they lost the will to fight each other.'

'The Great Leader,' Evie said quietly.

'The Great Leader.' Linus nodded thoughtfully.

'That's one word for him. Me, I prefer Dr Fisher. That was his name, before the Horrors, before the City, before any of this. That was his name when he took his ideas to various medical journals, to a number of conferences. And do you know what happened?'

'People didn't like the idea because they didn't want to get rid of the evil, because it didn't want to leave.'

'That's one way of putting it.' Linus shrugged. 'But what really happened was they laughed at him. Ridiculed his theories. Refused to publish him, wrote comic comment pieces about him, called him Frankenstein's successor. You know who Frankenstein was?'

Evie and Raffy shook their heads. 'No, of course you don't,' Linus said, smiling to himself. 'Well, that doesn't matter. What matters is that Dr Fisher refused to give up on his dream and tried to recruit people to be experimental subjects, to have pieces of their brain removed. Only it didn't go so well. And when the medical and scientific authorities found out, they struck him off and started court proceedings to have him put away. He wasn't, though. Put away, that is. He pleaded insanity. Got off . . .' He caught Evie and Raffy's blank stares and smiled again. 'Ah. Court case. Something else you don't know about. Okay, forget that. What happened was that he went underground. Off the radar.

Started to hang out with the kooks and the freaks, people who didn't laugh at him, people whose own great ideas had been thwarted too. People like me.'

'Like you?' Suddenly Linus had Evie and Raffy's attention. 'You knew the Great Leader?'

'We were friends,' Linus agreed. 'Of sorts. Comrades, really. We both had a dream. Both had an idea of how things should be.'

'What was your dream?' Evie asked breathlessly. 'The same as the Great Leader's?'

'No.' Linus shook his head. 'But . . .' He breathed out. 'You want to see my idea?'

They both nodded.

'Okay, come with me.'

He jumped up lightly and left the room; Evie and Raffy exchanged tentative glances then followed him back across the courtyard, through the corridor, past the Evils' tent, across another courtyard and into a guarded compound. Linus escorted Raffy and Evie through the entrance, down another corridor and into a huge room, which was full of computers.

Raffy seemed in awe as he looked around, while Evie stared uncertainly. The room was warm, full of the buzzing and whirring sound of computers at work.

'You have so many,' she breathed. 'How? How did you get them all here?'

Linus grinned. 'These are my babies,' he said, his eyes suddenly full of affection, of something almost approaching love. He turned to Evie and Raffy, his eyes glittering. 'My idea,' he said, 'was a system. A system that could make the world a better place, an ordered place, a place where no one wanted for anything because the system pre-empted that want. Where no one went hungry, or did badly at school, where no one was bullied and everyone found the person they were destined to be with. All because of the system.'

Evie looked at him dubiously. 'You mean . . . like the City's System?'

Linus shook his head and his eyes clouded over. 'I mean what the City's System was supposed to be like,' he said abruptly. 'The system that I designed. The system that I built and established.'

'You built the System?' Raffy asked incredulously.

'I built the System,' Linus confirmed. 'And for that I am sorry. For that . . .' He sighed. 'I will never forgive myself.'

Raffy walked towards the machines. 'May I?' he asked, approaching one of them.

'Of course,' said Linus.

Raffy put his hands on the keyboard and started

to type; screens emerged, data fields, rows of figures and letters that meant nothing to Evie.

'This is your system?' Raffy asked.

Linus nodded; for the first time since they'd met him, he seemed tense, anxious – as though he were scared of something.

'Wow,' Raffy breathed. 'This is . . . It's incredible.'

Linus grinned, his face suddenly like a little boy's in spite of the mass of lines that travelled across it, and Evie realised that he hadn't been scared; it had been Raffy's approval he had wanted, that had caused his jaw to tighten, his brow to wrinkle.

'What does it do?' she asked.

Raffy turned and pulled up a chair. 'See these codes? There's one for every person, interlinked with needs, desires, first-degree, second- degree, third . . . All prioritised, all factored into the communities' resources, people's time . . . It's incredible,' he repeated.

Linus shrugged bashfully. 'It's got its good points,' he said.

'So, then . . .' Raffy frowned, swung his chair round. 'How come there are no labels? If you built the City's System?'

'I built the original system,' Linus said, his mouth twitching. 'Not the System as it exists today. I did not build a system that labels people, that punishes them, that . . .' He looked down. 'The system I designed is not the System that exists in your City. That was built later, by others. Using my prototype. That's the problem with dreams, you see – they get distorted. No one has the same one. And dreams, when they become reality, are never what you anticipated, never what you hoped for.'

He turned away; Evie stood up and walked to his side.

'What about the Great Leader's dream?' she asked. 'That didn't get distorted.'

'Didn't get distorted?' Linus looked at her grimly. 'You really don't know anything, do you?'

Evie frowned, folding her arms defensively. She was getting tired of Linus with his meandering stories that never delivered the things he said they would. 'Yes we do. We know loads of things. And if we don't know everything, it's because you won't tell us.'

Linus looked at her carefully. 'Okay,' he said. 'Sit down. I'll tell you all about the Great Leader's dream, shall I?'

Evie nodded and returned to her chair next to Raffy, who she had to forcibly pull away from the computer screen.

Linus took a deep breath. 'Back to my story,' he said. 'So there we were, Dr Fisher and me, drinking lots of coffee and talking about how the world would be a better place if only we were allowed to run things. And then the Horrors started. You know why they called them the Horrors?'

'Because it was a war and war is full of horror,' Evie said.

Linus pulled a face. 'There had been wars before. Plenty of wars, plenty of death, cruelty and destruction. That never stopped anything. No, the Horrors were so named because all the soldiers were children and all the bombs were aimed at civilians. There was no combat, no strategy, just merciless killing with no end in sight. The people who started it weren't fighting for a purpose; they simply wanted to destroy everything and everyone, and they nearly succeeded. You can't fight an enemy like that; can't hide from them, either.'

'You hid,' Raffy said, his eyes narrowing. 'You must have – otherwise how are you here now?'

Linus laughed. 'Clever boy. Yes, I hid. Dr Fisher hid. We'd been hiding for years, it wasn't anything new for us. When we saw what was happening, we knew that this was our chance; that the only way to make sense of the horror, to make it mean something, was to build a new world of peace and hope. A place where people weren't evil any more, where their needs were looked after, and they could relax and just live instead of fearing every moment. That's all we wanted. That's all we were trying to do . . .'

His voice faltered and he cleared his throat. 'So we established the City.'

'You?' Raffy frowned.

'Me and Dr Fisher,' Linus agreed.

Raffy looked at him dubiously. 'Then why aren't you ever mentioned? How come you're not in any of the Sentiments?'

'The Sentiments?' Linus laughed. 'You actually listen to that crap?'

Evie was shocked; fear washed over her. She tried to push it away, but couldn't. Not entirely.

Linus noticed her reaction. 'Don't worry, your System can't hear me. It can't hear anything, not any more.'

'What do you mean?' Raffy asked uncertainly.

Linus sighed. 'Can I finish my story?'

Raffy shrugged. 'Fine, finish it.'

'Thank you,' replied Linus, affecting a deferential air. 'So we had some followers. The Horrors had ended and everyone was fighting over food, water, the basics. The world was disintegrating into mayhem and tribal warfare. So Dr Fisher and I set out our vision and people bought into it. They wanted a new way, a new chance. We colonised what had been the city of London before the Horrors, took over those buildings still standing and the resources that remained. There was a river; we had the base we needed to build on. And we had men to help us build, who built the wall, built homes, tirelessly and stoically. Men who believed in us and the dream we promised them. I started to build the System. And Fisher . . .'

He swallowed; his eyes started to dart around uncomfortably.

'And Fisher?' Raffy prompted him.

Linus looked down. 'Dr Fisher started his operations.'

'Removing the amygdala. The New Baptism,' said Evie. 'Everyone has it in the City.'

'They do, do they?' Linus asked, a hint of sarcasm in his voice.

'Yes,' Raffy said, frowning. 'You know that.'

Linus shook his head. 'What I know is that the men he operated on were turned into vegetables. Only he wouldn't admit it. He told me it would work, that he'd done it before, and when I discovered the truth, he made excuses – blamed the equipment, his helpers, anything. He told me it would work the next time, the time after that. On and on he went, and I didn't stop him. Not until it was too late. Not until . . .'

He broke off, apparently reluctant to continue.

'It did work,' challenged Evie. 'We're not vegetables.'

'No,' Linus conceded. 'But you haven't had the New Baptism either.'

'Yes, we have,' Evie said hotly. 'Just because we ran away doesn't mean that we're evil. Doesn't mean that we didn't have the New Baptism, because we did. I know we did. We have the scars. The ones that you opened up when you took us prisoner.'

Linus didn't reply.

'But . . .' Raffy said, his hand, like Evie's, moving to his forehead, to his scar. His eyes were flashing, full of anger. 'If the operations didn't work then why did he keep doing it? Why did everyone let him?'

'Because we were weak. Because we accepted his excuses. Because we wanted it to succeed as much as he did. He told everyone that the operation didn't work when people were too full of evil,' Linus said regretfully. 'And the ones who turned into vegetables he hid. We hid.' He buried his head in his hands, then looked up. 'Don't you get it? The people your Great Leader operated on . . . they're the Evils you're all so scared of. He created them. They were the people who believed in him, who worked for him. And he . . .' Linus stood up, took a few steps and leant over, his hands on his knees for a few seconds. Then he came back, apparently ready to continue.

'Eventually he stopped. He had to. But people believed in the New Baptism; they needed it, needed to believe that evil had been eradicated. So . . .' He was shifting awkwardly on his feet, unable to look either of them in the eye. 'So the New Baptism was faked. People thought they were having it. A little incision to the side of the head. At least I thought it was just a little incision . . .' He sighed. 'Point is, they were convinced. And it worked, too – the placebo effect.'

'Placebo?' Evie asked, her nose wrinkling.

'Tell someone you're giving them medicine and they'll get better, even if you're only giving them sawdust,' Linus explained. 'Tell people they're incapable of evil and they'll believe that, too.'

'So none of us has had the New Baptism?' Evie's hand moved to her head inadvertently. Her mind was racing. Could this really be true? All this time she'd been petrified that her amygdala was growing back and it had never been removed? Nor had her parents'? Nor had anyone's? 'Not even the Brother? Not even the A's?'

'Especially not the Brother,' Linus said darkly. 'And as for the A's . . .' He let out a long breath. 'We didn't have A's back then. The System wasn't built to grade people, to divide them up or pass judgement on them. It was built to make sure they had what they needed, that they were fulfilled.'

'So no one had the New Baptism at all?' Evie asked, still finding it hard to come to terms with.

'No one at all. Of course, Fisher didn't take it very well. The not being allowed to operate. He was convinced if he could just keep trying he'd figure it out. He didn't seem to understand that he was destroying people's lives. So we had to restrain him, lock him up. The Brother – he was just Mark back then – had been helpful; I thought he was a friend. I . . . I told him the truth. And he was great. He had all these ideas; he was going to reinforce the placebo with spiritual gatherings; he was going to be the spiritual leader of the City, keep people on the straight and narrow. He and I were the only ones who knew that the New Baptisms weren't real; the only ones who knew any of it. But then . . .'

'Then?' Evie prompted.

Linus stood up and started to pace about the room. 'I had a team of people trained on the System. I'd trained them all myself. The System was mine. I didn't care about anything else. But he just couldn't leave it alone – couldn't resist the power it afforded him.' His voice was bitter; his face suddenly full of anger.

'The Brother?' Evie asked, feeling the familiar prickle of fear on the back of her neck, the uneasy sensation of inadequacy, of never being good enough, that haunted her whenever she heard his name.

'The Brother,' Linus confirmed. 'He wanted to control everything. He brought in changes without telling me, introduced labelling – A, B, C, D. Said it was crucial to keep the order, said otherwise he'd have to come clean about the New Baptism. And I went along with it for a bit; I thought he was doing it for the best. We'd been talking about letting more people into the City; it wasn't growing fast enough and we needed more people to join us. So we sent out word that there was a safe community here, that people should come. And they came in their thousands – people were desperate after the Horrors; surviving was difficult. Very difficult. They thought they were coming to their salvation. And I was part of it. I helped spread the word.'

Evie closed her eyes. She could feel the warmth of her real father's chest, could sense the atmosphere of hope as they walked towards the City.

'But they only took the children,' she whispered, opening her eyes again to see Raffy staring at her worriedly.

She managed a smile to reassure him, then turned

to Linus. 'So what happened to them? To my real parents? Did they kill them?' She spoke the words flatly as though she didn't care, but it was only because she couldn't ask any other way, had to keep her emotions buried in case they consumed her.

Linus looked at her miserably. 'I didn't know,' he murmured. 'That you came that way. I didn't know.'

'So?' Evie persisted.

Linus didn't meet her eyes. 'It was the deal the Brother made with Fisher in return for power. Fisher – your Great Leader – was allowed to operate on the adults who came. He got to butcher people and the Brother . . . Well, he got something else. An army of Evils to terrify the City's citizens, to keep them enslaved, to make them so afraid that they would do whatever the Brother told them to do.'

Evie swallowed, forcing back the tears which pricked at her eyes. 'My parents are Evils,' she said instead. It wasn't a question, it was a statement. The people she had feared for so long were her own parents, the ones who had trudged for days in order to give her a better future.

'And you keep them locked up? You have my parents here?' She swung round, her eyes flashing suddenly.

Linus shook his head. 'No, Evie. We have a few here, that's all. The few that we have rescued,' he added gently. 'Most of them . . . Most of them are kept prisoner by the City. There's a camp a few miles from the City. That's where the Evils are kept. That's where the Brother has put them.'

Evie nodded tightly. 'And that's why you left?'

Linus sighed heavily. 'I wish,' he said. 'That's when I should have left. But I didn't want to see what was going on. I wanted to build my System, to make it perfect. I told myself that the Brother's tactics were short term, necessary. I told myself . . .' He let the sentence hang; his face looked tortured.

'So what was it?' Evie asked, cuttingly. 'It wasn't butchering my parents. What made you leave?'

Linus met her gaze, then looked down again, humbled. 'Two things. First, Fisher disappeared.'

'The Great Leader?' Evie asked, with an involuntary shiver.

Linus nodded. 'The Brother told me he'd escaped, but I didn't believe him. I suspected . . . foul play.'

'You think he killed him?' Raffy asked, suspiciously.

Linus nodded. 'That's what I deduced.'

'So you confronted the Brother?' Raffy asked then, leaning forward, his eyes engaging for the first time.

Linus's face twitched slightly. 'No,' he said, looking down again. 'To my shame. I thought he knew what he was doing. In some ways I was relieved.'

'Relieved that he'd killed the Great Leader?' Evie gasped.

'I'm not proud of myself. But I was relieved that such a dangerous man had been taken out of the equation,' Linus responded quietly.

'So what changed?' Raffy asked. 'What was the second thing?'

Linus's expression hardened. 'I found out that the fake New Baptism was more sinister than I'd realised. He was using the operation to put chips into people's heads instead. The ones I told you about. Chips to track them. Chips to link them to the System. My System. So I told him enough was enough. I told him he had to stop, that I was going to tell everyone that the New Baptisms were a lie, that the Evils were a lie, but that it didn't matter, that we would still have the City they'd dreamt of.'

Linus stopped pacing.

'And?' Raffy asked tentatively.

'And that was my last day in the City. That was when the Brother introduced a new label. K. He said it was for people whose amygdalas had grown back. But it wasn't. It was for people he decided were enemies of the regime. People who threatened him. People he had to get rid of straight away. K's were supposedly taken away for a second New Baptism, but that was just a lie like all the rest. K stands for Killable – as you know. The Brother didn't want to kill me himself; he knew someone would find out eventually. So he told everyone I was being reconditioned, then tied me up outside and left me for the Evils to kill. The Evils who he'd told me were being cared for, but who in reality he'd kept locked up in filthy conditions and treated like animals.'

'But they didn't kill you,' Evie whispered. 'You're still here.'

'No, they didn't kill me.' Linus turned to Raffy. 'They didn't kill me because your father came to my rescue. Your father saved my life.'

17

'My father?' Evie barely recognised Raffy's voice. 'My father saved your life?'

'Yes, son,' Linus said. 'He was one of the originals. One of the men who helped us build the City. He was a believer; he helped me build the System. But he could see things were changing, too. He was a quiet man, didn't lose his temper like I did. But he guessed about the New Baptisms; he didn't like what the Brother was doing to the System. Using it to police people, to scare them, instead of to help them. He found out that the Brother was sending his men after me and risked his life to help me to escape. Back then it was easier – I didn't have a chip in my head for one thing. But he knew how much the Brother wanted me dead and he made sure that didn't happen. And one day I'm going to make sure he knows how grateful I am.'

Raffy looked at him. He seemed stronger suddenly, like his back was slightly straighter. 'My father was made a K when I was four,' he said. 'If K really does mean Killable, then . . .'

'Your father was made a K? No, that's impossible,' Linus said quickly. 'That's impossible.'

'Not impossible,' Raffy argued in a low voice. 'I think I'd know.'

'But . . .' Linus's face creased into confusion. 'But I know he's alive.'

'And I know he isn't,' Raffy said. 'He was taken away. I remember it like it was yesterday. The police guard came for him. Told us he was dangerous, that he needed to be reconditioned, that he'd never come back because he was weak and the evil in him was too strong. My mother was there. She was shaking. She told me I had to be good, otherwise they'd come for me next. She said . . .'

He didn't finish the sentence; he couldn't. His whole body was shaking. Evie reached out a hand and he gripped it tightly. She remembered that night, too; remembered how afterwards Raffy had changed – everything had changed.

Linus reeled. His expression said it all: grief, guilt, anger, all etched into the lines of his face. 'When you were four?' he asked. 'So, what, twelve years ago?'

'Thirteen,' Raffy said, his voice slightly defensive.

'Thirteen. That's five years after I escaped.' Linus folded his arms and paced around again for a minute. Then he came back to Raffy, stood right in front of him. 'But if your father's dead,' he said then, his face anxious, his eyes intense, 'then who has been sending me messages all this time? Who told me to look out for you? Who's been telling me when people were being made K's so that we could get to them first, bring them to safety?'

Evie stared at him. 'So that's who you are? You're all K's? All of you?'

'Most of us.' A small shadow fell over Linus's face. 'We don't always get here in time. Sometimes the Evils . . .' He tailed off, cleared his throat. 'And sometimes we have to let it happen,' he added eventually. 'Otherwise they'd come after us. Otherwise . . .' He appeared to shake himself. 'The point is, your father told me about you. He told me to find you. How could he do that if he's dead?'

'You knew about us?' Evie asked incredulously. 'You knew we were escaping from the City? Then why did you take us prisoner? Why did you beat Raffy?'

Linus arched an eyebrow. 'That wasn't a beating. That was just so you wouldn't try to escape. Not until I'd got you here to safety. Until I was sure the City police guard had given up their search.' He turned back to Raffy. 'So who has been communicating with me? I need to know.' He gripped Raffy's shoulder, staring at him. Raffy looked back helplessly. 'I don't know,' he said. 'But I found a communication device. In the System.'

'You found the communication device? So it's been compromised?' Linus's eyes grew big with fear.

'That's why they made him a K,' Evie explained quietly.

'When did you find it? How? Who did you tell?'

'I found a glitch. Only it wasn't a glitch. I was doing maintenance on the System and I saw some weird code, some activity that didn't make any sense,' Raffy answered uncomfortably. 'Are you saying that my father planted it? That it was his way of communicating with you?'

Linus looked like he could barely hear Raffy, was barely aware of their presence. 'But it doesn't make any sense,' he was saying, shaking his head, his face still taut with worry. 'You found it last week? Who's been communicating with me? Who took over from your father?'

Then Evie looked at Raffy and over at Linus, and she took a step forward. Because she knew, she understood suddenly – understood everything.

'Lucas,' she said quietly. 'He knew. He's been doing

it all this time. He's senior in the government but he told me about Raffy. He told me Raffy had to escape.'

'Lucas?' Raffy snorted. 'Lucas was the one who kept telling everyone I was mad, who said that I hadn't found anything more than a glitch, that I was delusional . . .' As he spoke, he realised what he was saying, realised what Lucas had been trying to do. 'Lucas?' he stuttered. 'Lucas? All this time?'

'Who's Lucas?' Linus asked, his voice agitated. 'Tell me.'

'Lucas is my brother,' Raffy said.

'But it can't be him. He'd have been just a boy when your father . . .'

'He was fifteen,' Evie told him. 'He left school to go and work for the government. Everyone said it was because he was embarrassed about his father. Ashamed.'

'I thought he was ashamed,' Raffy said quietly. 'I've hated him all these years.'

'He wanted you to hate him.' Evie put her hand on Raffy's shoulder. 'He wanted everyone to believe that he *was* ashamed. So that no one would suspect.'

'Your father must have trained him up before . . .' Linus was shaking his head incredulously.

'Before they killed him?' Raffy asked, his voice choked with emotion.

Linus nodded. 'I'm sorry.' He looked at Raffy

sorrowfully. 'He was a good man. I can't tell you how sorry I am about what happened. But we'll avenge his death. Don't you worry about that. Tell me, is the device compromised? Does the Brother know about it now?'

Raffy shook his head. 'I don't know. I don't think so. No one believed me. Lucas told everyone I was mad. That I'd planted a glitch and was deluded about what it could do. He locked me up at home so I couldn't tell anyone else, so they couldn't talk to me.'

'Clever man, your brother,' Linus said grimly. 'And then what?'

'Then the System made him a K,' Evie said, a strange feeling spreading out from her stomach. Lucas. All that time. That's why the System hadn't known about her and Raffy. Hadn't Lucas said he'd known, that he'd protected them? He must have stopped the System from seeing them, from finding out. Everything he'd ever done had been for a reason. Everything. And all she had ever done was despise him. 'Then he came and found me and told me that we had to run. He'd been planning it for days. He'd been looking for my father's key.'

'Your father is a key holder?'

Evie nodded.

'So the key you've got is real?'

'Of course it is.' Evie felt it in her pocket, gripping it in her hand. All she could think about was Lucas, alone in the City, his cold eyes hiding the boy underneath. The boy who had watched his father being taken to his death, who had gone undercover and grown into a man protecting everyone except himself.

Linus exhaled thoughtfully. 'Okay, then,' he said. 'We need to talk to your brother. We need to talk to Lucas.'

Lucas saw the icon flashing the moment the connection came through; he had been waiting, hoping, worrying. It had been several long days and nights; the days spent with his usual mask on, the blank smile, the formal language, the cold authority that had served him so well all these years. But at night, his mask slipped; at night, the demons surfaced, telling him that he had let his father down, that he had left his brother to fend for himself, that he would never see him again, would never see Evie. Evie . . . He closed his eyes for a second and steeled himself, in case the news was bad, in case the worst had happened. Then, carefully checking as he always did that no one was near, no one could see or would suspect, he input the code to activate the device.

'Operator. Your message?'

'Are we safe?'

'We are safe.'

'A monster lives in the north, but where?'

Lucas smiled. It had been his father's idea to use passcodes based on the fairy tales and myths that he had told Lucas secretly when Lucas was small; their secret, not to be shared with anyone else. By the time Raffy was the same age, their father was dead. Lucas hadn't been able to bring himself to tell his brother the stories; he had been afraid that his mask would slip, that he would crumble. He had worried that Raffy would not be able to keep the secret, that in telling him he would risk everything. But how much had he denied himself and his brother? Too much? He felt a stray tear appear in his eye and brushed it away. Crying felt alien now, as though it was something only others did.

'Loch Ness.'

A pause. 'You are not who you have led me to believe you are. To know that you are friend not foe, tell me something only you would know.'

Lucas felt his body stiffen. He knew; Linus knew who he was. Which meant . . . He took a deep breath, told himself to stay calm, not to let relief flood his veins, not yet . . .

'If you have who I think you have, tell them to

look away now.' He waited. 'Ask them about the tree. Where they used to meet. No one else knew.'

There was a pause.

'Okay. And who am I?'

Linus looked at the screen, tried to work out what to say, how to explain what he knew and what he'd been told. 'My father told me that you are a good man, a man who can change the future. He told me to keep you informed. He told me to protect my brother. He told me to wear a mask and never take it off until I knew it was time. He told me that you would tell me when that time was.'

Nothing appeared for a few seconds. Then:

'Your brother and the girl are safe. It is nearly time. We have been preparing. I need information from you.'

'Anything,' Lucas wrote back, his eyes shining, his whole body feeling like a firework had just gone off inside it. And he told himself that it was because his brother was safe. He told himself it was because it was nearly time. But he knew there was something else. Something that had always been there, always kept him going, even though it had always been hopeless, even though he had been deluding himself. Evie. His Evie. He sighed deeply.

Raffy's Evie.

The thought winded him, just as the discovery of

their little meetings in the tree had made him feel like his insides had been hollowed out. They were with Linus, together; they would always be together and Lucas would always be alone.

But that's where the mask came in. That's where the mask really paid its way.

'I will supply whatever information you need.'

'The time is approaching. Code 32. There is a full moon next Wednesday. We have a City key now. I'll be in touch. Message over.'

The icon disappeared and Lucas stared at the screen where it had been, offering such hope, his only connection to the man he'd worked for for so long. Then he stood up, his expression clearing to a blank as he left his office and walked down towards the System Operator Unit. Next Wednesday, Code 32. He would be ready. He would be waiting.

Evie's emotions were whirling as Linus closed down the communication device. 'That was really Lucas?' she asked.

'It really was Lucas,' Raffy said, his eyes gripped by the screen. He turned to Linus. 'So what's happening next Wednesday? What did you mean about it being time?'

'I meant,' Linus said, his familiar smile finally

reappearing, 'that it is time we paid your City a visit. Time we shook things up a bit.'

'We're going back?' Evie asked, her heart thudding loudly.

'No, we're not,' said Raffy. 'I promised we'd never go back. I promised Evie.'

'I want to go back,' Evie insisted, her voice low.

Raffy stared at her. 'You want to go back?'

'That's settled, then,' Linus exclaimed. 'We've been waiting a long time, but I think we're ready.'

'Ready for what?' Raffy asked.

'Ready to avenge your father's death. Ready to show the Brother up for what he really is. Ready to save Lucas and free the people of the City, to make it the place it was always meant to be.'

'But the police guards . . .' Raffy protested. 'How are we going to—'

'Don't worry about the police guards,' Linus interjected. 'We're going to take some friends with us.'

'Friends?' Evie asked cautiously. 'Which friends?'

'The Evils.' Linus smiled. 'Now come on, we've got work to do.'

18

It is cold, it is dark. She feels strange arms around her; her throat hoarse from crying, she is silent now. She feels her head fall forward; feels her eyes closing. She wants to sleep. But she forces them open again. She cannot sleep now, she knows that.

A door opens and a light shines out of it; as it closes behind them she is enveloped in a suffocating warmth. She is put down; she is on a chair. There are people looking at her; a crowd of them, she doesn't know how many. They are staring, pushing forward. She doesn't look at them. She looks down at her feet; it is something that she has learnt to do. Only make eye contact when you know what is happening, when you know that you are safe. She has seen violence in her life; she has seen men killed in front of her, seen savages taking human bodies for meat. Her parents tried to tell her that she was mistaken about what she saw, but she is wiser than her years. She knows.

'Delphine. Ralph. Would you come with me, please?' The man speaks; a couple leave the crowd and walk towards him. They talk in hushed voices. Then the couple approach Evie.

'Evangeline?' The man is the first to speak. He crouches down to her level. 'Evangeline, I am so glad you are here. I'm your father. This is your mother. We have been waiting for you.'

Evie is startled. She was prepared for many things, but not this. She breaks her rule; looks up. Their eyes lock.

'My father,' she says. 'My father is . . .' She trails off; she doesn't know how to finish the sentence, doesn't know where her father is.

'I am your father, Evangeline,' the man says gently but firmly. 'The man you came with will be looked after. He needs our help, and you want us to help him, don't you? You want us to help all the people you came with.'

Evie nods. The warmth is permeating her bones; it is intoxicating. She has not been warm for so long.

'Are you hungry, Evie? Shall we go and have some food?'

This time it is the woman speaking; her eyes are

scrutinising her, making Evie feel self-conscious. She nods again. The woman looks pleased. She holds out her hand and Evie takes it.

'Good,' says the man who carried her into this room. 'Good. Now, please wait here. There are more. Please be patient . . .'

It was Wednesday morning. Evie woke up and looked around. She was in a smallish tent with cream canvas walls and ceiling; under her was a mattress with cotton sheets; next to her was Raffy, deeply asleep still, his rhythmic breathing providing a slow tempo beat. They were alone; since arriving here there had been no more talk of being captive, no more ropes, no more threats. And yet Evie was more afraid now than ever before. Not for herself so much; she had stopped worrying about her future as soon as she'd learnt the truth about her past. But for all of them. Raffy. Lucas . . .

'Morning.' Raffy opened his eyes and the customary lopsided grin appeared on his face, making Evie laugh in spite of herself. The same grin that had greeted her in their tree for so many years, the same grin that had reassured her, comforted her, teased her for what felt like her whole life. Raffy had been the one constant, the one person she could rely on, talk to and confide in. Yet now, here, beyond the City walls, where they were free to be whoever they wanted . . . Somehow things felt different.

'Look,' he said, looking around. 'We're all alone.'

He grabbed her and pulled her towards him in a bear hug; but as she moved she turned so that she was facing away, his face meeting the back of her neck instead of . . .

Instead of her lips?

She frowned. They used to kiss all the time, in the City. Kisses that were full of hope, desperation and longing. Kisses that bound them together even whilst they were being torn apart. Kisses that spoke of their solidarity, their fervent belief in each other and their rebellion against the life that had been set out for them.

But since they had been here, since they had arrived at Base Camp, their lips had not so much as brushed each other's.

Evie knew that it was not Raffy's fault; she knew that it had not been he who had turned his head, changed the subject and given a hug instead, made a joke. What she didn't know was why.

She closed her eyes and took a deep breath; she had dreamt of lying like this with Raffy, had dreamt of a world where such a thing was possible. Now, somehow, his arms felt claustrophobic around her; his breath tickled her neck; he was suffocating her, pulling her down when she needed to . . .

Needed to what?

And then she knew what it was she had to do. There was a secret that was weighing her down, coming between them.

'Raffy,' she said quietly. 'There's something I have to tell you.'

'There's something I have to tell you, too.'

'There is?' Evie looked at him apprehensively.

He grinned. 'I have to tell you how much I love you. I have to tell you how beautiful you are.' He pulled her towards him again, kissed her, and Evie found herself kissing him back. As she arched towards him, he pulled off the old T-shirt she'd been sleeping in, pulled off his own shirt and her skin against his felt so exquisite, so dangerous, so right. And as she lay down, his eyes sought hers and looked into them so intensely, so deeply, that she felt perhaps he could see, perhaps he knew already, perhaps he had accepted it and forgiven her. And then she knew that he must, because he was inside her, because they were as one, and the ripples in her body were consuming her, making her cry out and grasp onto Raffy like a life raft, like her salvation. And then she was crying, tears of joy, but also something more, and as Raffy kissed them away, more came to take their place until her cheeks, her neck, the pillow beneath her head were wet.

'Don't cry, Evie. Don't cry,' Raffy whispered. 'Everything's going to be okay. Everything's going to be fine.'

And Evie nodded, because she wanted to believe him. She needed to believe him.

'So what was it you wanted to tell me?' He grinned, rolled off her and kissed her again. 'My beautiful Evie. What was it?'

She closed her eyes. Then opened them. 'I need to tell you something that happened. The night we ran away,' she said, her voice wavering.

Raffy's face darkened slightly. 'Look, I know what happened that night,' he said, turning away. 'I know I got Lucas wrong. I know you did what you had to do. I . . .' He swallowed, turned to face her again. 'Look, it doesn't matter, does it? We're free. We're here. We have each other.'

Evie nodded. Perhaps he was right. Perhaps it didn't matter. But she knew it did. He loved her, but he didn't know everything. The love wasn't real. Not yet.

'I kissed Lucas,' she whispered.

Raffy laughed. 'I know. I saw you. It wasn't the night we ran away. It was at work. I saw you, remember? I didn't like it, but you were matched to him. You didn't have a choice. I know that.'

Evie shook her head. 'I don't mean then. I mean I kissed him when he came to my room. When he told me you and I had to run away.'

Raffy didn't move. His face didn't change. For a second, a blissful, beautiful second, Evie thought that maybe she'd been worrying too much, that Raffy understood, that he could see that a kiss meant nothing . . . And then she saw his eyes, saw that they had gone black, and that it was not understanding that kept his face still, but anger – thunderous, consuming fury.

'You kissed him?' He stared at her, his eyes narrowed to slits, his expression cold as ice. 'You kissed Lucas?'

'I . . . I don't know how it happened,' Evie heard herself say. 'I didn't mean to. It just . . .'

Raffy stood up. 'I trusted you,' he said. 'I trusted you more than anyone else. I didn't care if there wasn't anyone else in the world, so long as there was you. And now . . . Now I find out you kissed my brother?'

Evie stood too, pulling a sheet around herself, holding her hands out to Raffy. 'I'm so sorry. I wanted to tell you, to explain. I love you, Raffy. Only you. But I had to tell you, I had to—'

'You love me? You don't know what love is,' Raffy spat, pulling on his ill-fitting clothes, lent to him by Linus. 'I don't even know who you are any more.'

Evie tried again – to touch him, to make him look at her, to forgive her, but he shrugged her off. 'I'm . . . I'm going for a walk,' he said angrily, marching out of the tent.

'A walk? Where?'

'Anywhere,' she heard him say as he disappeared outside, leaving her to fall back onto the makeshift bed, a crumpled mess, curling up next to her tear-stained pillow.

It took Evie half an hour to leave the tent herself. Half an hour of listlessness, pacing, rehearsing conversations in her head and falling back down on the bed in hopelessness and despair. Eventually, she dried her eyes and dressed herself, then went to the communal tap beneath the rainwater containers to splash water over her face. She had never felt so alone. And she had no-one to blame but herself. Would Raffy ever forgive her? Would his dark eyes turn soft again? She knew too well how long his anger could last, how slow he was to forgive. He had never forgiven Lucas; now he may never forgive her.

She scanned the camp but there was no sign of Raffy; no sign of anyone. Evie suspected that he and Linus would be sitting at the computers working through programming code, while everyone else would be in the food tent having breakfast. But Evie wasn't hungry, couldn't contemplate eating. Instead she navigated her way through the various tents, trying not to think too much about what she was doing and to think instead of practical things, of normal things. Like tents. Tents were the only suitable accommodation for them, Linus had told her and Raffy the day before. Tents offered protection but they were portable, easy to dismantle in a hurry. The City could build for permanence, with its wall around it and its dominance of the river, but Base Camp had to be moveable, had to be flexible and adaptable. Sometimes strength meant knowing when to run away, he'd said. And the words had stayed with Evie, though she wasn't sure why.

She moved past the tents, telling herself that she was just exploring, finding her way around. But she knew she wasn't. She knew exactly where she was going. She had lost enough people. She had lost enough love.

And then she was there, outside the tent she'd seen for the first time the day before, the tent that had filled her thoughts ever since.

'These are the lucky ones,' Linus had told her. 'These are the ones we managed to rescue. The others . . .'

He hadn't finished the sentence, had simply walked

on. But later she'd made him finish; later, over supper, she'd asked him everything. She'd seen a wary look in his eye, but she had also known he would tell her, because it was in his nature. And so he'd described how the Evils were kept in another camp, set up by the City. How the guards looking after them (his voice when he spoke these words heavy with sarcasm) beat them, mutilated them and raped them, because they had no rights, because they were evil incarnate, and because the guards had no other entertainment. He'd told her that every so often the Evils were brought to the City at night and let in to cause havoc and destruction, so that the people would continue to fear them and what lay outside the City walls. So they would believe that Man without the New Baptism was destined to become like the Evils: lawless cannibals who wanted only to destroy.

'I'm sorry,' he'd said quietly, reaching out and squeezing her hand. 'But you asked.'

And she'd nodded gratefully because he'd told her the truth and hadn't hidden things from her, like everyone else had her whole life. But inside, she'd felt a rage stronger than anything she'd ever experienced before; an anger that had consumed her, that consumed her still. Their lies. Their terrible, terrible lies. All her life she had feared being evil, had feared that she had evil within her and that she would let down her parents, let down the Brother. All her life she had been flooded with guilt at every transgression, every illicit meeting with Raffy, every less-than-generous thought about Lucas. And now . . . Now she knew the truth. That she was the daughter of Evils, that the Evils were not evil, but were victims of the City's cruel regime. That evil lived not outside the City's walls but within it, throughout it, with its secrets and its brutality.

She pressed her nose against the plastic window; inside she could see the people resting on mattresses just like the one she and Raffy had shared. But would never share again. She felt a desperate longing consume her, felt a miserable tear sting her eyes, but she forced her consciousness back to the present. Not now. Not now.

Many of the Evils' eyes were open; they were awake. But they would never really be awake again, Evie knew that. Their awareness had been taken from them. Their future. Their children.

A woman sat up slowly on her mattress and caught Evie's eye – the same woman who had caught her eye the first time Evie had seen them. The woman whose kind face had stirred something deep within Evie which had stayed with her. As Evie gazed at the woman, she felt herself grow warm. The woman smiled, waved and walked towards the window. Mesmerised, Evie reached out, pressing her hand against the plastic; the woman did likewise. She looked to be in her forties; a little younger than the woman who had pretended to be Evie's mother back in the City. She was more beautiful, too – even if her eyes were shadows, even if her mouth fell slackly and her movements were awkward. Her eyes had a sadness to them that Evie recognised, one that she had seen reflected back at her in the mirror every day of her life.

'Evie?' She started at the sound of Linus's voice; he was behind her and she had no idea how long he'd been there. Then again, she had no idea how long she'd been there either. 'It's time for breakfast, if you're hungry.'

'Not really,' Evie whispered. She could feel the woman's hand through the plastic.

'Come anyway. If you don't mind?' He put his arm around her to guide her away; Evie knew she was powerless to resist. She gave the woman one last smile, then turned to follow Linus.

'We look after them here,' he said as they walked. 'They're as happy as they're able to be.'

'I know,' Evie said, her voice slightly strangled.

'And we're going to stop what's happening.'

'I know,' Evie said again. But stopping it wasn't enough for her, she realised suddenly. It was too late for that. Because no one had stopped it from happening to her parents. Because no one had stopped it from ripping her life apart.

'Morning! Sleep well?' Martha was sitting next to Raffy and smiled brightly – too brightly, Evie found herself thinking. Had Raffy told her? Did she know that Evie had betrayed him? Did she judge her as Evie judged herself?

'Very well, thanks.' She smiled, then sat down opposite them. Raffy wouldn't look at her; he turned his shoulders just slightly so that he was facing away from her. Linus disappeared off to the counter and returned with some porridge and dried fruit.

As he sat back down, Raffy stood up. 'See you later,' he muttered as Evie stared after him.

'This'll set you up for the day,' Linus said, putting the porridge in front of her, his face once again creasing into the smile that Evie felt she'd known for years, not days.

She took it gratefully and started to eat, surprising herself when she found that she was hungry after all.

'Is everything okay?' Martha asked, concern filling her eyes. 'You don't seem yourself.'

'I'm fine,' Evie lied. She turned to Linus. She didn't

want Martha's concern. She wanted distraction. She wanted not to think about Raffy, not to feel the huge, painful hole in her heart that was of her own making. 'Where do you grow all your food?' she asked. 'Where are your animals?'

Linus exchanged a wry smile with Martha. 'We grow what we can around the back. And we've got a few goats. But largely we're foragers.'

'Foragers?' Evie asked, her brow wrinkling.

'He means we search for food,' Martha said.

'You mean like berries, that sort of thing?'

Linus grinned. 'Berries, squirrels, City grain . . .'

'City grain?' Evie asked doubtfully. 'But how do you carry it all the way from the City?'

She looked at Linus, saw a flicker of something in his eye and felt herself flare up. 'If you don't want to tell me the truth, that's fine,' she said bitingly. 'I mean, why should you? No one else ever has.'

Martha stared at her, her eyes wide with surprise, but Linus just put his hand over hers and pressed it gently. 'Evie, we're not keeping secrets from you. Martha and I were exchanging a private joke, but not a secret one. There are things you don't yet know about your City. I know it sells itself as being self-sufficient, but the small patches of land within the City walls can't sustain the population.'

'So then where do they get their food from?' Evie asked, but even as she did so, she realised she knew the answer. 'The camp,' she murmured. 'They make the Evils work.'

'We prefer to call them the damaged ones,' Linus said, his voice soft, 'but yes. In a nutshell.'

'And you steal the food?'

'We . . . assist with distribution,' Linus said, his eyes twinkling slightly.

Evie looked down at the porridge in front of her; suddenly she wasn't hungry any more. She pushed her bowl away.

'You don't want it?' Linus asked, a note of concern in his voice.

'You're using them too,' Evie retorted. 'They're feeding you as well as the City. I think I'd rather forage for berries, if it's all the same to you.'

Linus scraped back his chair. 'You could look at it like that,' he said.

'There's another way?' Evie asked stiffly.

Linus shrugged. 'The damaged ones are working for the City. They don't get a choice in that. The ones we've saved, the ones who are here, they don't work; they are cared for. We're not part of the regime. But we do mess with it. We do steal the food because it upsets the Brother, because if there are food shortages it will call into question the Brother's leadership. Because we need food to feed the people we rescue and to fight the evil that has corrupted the City.'

He spoke quietly and gently but she knew that he felt far from calm. Evie watched him carefully, wishing she could speak so articulately, so calmly when inside she felt like a tornado was whirling.

'We steal the food,' Linus continued, his eyes not leaving Evie's, 'because when we do, the guards who rule the mutilated ones with a rod of steel, who treat them with cruelty and contempt, are punished for the theft, and it's one way of bringing them to justice. But the real way of achieving justice is to win the war that we're waging. The real way of achieving justice is to take the City back, to tell its citizens the truth and to stop the Brother once and for all. And for that, we need strength. I'm not at Base Camp to build a new city or to establish farms. I'm here to wage a war.'

He reached into his back pocket and pulled something out – a gun, the same gun Evie had seen him with the first time she'd met him, when he'd captured her and Raffy, when she hadn't known who he was or what he wanted. He watched her watching the gun, then put it away again. 'How about you, Evie?' he asked then. 'Are you here to wage a war?'

The question hung in the air for a few seconds with

neither of them moving. And then, slowly, deliberately, Evie pulled the bowl towards her again and took a mouthful.

'Atta girl!' Linus grinned. 'Now hurry up because we've got work to do. You and Martha are on logistics and timetabling. Who's going to be where, when and how. We're going in tonight and we're going to surprise everyone. The City won't know what's hit it, but we have to be absolutely prepared and ready. Okay?'

'Okay,' Evie agreed, feeling Linus's gaze on her. Suddenly she didn't feel so alone anymore. She realised that she was part of something. And she still needed to earn Raffy's forgiveness, still felt a hole right in the centre of her, but she had something new to mask the pain a little; she had a purpose. 'Okay. We'll be ready.'

19

The Brother looked at the screen in front of him, trying to suppress his rage, trying to learn from Lucas and maintain a cool exterior even though inside he was at boiling point. Such betrayal. Such terrible, brutal betrayal. He should have known. He blamed himself. No he didn't. He didn't blame himself at all. Blame was irrelevant, anyway. What mattered was retribution, justice, defeat of those who thought they could challenge him and everything he'd worked so hard to build up. He was the Brother and they were . . . nothing. Savages. Pathetic weasels. And all in thrall to Linus, that pitiable, snivelling man who thought that he could change the world by giving people what they wanted. People didn't know what they wanted! People could never know. They needed to be told what they wanted. They needed to be led. And the Brother had led them. He had led them well. They were safe. They were ordered. They were happy . . .

The knock at his door made him jump, but he quickly composed himself. It was exactly on time; rather weaker than Lucas's knock, rather too hesitant for his liking, but he could work on that.

'Ah, Sam. Come in.' The young man looked apprehensive, worried. He believed he was in trouble, the Brother realised, and the thought made him smile. 'Please, sit down,' he said, motioning to the chairs on the other side of his desk. Sam sat in one gingerly, his leg muscles obviously tense, his entire body leaning forward.

'You have worked in the System Unit for how long now?'

'Five years,' Sam said.

The Brother nodded slowly. 'And I understand that you are quite the technician?'

Sam reddened. 'I do my best,' he said awkwardly. 'Lucas has taught us all well. I do my best,' he repeated.

'And that is all I ask,' the Brother said, smiling kindly, the smile he bestowed on his congregation at the Gathering.

'At least, that is all I ask usually. But sometimes more is required. Sometimes we are called upon to do much more, to rise to an occasion, for the better good, to serve our great City. Do you think that you, Sam, are up to such a task?'

Sam's eyes grew large; his legs were jittering up and down as though they were not under his control at all. 'I . . . I will do whatever I can,' he managed to say. 'Anything for our great City, Brother.'

'Good,' the Brother said, smiling again. 'Because sometimes things happen. Terrible things. Sometimes we discover that evil is all around us, in places we never suspected. Sometimes we realise that the System is testing us, that we must act to show our devotion to good.'

'Yes, Brother,' Sam said, though the Brother could see from his expression that he had no idea what he was talking about.

'Then it is decided,' the Brother declared with a nod. He leant forward. 'I have a system change for you, Sam. A system change that you must share with no one, do you understand?'

'Of course,' Sam replied.

The Brother handed him an envelope. 'Open it,' he said. Sam took it gingerly; his hands were shaking as he clumsily managed to rip it open.

'Now read it,' demanded the Brother. He watched carefully as Sam's eyes became saucers and his shaking became so pronounced that the Brother wondered if he was going to fall off the chair. 'You see what I mean when I say that you are to tell no one?'

Sam nodded. 'Lucas?' he whispered, his voice incredulous, desperate. 'But how . . . I . . .'

'It is not for us to ask such questions,' the Brother said firmly. 'It is for us to demonstrate our commitment and resolve. To be strong. To accept. To realise that we must be ever more watchful. Do you understand, Sam?'

Sam nodded miserably.

'And such a strong, brave deed will be rewarded,' the Brother continued, standing up to let Sam know it was time to leave. 'I will soon be without my second in command, my System chief. I will need someone to fill that position, Sam. Someone I can rely on.'

Sam met his eyes, understood what he was saying.

'You can rely on me,' he stammered, closing the file, standing up and walking towards the door. 'Thank you, Brother.'

'And thank you, Sam. I think a more positive system change will soon be generated in your favour. I think you'll enjoy being an A.'

He smiled to himself as he saw Sam's posture straighten slightly and a new confidence suddenly take hold.

'Thank you, Brother.' Sam hesitated at the door; his voice was almost a whisper.

'Thank the System,' the Brother said. 'As you know, I can only guide. It is the System that rewards those who show loyalty and goodness.'

Sam nodded nervously then left the room, leaving the Brother alone again. He let out a deep breath, put his hands up to support his head, then closed his eyes for his mid-morning nap.

Evie barely saw Raffy all morning; he was holed up with Linus in the System room, or he was just avoiding her. Probably both, she figured. She, meanwhile, had been with Martha, meticulously planning by the minute their invasion of the City. The word 'invasion' seemed strange to her – to invade the place she'd always considered home. But she knew it wasn't home, had never been home. Linus wanted to destroy the System that had changed the whole nature of the City; she found herself wanting to destroy the City itself.

But then she forced herself to remember that not everyone in the City was corrupt. She was angry at herself and it was making her angry with everyone and everything. She had to suppress her anger, had to suppress the voracity of the hate and rage that threatened to consume her when she let them off their leashes, when she allowed herself to feel instead of blocking her emotions and concentrating on the job at hand, pushing out of her head the knowledge of what had happened to her parents, the parents who had loved her, the parents who had brought her to the City for a better life.

The City of the good.

How hollow that description sounded now.

How empty everything seemed now.

'So, after we've been to the damaged ones' camp at 1800 hours, we start the march towards the City. We'll need to bring everyone simply to keep the damaged ones in some kind of order, but as soon as we get to the City, as soon as the damaged ones enter, only ten of us go through the gate; the rest drop back and hide outside the wall.'

'What will happen to them?' Evie asked Martha.

'They'll just stay hidden until they hear from us that—'

'Not them,' Evie broke in. 'The damaged ones. The Evils. What's going to happen to them?'

'They will divert the police guard away from us so that we can—'

'So we're using them, just like the City uses them,' Evie interrupted stonily.

She hated herself suddenly, hated herself for being undamaged, for sitting here in Base Camp planning something when they could do nothing, could think nothing, could feel nothing. She hated herself, but she hated the Brother more, the Great Leader, the people who had made it happen.

Martha looked at her in concern. 'We are working together,' she said patiently. 'If we get in, if Linus and Raffy disable the System and change it for good, if we can let everyone know what's been happening, then there won't be any more Evils. There won't be any more damaged ones. We need their help to get in. I think if they knew what the City had done to them, they'd be on our side. Don't you?'

Evie pursed her lips. 'But being on our side doesn't mean being happy to be used as target practice,' she said. 'Being on our side doesn't mean being happy to be used as a decoy.'

She wanted to see Raffy; needed to, like an ache. She wanted to see him look at her again the way he'd looked at her this morning, to feel whole like she'd felt when they'd made love and to feel that surge of hope, of belief. She wanted the sun to return, to warm her bones. But instead, all she could see was shadow.

'No, it doesn't,' Martha agreed. 'But sometimes war means that we face difficult decisions. The damaged ones in the camps are treated terribly. Inhumanely. If we are successful, those who survive the attack will be cared for properly. And there will be no more. There will be no more butchery. That has to be worth it, doesn't it?'

Evie nodded silently. It was a logical answer.

Then again, the City was full of logic. Logic and systems and order.

The opening to the tent swished back and Raffy came in, making Evie's heart jump, making her stomach constrict as she looked at him, her eyes full of hope. But he didn't return her gaze. Linus walked in behind him. 'How are things going?' he asked.

'Great,' Martha smiled. 'How's Raffy getting on with the System?'

'He's a natural,' Linus said proudly.

Martha raised her eyebrows. 'A natural, huh?'

Raffy grinned at her. 'Linus's System is awesome!' he said, sitting down as far away from Evie as he could. 'He's made a virus that's going to completely disable the City's System so we can rebuild it like it's meant to be. It's so amazing. It can tell when someone needs company, or when someone's unwell; it can even create games for when you're bored. If every house had a computer it could make sure everything's taken care of. Can you imagine?'

Raffy's eyes were shining and Evie found herself smiling at him, but he didn't see her. Or perhaps he chose not to.

'So what have you two been doing?' Linus asked.

Evie tried to hide the hurt that pulsated through her heart, her head, her whole body. Raffy would never forgive her. She had lost him, just as she deserved to. 'We're just working through numbers,' she said.

Martha shot her a little smile. 'We've organised the backpacks, we've got the timetable down, assuming that we're at the damaged ones' camp by 5 p.m. and out again by 6 p.m.'

'That sounds about right,' Linus agreed. 'So arriving at the City as it gets dark?'

'And at the point that most people will be at home,' Martha said.

Linus smiled. 'Exciting, isn't it?'

He looked at Evie, who tried to seem enthused. 'Yeah,' she managed to say.

'Well,' Linus went on, rubbing his hands together, 'going by Martha's timetable, we must be leaving here at what, 3 p.m.? 4 p.m.?'

'3.30 p.m.,' Martha said.

'So then I think lunch is our next big priority.' Linus smiled. 'Can't have growling stomachs, can we?'

'We certainly can't,' Martha grinned back, standing up. 'Evie, you want to come with me to the kitchens and see if we can convince someone to cook for us?'

'Sure,' Evie said, jumping up. Raffy moved back

slightly as she passed him, as though recoiling from her, and it felt like a punch to the stomach.

'So, kitchens,' Martha said once they were out of the tent. Evie hesitated.

'I'm just . . . going to the loo,' she said.

'Okay,' Martha called back. 'See you in a bit.'

Evie didn't move for a second or two, then she took a deep breath, checked that no one was looking and started walking away from the kitchens, away from Raffy and Linus, away from the bathrooms. She was going to finish what she had started. She had nothing else now.

She walked down the covered walkway, past the sleeping tents, past the System tent until she was there, outside the damaged ones' tent again, looking in hopefully through the window. And immediately the woman appeared, as though she'd known Evie would come, as though she'd been waiting. She walked towards the window, and Evie stretched out her hand and felt her pressing against the plastic, and she felt something more powerful than hatred, more powerful than anger. She knew. She knew deep down who this woman was.

She walked towards the door and smiled at Angel, who was standing guard outside, 'protecting the damaged ones' as Linus put it. 'I think Martha needs your help,' she said. 'Planning for tonight. She said she needs some logistics information.'

Angel frowned. 'Now?'

Evie pulled an uncertain face, moved towards him, lowered her voice. 'She said she needed some expert guidance on transporting the damaged ones. I can stay here if you want. While you go and see her?'

Angel looked unconvinced; Evie steeled herself.

'Or I could tell her you can't come?' she suggested. 'Only she's really busy. So's Linus . . .'

Angel looked around anxiously. 'I don't know,' he breathed. 'I don't know about leaving them.'

'For five minutes? I'll be here,' Evie said, a note of irritation in her voice. She eyed the ring of keys in Angel's hand; then her eyes travelled to the padlocks and chains keeping the doors to the tent closed. Protected? They weren't being protected. They were being kept prisoner.

'Okay.' It took Evie a couple of seconds to realise that Angel had relented. 'Okay. You stay here,' he said.

'Of course.'

'I won't be long.' He started to move; Evie dug her nails into her palms to give her courage.

'Shouldn't you give me the keys?' she asked.

'The keys?'

'In case something goes wrong. I'm not going to use

them, obviously, but I thought the keys had to stay next to the doors at all times. Isn't that what Linus said?'

Angel shook his head, 'I shouldn't,' he said.

Evie's eyes narrowed. 'Look I'm not asking for your gun. Just the keys. Just in case. We're on the same side, Angel. Don't you trust me?'

Angel paused, his face full of thought, full of anxiety. Eventually he nodded, walked back over to Evie and handed her the bunch of keys. Then, heavily, reluctantly, he headed down the walkway, only turning once; Evie offered him a smile when he did, taking up the exact same position he'd been holding for the past few hours.

Only when he'd turned the corner, only when she was sure that he wasn't coming straight back, did she move towards the door, taking out the keys, trying one, another, another, until she found the right one. Until the padlocks were coming off, until she was opening the tent door and going inside.

The woman was waiting for her, arms outstretched. Evie could see the look in her eyes, the same look she knew she had in her own.

'Mother.' She whispered the word as the woman took her hands, felt her arms, clasped her to her bosom. Her movements were jerky and seemed hard to control but Evie didn't care; she didn't care about anything any more – not the System, not the Brother, not Linus and his plans. She had found her mother. She had found the woman who had borne her, raised her, who had trudged for miles to find somewhere safe to live, whose life had been changed irreparably by the Great Leader and his cruel, abominable experiments on her brain.

'My name is Evie,' she managed to say through her tears. She could see a crowd gathering; the other damaged ones were walking towards them curiously, their rolling eyes not scary to Evie any more because she was one of them, because they were not evil but the result of it. 'My name is Evie and I think I'm your daughter.'

At this the woman moved her hands to Evie's shoulders, pushed her a few inches away, then smiled. It was not a warm smile; it was a manic, crazed smile, but Evie saw the beauty in it. She saw beyond the wild, staring eyes to the soul that lay beneath. The lonely, desperate soul of a mother scorned.

'They lied to us. They lied to all of us,' Evie told her, her eyes imploring her mother, willing her to understand. 'But I found you. I'm here now. You're safe.'

'Safe,' her mother said, the word just decipherable.

'Safe,' Evie repeated excitedly, their first real communication, the first sign that she was being understood. 'I'm not going back to the City. I'm going to stay here with you. I'm going to look after you. I'm going to—'

The movement was too quick for her to respond to, too unexpected to be prepared for. Evie wasn't even sure how it had happened, but she suddenly found herself in a vice-like grip, her mother's arm pressed against her neck, her mother's elbow digging into her clavicle. Evie forced herself to stay calm; her mother was afraid. She needed reassurance. Other damaged ones were moving towards the door; Evie realised too late that she had failed to lock it again, that they were opening it, shrieking in delight as they tugged at the zips. Soon there was a stampede as they started to tumble over each other.

'You're safe,' Evie said again, trying to avoid being trampled. 'You don't have to hurt me. I'm on your side. I'm here to help you. I'm here to—'

'City,' her mother screamed. 'City!'

'No,' Evie said, trying to loosen her mother's grip as her hand pressed against Evie's vocal passage, making her gasp for air. She had to reach the door before the others got out. Had to calm her mother down. Perhaps mention of the City had brought back terrifying memories. 'No, we're not in the City. You're safe here. You're—'

'City,' her mother screamed again as the door opened and damaged ones spilled out, their howls echoing around the covered corridor and reminding Evie of the Evils' howls heard from her bedroom as a child. She managed to suppress her fear, reminded herself that it was different, that they were different, that *she* was.

But her mother's grip was becoming too tight to bear; her oxygen supply was diminishing, and the other damaged ones were all leaving the tent. Evie gasped; heard voices, heard more angry howling from the damaged ones. And then the door opened again and Angel walked in, flanked by Linus and Martha; behind them other men were bringing the damaged ones back in, their hands behind their backs as they struggled and kicked out.

Evie's mother looked up, pulling Evie with her and making her cry out silently in pain as the pressure against her throat intensified. 'City or die. City or she die.'

'Annabel, let go of the girl.' It was Linus speaking, but Evie could barely hear him. Her mind was going dark; stars were appearing in front of her eyes. He and Angel approached; Evie's mother tightened her grip.

'Take me City or she die,' she said.

'You're not going to the City, Annabel,' Linus said,

and then Evie felt her neck being crushed and she knew for certain that she was dead, that the blackness was final, that everything was over. Then suddenly the pressure was released and she gagged, and someone's arms were around her and she was being sick and gasping frantically, and she was alive, and the pain around her neck made her cry out but still she pushed the arms away because she knew they weren't her mother's arms, knew that she had to find her, explain again . . .

She whipped round, her eyes searching through the confusion of men, damaged ones – and Raffy running towards her.

'Evie!' he shouted. 'Evie, are you okay? What happened? What . . .'

She shook her head. 'My mother,' she tried to say, but her voice had forsaken her. 'My mother . . .'

'Your mother? You think this is your mother?' Linus cried; behind him Evie saw Angel holding her mother. All the light had gone out of her eyes; she was limp.

'What have you done to her?' she asked angrily. 'What have you done?'

'Sedated her,' Linus said, his eyes seeking hers, refusing to let her look elsewhere. 'You thought she was your mother?'

'I know she is,' Evie said bitterly. 'I'm going to look

after her. I'm going to take care of her. Stop you giving her drugs every time she gets angry. We're going to look after each other.'

'You think she's capable of looking after you?' Linus sighed. 'Okay, Angel, take her to her bed. Evie, come with me please.'

He didn't wait for a reply; he took her by the arm, led her out of the tent, sat her down and gave her some water. 'You want to save that woman? You want to look after her?'

'She's not that woman. She's my mother,' Evie insisted, slumping over. Tears of frustration, anger and loneliness were running down her face. 'I know she is. Why won't you just admit it? Why do you care, anyway? No one else does.'

'I care because it's not true,' Linus said, sitting back and putting his arm around her; she stiffened and he withdrew it.

'How do you know?' Evie swung round to face him, her eyes flashing angrily. 'How do you know?'

'Because she only came to us a year ago.' Linus looked pained, suddenly, his eyes darker. 'Because . . .' He stopped, put his head in his hands briefly, then turned to Evie again. 'Evie, she's not your mother. I know that. But even if she was . . . even if we found her . . . You have to understand. The damaged ones are not human, not as we are. When the amygdala was removed, it was supposed to remove the evil from people's brains, but in reality, it removes everything. All morality. All idea of good and evil, cause and effect. The damaged ones are . . . damaged, Evie. Irreparably damaged. Annabel is one of the more advanced, or the less brutalised, whichever way you want to look at it. She has desires, which is more than can be said for the others.'

'Desires? So that makes her human,' Evie whispered. 'That makes her like us.'

'No,' Linus disagreed. 'No, it just makes her dangerous. Because she has only one desire. And that desire is to go back to the City. She thinks that we stole her away, that we're keeping her from the place she struggled for so long to get to. She doesn't know what happened to her there. She doesn't know that they tossed her out.'

'I can explain,' Evie said uncertainly. 'I can make her see . . .'

'She was going to kill you,' Linus stated, his voice serious, his eyes suddenly staring at her intently. 'She was going to kill you. That's how much she wants to go back to the City. Do you see? She lured you in as bait.'

'No.' Evie shook her head, tears streaming down her face. 'No.'

'Yes,' Linus said, putting his hand on hers. 'That's why we need to go back to the City. That's why we need to change things. Fight back. For your parents. For all the other damaged ones. For all the D's and the K's and for all the misery the Brother's System has caused.'

'And my parents?' Evie asked defiantly.

Linus breathed out slowly. 'Your parents, if they are still alive, are incapable of being your parents.'

'No.' Evie shook her head. 'No, that's not true. You just want me to think that so I'll help you with your plan. So I'll give you the City key. Well I won't. Not unless you set my mother free.'

Linus looked at her, his eyes crinkling. 'Evie, we have the key. You think it's been in Raffy's rucksack all this time?'

Evie glared at him. 'You have it?'

'We've been planning this a long time,' Linus replied. 'Your key, Lucas, these are the ingredients that urged us forward. But not by much. We've been ready. We've been waiting. Are you with us? Are you going to come? Fight? Change things?'

Evie looked at him, took in his nut-brown, lined face, his twinkly blue eyes, the kindness, the strength and the pain etched across his features. Then she looked back at the damaged ones' tent, where Angel stood outside and Raffy stood next to him, looking at her anxiously, giving her a little smile when he caught her eye.

And she nodded, a small movement that could have easily been missed. But Linus didn't miss it.

'Atta girl,' he said under his breath, the words more encouraging this time, as his arm moved back around her and gave her a squeeze. 'And Evie, you're not alone. There's no reason to feel that. We're with you. Your friend Raffy is with you, even if it doesn't feel like it right now. And . . .' He stood up. 'And I imagine Lucas will be happy to see you, too.' He winked, and Evie felt a strange sensation, like somehow Linus knew something. But he couldn't. It was impossible. And before she could think about it any more, he was gone. When she looked up she saw Raffy hovering, a few feet away, his expression unreadable.

'Everything okay?' he asked, his hands in his pockets.

'Everything's fine,' she managed to reply.

Raffy nodded, then slowly walked towards her and sat down at her side. He didn't touch her, didn't talk to her, but he sat there. And for that, Evie was more grateful than she could put into words.

20

Dirt, dust and grime in her eyes, in her nose, choking her. A hand around hers, pulling her on, reassuring her. A rock catches her unawares and she falls, her face pressed into the ground; she lifts her head and wipes her forehead – there is blood on the back of her hand. Her lip begins to quiver but before tears can come she is swept up; her arms wrap around a familiar neck and the journey continues.

The rhythm of his walking calms her; she feels safe. His body is warm; she nestles into him. She can smell him; sweat, hunger, determination, love. 'Nearly there,' he murmurs into her ear. 'Nearly there, my darling.'

'Just you wait,' he says as she drifts off to sleep. 'We're going to the land of plenty. Of peace. We're going to be so happy, Evangeline. You just wait and see . . .'

A vision. Light. Men coming towards them. They are safe. She is safe. She sees the smiles on the faces of her father, her mother; their eyes lit up. They squeeze her hands. 'We are here, Evie. At last we are here. We told you, didn't we? We told you we'd find it . . .'

And then one of the other men comes towards her and tries to take her. And her father tries to hold onto her. 'What are you doing? This is our daughter. She is with us. We are together. We are—'

But the man is not listening; he does not see them, does not hear her mother's cries. He takes Evie and marches away; she can still hear her parents' frantic questions, asking where she is going, when they will see her next. She hears them shouting her name, telling her they will see her soon.

The man smiles at her. 'Forget about them,' he says. 'They are not worth thinking about any more. Come with me . . .'

She is in a room. It is cold, it is dark. She feels strange arms around her; her throat hoarse from crying, she is silent now. She feels her head fall forward; feels her eyes closing. She wants to sleep, but she forces them open again. She cannot sleep now, she knows that – the man has told her, the man who smiles but with danger in his eyes. He has told her that her parents do not exist, that the people she travelled for so long with, the people whose hope and stories of salvation kept her strong when she felt weak, who gave her the motivation to keep walking when all she wanted to do was curl up, give up, are no longer here. That they have gone. That they have deserted her, just as they always intended to.

The people stare at her. She looks down at her feet; it is something that she has learnt to do. Only make eye contact when you know what is happening, when you know that you are safe. She has seen violence in her life; she has seen men killed in front of her, seen savages taking human bodies for meat. Her parents have tried to tell her that the world can be a beautiful place, but she is wiser than her years. She knows that it is not.

'Delphine. Ralph. Would you like to meet her properly?' A couple approach Evie.

'Evangeline?' The man is the first to speak. He crouches down to her level. 'Evangeline, I am so glad you are here. I'm your father. This is your mother. We have been waiting for you.'

Evie is startled. She was prepared for many things, but not this. She breaks her rule; looks up. Their eyes lock.

'My father,' she says. 'My father is . . .' She trails off; she doesn't know how to finish the sentence, doesn't know where her father is.

'I am your father, Evangeline,' the man says gently but firmly. 'The man you came with will be looked after. He needs our help, and you want us to help him, don't you? You want us to help all the people you came with.'

Evie nods. The man offers her food and water; she takes it hungrily.

'Is she diseased? Is there anything wrong with her?' This time it is the woman speaking; her eyes are scrutinising her, making Evie feel self-conscious.

'She is not diseased, Delphine. She is three years old. She is the daughter you have longed for, is she not?' The first man stares at Evie. 'You are the daughter that this lady has been longing for, aren't you? You will be a good, loyal daughter, to her and to the City? Won't you?'

Evie nods. She knows that her parents are gone. She knows.

'I will be a good daughter,' she says, her voice quiet, husky.

'You will when you've had the New Baptism,' the woman retorts.

'She will have it in the morning,' the first man reassures her calmly. 'With the others.'

'She's perfect,' says the man who calls himself her father. 'Delphine, come on. There are people waiting. Let's take her home. Let's take her.'

The woman looks her up and down one more time, then nods. 'Yes,' she says. 'She'll do.'

She holds out her hand and Evie takes it.

'Your name is Evangeline?' her new father asks her. Evie nods. 'I think we'll call you Evie,' he says.

'My parents call me Evie,' she whispers.

The woman stops, grabs her shoulders. 'We are your parents,' she hisses. 'You do not have other parents, do you understand? Only evil children talk about other parents. Only wicked, terrible children who are punished for their wickedness. We are your parents. Forget the people you came with, just as they have forgotten you. Do you understand? Do you?'

Evie nods. She does understand. Suddenly, as she wakes up, she understands everything.

They walked in silence, Linus at the front with Martha, then Raffy and Evie, and three other men. The damaged ones were being brought separately in a transporter by Angel and five other men who would meet Linus and the others a mile from the City.

The plan was simple enough. Let the damaged ones into the City via the East Gate, wait for the uproar to start, then sneak round to the West Gate where Lucas would be waiting. Then it would be straight to the government building where Linus and Raffy would get to work, changing the System back to what it was always meant to be. Meanwhile Evie and Martha would send out new System changes, making everyone an A, telling them in their letters that the labelling was a farce, that it was over, that a new dawn had begun. Lucas and Angel would take the Brother, make sure that he gave the order for the letters to go out, and make sure that his reign came to an end as soon as everyone knew the truth.

And then . . .

Then, Linus had told Evie gently, she and Raffy could choose what they wanted to do. She, Raffy and Lucas, he'd corrected himself, bringing a flush to Evie's cheeks. They could stay in the City, he'd said. They could come back to Base Camp. They could go and join one of the other communities, the other cities that he'd told them about. Evie had asked him if he was going back to Base Camp, but he hadn't answered; he'd just smiled, his face creasing even more than usual, his blue eyes twinkling as though they were sharing a private joke, even though Evie didn't know what the joke was or why it was meant to be funny.

'Do you think that you can ever really get rid of evil?' she'd asked him. 'I mean, if the New Baptisms had actually worked?'

Linus had looked at her, the smile still on his face,

but his eyes sad. 'I'm not sure evil really exists,' he said, his voice low and quiet. 'I think people can do terrible things if they're pushed or ignored or angry, if they feel hopeless and helpless and desperate enough.' Then he'd looked her right in the eye. 'But you, Evie, you are not evil. Do you understand? Whatever you've been told, whatever you've been led to believe. You. Are. Not. Evil. And nor is Raffy. You have to remember that. You have to hold on to that. You promise?'

And Evie had nodded, and she'd wanted to believe him, but she couldn't be sure. Because the anger inside her was still raging and there were terrible ideas in her head that she couldn't suppress – didn't want to suppress. But she didn't tell Linus. She just managed a little smile, then walked over to Raffy because it was time to leave, because it was time . . .

Lucas stared at the computer screen, at the message from Linus, and he took a deep breath, trying to contain his fear, his excitement. It was happening. After all this time, it was finally happening. He looked around; he knew no one was watching, knew no one suspected, but his reflexes were on high alert, as they always were, as they had been for most of his life. Soon he could be free. Truly free. His promises to his father would be met; he could live again.

Carefully, he closed the message, wiped the device, removed all traces of it from the System. Then he stood up, wavering for a moment as his legs nearly gave way beneath him, the enormity of what was happening hitting him like a tornado. But immediately he regained his balance, his poise. This was no time to be allowing emotions to surface; there would be time for that later. Right now, he had to focus, to concentrate. There were things to do. The key to the West Gate had been secured; he had visited Greer, the key holder, on the pretext of discussing security, and had easily secreted it out of the house. But he had to get it to the gate at the right moment, had to time it perfectly. Then he had to secure access to the government buildings for Linus and Raffy, for Evie and Martha.

Evie.

He shook himself. He was ready. Everything was ready.

He walked towards the door, took one look back, then opened it. And his face fell.

'Lucas,' the Brother greeted him, standing just outside with Sam, Lucas's deputy, at his side. A little smile of quiet triumph played on his lips. There were police guards behind him; they stared at Lucas with menace in their eyes, the usual respect and deference gone. 'Are you going somewhere? Only I hoped we might have a word.'

His eyes met Sam's, who quickly looked away. And then Lucas knew.

'Might I shut down my computer first?' he asked.

The Brother shook his head. 'I don't think that will be necessary,' he said, his eyes suddenly very hard. 'I think it would be best if you came straight away.'

The guards stepped forward. Lucas closed his eyes for just a second, allowing himself just the briefest moment, then he steeled himself and nodded.

'Of course,' he said formally, his eyes glazing over, his mask, his constant companion, covering his face once more. 'Whatever you say, Brother.'

The heat was scorching as they walked, merciless as it beat down on top of them, their hats no match for its relentlessness.

'Drink,' Linus said every half an hour or so. 'Keep drinking. We have a long way to go.'

After four hours they stopped for some food – some sandwiches and hard cakes that felt heavy in Evie's stomach.

'Now we rest for twenty minutes,' Linus told them. 'And then we must move again if we're going to get to the City for sundown.'

Raffy and Evie headed for the shade of a sparse tree and sat against it heavily. They had barely spoken in over a day, had existed together but separately. It was a purgatory that Evie had come to accept, even to appreciate. Because anything was better than being alone. And because she understood – she knew that she deserved it.

'You scared?' Raffy asked.

Evie turned to him, her expression curious. She was many things, but it hadn't occurred to her to be scared.

'Not scared,' she said. 'I'm just . . .' She searched for the right word and floundered. There was no word, nothing that could encapsulate how she felt – how apprehensive, excited, driven, angry, determined. And then she realised that she *was* scared. She was scared of failing. 'Maybe a bit,' she conceded.

'Me too,' Raffy admitted quietly.

'Okay,' Linus said, walking over. 'Time to get going. You guys okay? Need anything?'

'We're fine,' Raffy said, standing up, and a few seconds later, as though it were an afterthought, holding out his hand to Evie awkwardly.

'Fine,' she agreed as she did her best to pull herself up while at the same time accepting his offer, not wanting to agitate him, not wanting to turn down any suggestion of warmth between them.

'Good,' Linus declared. 'No stops now until we meet with Angel and the damaged ones a mile from the City.'

Lucas was led out of the System building and through a covered passage, used only for dissidents and prisoners, which led to the hospital.

'Is someone going to tell me what's going on?' he asked eventually when he was led into a room, forced into a chair and then chained to it, his hands behind his back.

'What's going on? Oh, Lucas. I think you know what's going on. Your plans are being ruined. That's what's going on. You've been discovered, you traitor. All these years I have depended on you, trusted in you, and all along you were planning to betray me. Well, I too am capable of duplicity, Lucas. I too can spy and watch and keep tabs. In fact, I am rather good at it, as you should have realised before you decided to take me on. So this is what's going to happen. You will be made a K as of tomorrow. The System change is already in progress. Your friends, when they arrive, will be met by an army of police guards who will kill them all before they so much as set foot in the City. I am sorry that you let evil into you, Lucas. I am sorry that it has come to this. Which is why you will be given the New

Baptism. Everyone deserves a second chance, Lucas, even you.'

'The New Baptism?' Lucas stared at him in alarm. 'But if I'm a K, you should—'

'Leave you to be mauled by the Evils? Oh, Lucas, you have been listening to gossip again.' The Brother smiled, playing with him. 'Everyone knows that K's are reconditioned. We are a forgiving society, after all. We protect our flock. And anyway, you are too consumed with evil to be safe. I cannot risk having evil of your scale present, even beyond our walls.'

Lucas wrestled against his chains. 'You can't do this,' he shouted. 'Sam! Do something! You know me. You know I'm not evil. Help me. Get me out of here.'

But Sam refused to meet his eyes; instead he walked towards the door. He believed the Brother, Lucas realised with a thud. Believed that Lucas was evil, that K's were reconditioned, that everyone had the New Baptism – believed everything he had ever been told. Just like Lucas had, before his father had revealed the truth. 'Shall I inform the police guard?' Sam asked the Brother.

'Tell them sundown,' the Brother said. 'That was the time you agreed in your last message, wasn't it?' he continued, smiling at Lucas.

Lucas closed his eyes.

'Sundown it is,' Sam said, leaving the room.

'Well, much as I'd love to stay and chat, I have a few things to be getting on with,' declared the Brother. 'Guards, keep him here. Don't take your eyes off him. Do you understand? This man is very dangerous and very evil. Do not listen to what he has to say because he will do his best to corrupt you.'

The guards nodded.

'Goodbye, Lucas,' the Brother said then, sweeping towards the door. 'Goodbye.'

'Okay. We wait here.' It was just beginning to get dark; the cool air felt light on the back of Evie's neck but the hairs on it stood up as they stopped. No one was talking; there was nothing to say. Everyone was concentrating, focusing; Linus was pacing up and down, making everyone feel slightly on edge – as though the tension weren't high enough already. And then, they heard it. The sound of wheels driving through the dust. A sound rarely heard and barely understood by Evie and Raffy. The sound got louder as the wheels rushed towards them, a low hum that got somehow higher as it got nearer. And then the van appeared in front of them, looming huge on the horizon. But as it got closer, another sound could be heard; a sound that made everyone stop, glance at each other, then look away quickly. A wailing, a crying, angry grunts that were instantly recognisable, that filled Evie with terror and repulsion then shame for feeling such things about her own people, about those whose lives had been damaged irreparably by the cruelty of the City.

The van stopped a few metres away; it was huge, far larger than anything Evie had ever seen on wheels, or seen moving full stop. As big as a house, she found herself thinking. Or at least one of the Base Camp tents. And then the doors were opening and the wails and grunts became unbearably loud as Angel got out and the damaged ones in the back started to shout, crying out and moaning, their faces clearly visible through the glass. Evie felt her eyes fill with tears which she was helpless to control. Linus walked over. 'They are not who they were before,' he said gently to her, so quietly no one else could hear. 'Remember that. And if they were, they would be with us. Every step of the way.'

Evie nodded and felt Raffy's hand tighten around hers. She squeezed back as hard as she could, hoping to tell him everything with that one movement, but then he let go and everything was cold again. She didn't want to look at the damaged ones, but she couldn't help it. She had to see them, each of them, with their staring eyes, their convulsing bodies, their terrifying screams and moans. The Evils. The feared ones. They seemed more afraid than anyone she had ever seen in her life, even Raffy's father the day he was taken away. She watched them, then slowly turned away as Linus gave the signal to start walking. But as she walked, she could still see them in her mind's eye. Could still see the people who had carried her to the City, believing they were being offered a second chance. The people who had believed in the Great Leader, who had offered themselves up like sacrificial lambs. They were the real killables. They had been disposable. Used once, then again and again by the Brother and the Great Leader to serve their despicable ends.

And now they were being used one more time. For her ends. For Linus's.

'You okay?' Raffy asked, looking at her anxiously.

She shook her head. 'I can't do this,' she replied, welling up. 'I can't let the damaged ones go to their deaths.'

'Their deaths?' Linus asked, looking slightly taken aback.

'They're decoys. The police guard will kill them, you know they will.'

'I know nothing of the sort,' Linus said, his face serious suddenly. 'You think I'd let the police guard lay a hand on them? No, Evie, they've suffered enough. They're just going to shake things up a bit, get some revenge for what they've been through. We all are.'

'Really?' Evie asked dubiously.

'Trust me,' Linus said, winking. He waited for Evie to nod, then started to walk. 'Okay, everyone, let's go.'

21

'Okay. Angel, you head to the East Gate with the damaged ones. Everyone else, you come with me. Now remember. We're in the City for one hour maximum. We change labels, we disable and reprogramme the System and then we go. Understand?'

Everyone nodded, then they watched in silence as Angel and his men got back into the van and drove off, the wails and groans of the damaged ones inside echoing through the still night until they could barely be heard.

'Lucas is going to be at the gate?' Raffy asked as they started to walk again. There was an edge to his voice that Evie suspected only she noticed and her heart sank. He was angry again – an anger that would only increase when he saw Lucas.

'That's the plan,' Linus said, swinging his hands by

his sides as though he was taking a little stroll instead of marching into battle.

'What if they've changed the locks on the East Gate? I mean, they know Evie and I took the key.'

'They haven't. There's no need to. The gates are bolted from the inside.'

'So how are the damaged ones going to get in?'

'Lucas has opened the bolts,' Linus said, stopping to turn to Raffy. He sounded impatient, but Evie could see his eyes twinkling in the moonlight. 'Raffy, I've told you. All you have to concentrate on is the System when we get there. Reprogramming it. You can do that?'

'Of course I can,' Raffy answered gruffly. 'I showed you. A thousand times.'

'I know you can. I trust you. So try trusting me.' Linus winked before turning back to the front to continue marching.

Raffy opened his mouth as if to say something, then appeared to think better of it. Evie knew how he felt; she felt it too: anxious and in need of answers, reassurance, promises. And Linus seemed too confident, too relaxed, like he didn't understand what they were doing, like he wasn't taking it that seriously.

She shivered, the cool air bringing up little goose-bumps on her arms. Then the shiver intensified as she saw a wall on the horizon. The City wall. They were here. They were just minutes away. She glanced at Raffy, who held her gaze for a second or two, then shoved his hands in his pockets. 'Looking forward to seeing Lucas?' he asked pointedly, and his voice was so cold it felt like a stab to Evie's chest.

She looked away, her eyes travelling over to Linus, to where the glint of a gun could be seen on the holster around his waist.

Linus reached the gate first. He stood for a few moments as though unwilling to go any closer.

'What are you waiting for?' Raffy asked impatiently. 'Let's go in.'

'I'm waiting to hear that the damaged ones are inside the City walls,' Linus said, raising his eyebrows. 'And I'm waiting because sometimes it's important to wait, to consider, to reflect. A moment of calm before the storm. Ever heard that saying?'

Raffy shook his head.

'Okay,' Linus said smiling slightly. 'Well, I'm also waiting because we don't have a key to this gate, remember. I'm waiting for Lucas to let us in.'

Raffy pulled a face and thrust his hands further into his pockets. Evie walked over to Linus.

'How will he know we're here?' she asked. 'Don't you need to knock or something?'

'Knock?' Linus laughed. 'These gates are ten inches thick. You think he'd hear me knocking? Just be patient.'

Now it was Evie's turn to redden. 'I'm just asking,' she said, sticking out her bottom lip. 'You know, Raffy and I want to change things just as much as you do. We're just trying to help. There's no need to laugh at us.' Linus stepped towards her.

'I'm sorry,' he said gently, putting his arms around her, just as she'd hoped he would. 'That was unfair of me. Lucas will know we're here because he will hear the damaged ones.'

Evie reached her arms around Linus, resting her head on his chest. 'I'm sorry,' she said as she slipped her hand into his pocket. 'I'm just . . .'

'No need to explain,' Linus whispered. 'We're all just . . . But we're going to do this. You have to believe that.'

'I do,' Evie whispered back.

She glanced over at Raffy, who was looking at her with disdain. Then they heard the wailing, the terrifying moans as the damaged ones rampaged through the streets, the smashing of windows, the screams of terrified people.

'And now,' Linus said, as Evie stepped back, braced herself, 'now the gate should open.'

*　　*　　*

Lucas stared down at the chains around his ankles and around his wrists. Chains so tight there was no way of releasing them, chains that chafed his skin, causing it to bleed.

He could hear the damaged ones outside, could hear the havoc they were creating, the fear as City dwellers ran for their lives. Linus would be at the gate now, waiting for him, waiting for it to open. Raffy, Evie too, depending on him.

He let his head fall back and closed his eyes.

Linus was pacing up and down; everyone was exchanging worried glances, not daring to say anything, not daring to ask why the gate wasn't opening. It had been five minutes since they'd heard the damaged ones within the City walls. The police guard would be called out; the disruption would not last for long. They should be in by now, making their way to the government building. Lucas should be opening the gate.

Little knots of fear were working their way up Evie's back as she stood, shivering, stiff and cold; waiting, watching, hardly daring to breathe, certainly not daring to think the unthinkable, that something had happened, that everything Linus had promised them was in jeopardy. She closed her eyes, reached into her pocket and felt the cold steel pressing against her leg. Stolen, hidden, her little secret.

They had to open the gate. They had to. Suddenly, without warning, she ran at it, pounding on it with her fists. 'Let us in. Lucas, let us in,' she shouted. 'You have to let us in now. Otherwise it will be too late. You have to let us in . . .' She was sobbing, the tears cascading down her cheeks, and Raffy ran to her, tried to pull her away, but she wouldn't let him. Instead she took his hands and slammed them against the gate over and over until he, too, was pounding it, kicking it, shouting out, calling for Lucas. Even though they knew he wasn't there, couldn't be there – even though Linus was looking at them with pain in his eyes because he knew too, because he had to know . . .

Then, suddenly, without warning, they heard a creak and Evie and Raffy fell forward as the gate slowly opened. As they tumbled through, a face appeared, a face that Evie recognised but not one she expected to see.

'Mr Bridges,' she said, her voice strangled. 'What are you . . . ?'

'Lucas sent me,' he answered, his voice anxious and low. 'I'm sorry I'm late. There's a bit of commotion. The police guard . . .' He looked around, his eyes large and fearful. 'I've got a message for someone called Linus.'

'That's me,' said Linus, stepping forward and clasping Mr Bridges' hand. 'You must be William.'

'William. Yes, sir. William Bridges at your service.'

'Tell me your message then get yourself home,' Linus said gently. 'And know that I am more grateful than I can say.'

Mr Bridges nodded anxiously. 'He said the labels . . . Lucas said you were going to stop the labels. He said . . .'

'We're here to stop more than labels,' Linus told him grimly. 'There's no need to live in fear any more. No need, do you understand?'

Mr Bridges nodded but he looked unconvinced. 'It's my family,' he said. 'I don't mind them coming after me, but my wife, my children . . . They're good people. I don't want to bring more shame on them. I don't want—'

'You're doing a good thing, William,' Linus said seriously. 'You're protecting your family's future. Remember that.'

William looked down. Then he whispered his message in Linus's ear, shot him one last look of hope mingled with desperation, and then he was off, a dark shape blending into the shadows of the night as he ran back through the streets. Evie watched him go, her mouth open.

'Where's Lucas?' she asked Linus. 'Did you know he wouldn't be here?'

'Yeah, where's Lucas?' Raffy asked bitterly. 'Evie's really desperate to see him.'

Evie felt her cheeks burning but she forced herself to stay silent.

'Lucas is a bit tied up,' Linus said, looking at the shadows that Mr Bridges had disappeared into. 'He said that he was getting William here to let us in. And William has just told me all I need to know about what to do next. But now isn't the time for talking. Now we have work to do.'

22

They ran through the shadows. Evie had never seen the City like this; police guards were on every corner. All around was panic; people running, guards chasing them. And then, as Evie and her group turned a corner, they saw them: the damaged ones. They were advancing towards her, towards Linus and Raffy, running like beasts, their teeth bared, snarling as terrified City dwellers scattered. Guards arrived, batons in hand, to beat them down, and Evie ran towards them screaming, 'No,' but Linus pulled her back.

'Angel will look after them,' he said, his voice low. 'Have faith.'

And Evie tried to have faith, but the guards had nearly reached them, their batons outstretched, and people were screaming at them to kill the Evils, to rid the City of their corrupt and wicked influence.

Suddenly, a light shone out, so bright that Evie's eyes closed against it and everyone stopped running for a moment. By the time it went off and Evie could see again, the damaged ones had disappeared and only their moans could be heard as they ran through another street, the police guards chasing after them again.

Evie watched open-mouthed as she realised what was happening. Because they weren't moaning. They weren't wailing. They were laughing. They thought it was a game. They were okay.

Linus saw the look on her face and winked. 'A few more minutes of that and they'll be out of the City,' he said to Evie. 'I told you they wouldn't get hurt. Come on. This way.'

He walked purposefully and Evie and Raffy jogged after him with Martha behind them. If anyone noticed them in the darkness it wasn't apparent; people were scurrying to their women, to safety, heads down, expressions grim, their entire focus escaping from the Evils. Evie tripped after Linus; it took them just a few minutes to get to the government building where she had spent so much of her time.

'Hasn't changed,' Linus said grimly, then walked right past it.

'Where are we . . . ?' Evie called after him, but

stopped before finishing the sentence because she saw where they were going. Into the Hospital. Linus stopped outside, motioning for them to follow him.

'Lucas is in here,' he announced. 'We get him out first.'

He started to march again and Evie and Raffy raced behind him, Martha once more bringing up the rear. The building was deserted; the lights were off and an eerie silence filled the air. 'This way,' Linus muttered. 'If I know the Brother, he'll have Lucas where he had everyone else. Where Fisher did his butchery. Where . . .'

He stopped outside a door and took a deep breath. It was the first time Evie had ever seen him pause, the only time she'd ever seen him look . . . vulnerable. Then he turned the handle. The door was locked. 'What did I say?' he cried, a half smile returning to his face. 'I knew it.' He took a few steps back, ran towards it and kicked; nothing happened.

'What about using these?' Raffy held out a bunch of keys.

Linus stared at it.

'They were behind the reception desk. I figured someone left them in a hurry before going to the Meeting House.'

Now Linus's smile was filling his face, creating even

more lines if that were possible. He took the keys, clapped Raffy on the back and opened the door. Everyone followed him through, a sharp intake of breath audible from each of them as they did so. They were in a large room containing four beds. The room smelt of disinfectant, but there were red patches on the floor that looked like . . . Evie shivered and looked away. She was desperate to ask where Lucas was but something stopped her – the memory of that kiss, the confusion buried deep inside her. Instead she stood silently, watching as Martha walked up and down, touching the beds, pressing her hands to them one after another.

'This is where they had him,' she whispered. 'This bed. I remember.'

'Had who?' Evie wanted to ask, but somehow couldn't. She watched as Linus moved over to her and put his hand on her shoulder. 'A lot of terrible things were done here. Are you okay?' he asked gently.

Martha nodded. She wiped at her eyes, then turned towards him, a look of determination on her face. 'I'm fine,' she said. 'Let's do what we came here to do. Let's change things once and for all.'

'Good girl.' Linus squeezed her shoulder. Then he walked towards another door. 'Let's see if one of these keys opens this door, shall we?' He looked through the bunch Raffy had given him. 'This looks like the ticket.'

He tried one key, then another. The second one worked; the door swung open, revealing a small, window-less room.

'Used to be a store cupboard,' Linus said cheerfully. 'So you're Lucas?'

Evie followed him in to see Lucas, on the floor, tied up and gagged. His face was black with dust, but when he saw her, his eyes lit up, eyes so different from the eyes she'd known for so long. And as Evie held his gaze, she found herself staring at the face she had seen for the first time in her bedroom all those days ago, a face that knew pain, despair, hope and everything in between, and she felt something shift inside her – some-thing that unsettled her, scared her. But before she could make sense of it, Raffy appeared at her side; instinct-ively she looked away, her cheeks reddening.

'Let's untie you, shall we?' Linus suggested, bending down. Martha joined him; only Raffy and Evie hung back. Minutes later, Lucas was free. He stretched, rubbed at his raw wrists and ankles, then embraced Linus.

'You came,' he said, his voice hoarse. 'I knew you'd come.'

'Of course we came.' Linus grinned. 'But now we've got work to do. As have you. You're ready for what needs to happen?'

Lucas nodded. 'Everything's set up.'

'Then wash your face, have a drink, and let's go.' Linus walked out of the airless room and back through the dormitory. Lucas half limped after him; every so often he turned, trying to catch his brother's eye, but Raffy would look only at his feet. Evie caught his gaze once or twice but each time forced herself to look away, even though as soon as he'd turned once more, she would track him again – watching him, his back, the way he moved . . .

'Bathroom's that way,' Linus said, pointing Lucas down the corridor. Lucas nodded gratefully and limped towards it. A minute or so later he re-emerged, his face clean, his hair its usual luminous hue.

'Okay,' he said, his tone businesslike once more, his eyes full of determination. 'I'll leave you here. See you in . . .' He pulled back his sleeve, looked at his gold watch. Evie saw Raffy's eyes narrow. 'Forty-five minutes. Good?'

'Good,' Linus agreed. Lucas walked quickly out of the building; moments later, Linus, Martha, Raffy and Evie followed, turning right then right again, into the government building that was next door. Linus pushed at the door; it was unlocked. 'Inside. Quick,' he said, opening it so that everyone could get in before closing it and locking it behind them.

'Right. Raffy and I'll be on the second floor. Evie, you know where you're going?'

Evie nodded silently.

'Come and find us when you're done.'

Evie took Martha up the stairs to Floor 4, to the place she'd worked in, the place she had spent so many hours changing reports, changing people's lives, enforcing the System's draconian labels, and she shuddered. Then she steeled herself and turned on her computer and Christine's, showing Martha how to input a change. There were no reports to guide her, no 'reason codes', but she knew them off by heart anyway.

'So we're changing them all to A?'

Evie nodded. If what Linus and Raffy were doing worked, there would be no labels any more. But just in case, they were making everyone the same. Because the Brother might try to make the System work again. But he couldn't, not if all records of former labels had been destroyed, not unless he said that the System had got it wrong, that the System had been corrupted. And if it had been corrupted, then no one would believe it any more. Then no one would believe anything any more.

'Except for the Brother,' Martha said wryly. 'We'll make him a D, shall we?'

Evie smiled, the first smile to cross her face since

they'd left Base Camp earlier that day. 'D sounds good,' she said. 'If I can identify his report, that is.'

Martha smiled back and they got to work.

The Brother stared out of his window in alarm, his breath short, his heart thudding in his chest. He'd heard the reports and now he could see for himself the Evils rampaging through the streets below, their hideous moans and screams sending shivers down his spine. But it made no sense. They were coming tomorrow. Tomorrow. He had seen the messages Lucas had sent, had seen the replies. It had been set for tomorrow.

He picked up his phone, then put it down again, pacing around his room. He had to think, had to work this through in his head. Lucas could not have sent a message – the device had been disabled and he had been locked up. No one else could have sent a message. If Linus was here a day early, it could only be because . . . But no, that was impossible. That was—

There was a knock at his door. An unmistakable knock – cool, efficient. But this time no one waited for him to call out; the door opened and Lucas appeared, a thin smile on his face.

'You? How?' The blood drained from the Brother's face. 'I don't understand . . .' He raced to the door, looked outside for the guards, for Sam, for . . .

'They've gone,' Lucas said with a little shrug. 'You sent them away, gave them errands to run.'

'Errands?' The Brother began to tremble. 'Errands?'

'We're in a state of emergency here,' Lucas said coolly.

'But how . . . how . . . ?' The Brother stared at him, bewildered. 'How could I have, if I didn't . . .'

'Come now.' Lucas shook his head, frowning. 'You don't think I have recordings of your voice? You don't think I can transmit from your line? Brother, you underestimate the System that you like to think you control. You have always underestimated its capabilities. And now . . .' He pulled a little face. 'Now it's a bit too late.'

'No.' The Brother shook his head vigorously. 'No. Guards. Guards!' he cried out.

'There's no use, there's no one there,' Lucas said icily. His eyes were impenetrable, but for once he looked like he was actually enjoying himself, as though he had been building up to this moment for a long time. Perhaps he had, the Brother realised with a jolt. 'You think you've been oh so clever, but you haven't. You've been played.'

'Played?' The Brother's eyes narrowed, his fear turning to anger. 'What do you mean?'

'I mean that you've always believed people are less

capable than you, less capable of running their lives, less capable of understanding human nature,' Lucas said, walking towards him threateningly. 'You were watching me, Brother, but you forgot that I have grown up in a City where everyone is watched all the time, where I factor in being spied on.'

The Brother stared at him. 'You set me up!' he gasped.

'I fed you the information I wanted you to hear,' Lucas said evenly. 'And now, Brother, you will ring the Gathering Bell. You will call your people to the Meeting House, safe from the Evils.'

'To the Meeting House? Are you mad?' the Brother asked angrily. 'I don't think so.' He moved towards Lucas. 'My guards will hunt you down, Lucas. You might have won a little battle, but you will not win the war. You will never win.'

'The thing is,' Lucas said, taking a gun out of the back of his trousers, 'I'm not interested in winning. And that's why you don't have a chance of beating me. Move, please. We don't have much time.'

'So, you and Raffy.' Martha turned to Evie. 'Everything okay between you?'

Evie flushed. 'Fine,' she said dismissively, staring at the screen in front of her. She'd discovered a way of highlighting hundreds of names at a time and changing their labels and she didn't want to stop. She had been enjoying the concentration, the thinking about something else, the not feeling tortured, miserable, uncertain and scared.

'Only it seemed to me like maybe things weren't so fine,' Martha said thoughtfully.

Evie closed her eyes and exhaled. 'Maybe not entirely fine,' she conceded.

'You want to talk about it?'

Evie shook her head. Then she nodded. Then she shook her head again.

'I was in love once,' Martha said, her eyes suddenly becoming rather misty, a little smile appearing on her face. 'It isn't always easy. Often it's really quite hard. But it's worth it. You and Raffy . . . You mustn't give up on each other. We all need someone.'

'Once? What happened?' Evie asked, hoping to divert the conversation away from her and Raffy as she changed 350 labels to 'A'.

'The City . . . ' Martha said quietly, looking back at the screen in front of her. 'The City took him away from me.'

'The City?' Evie asked curiously. She'd known that everyone at Base Camp had at some point come from the City, but somehow she'd never really imagined them there, never thought that they had lived as she had, within the rules and strictures. 'Were you not matched to him?'

Martha smiled sadly. 'It wasn't really like that,' she said. 'I was a . . . latecomer to the City. I'd been brought up in a small community a few miles away. We'd survived, but not much more than that. Food was a struggle. Water more so. Then the water dried up completely. We tried to find a new supply, but . . .'

'But the City had taken it,' Evie finished, looking down, guilt flooding her veins because it had been her City, because she had celebrated like everyone else when new dams were built.

'But the City had taken it,' confirmed Martha. 'So we did what we had to do. Daniel and I came here. We offered our labour in return for entry to the City. We submitted to the New Baptism.'

She paused; the pause went on and became silence. Evie looked over at Martha and realised that tears were falling down her face.

'And what happened?' she prompted gently, standing up, moving towards Martha and putting her hand on her shoulders, doing her best to comfort the woman whose own past, own pain, she had never even considered before.

'They said they'd look after us. I was pregnant with

our first child. They said I would be cared for. But they took Daniel away. For the New Baptism. They said I'd see him afterwards, but . . . I couldn't wait. I had to see for myself. I was in the same hospital; I sneaked into the New Baptism area. That's when I saw him. Saw all of them. Mutilated. Brain-damaged. He didn't know me. He was gone. They'd taken him . . .' She let her head fall forward, wrapped her arms around her shoulders.

Evie felt tears prick at her own eyes. 'The bed,' she whispered. 'The bed in the dormitory.' Martha nodded. 'What did you do?' Evie asked then, her voice barely audible.

'I ran,' Martha said. 'I knew I'd be next, so I ran back to the gate. I hid and waited for the gate to open again for new people. I should have warned them, should have told them to leave, but I didn't. I thought only of myself. I ran, as far as I could. I hid in the forest. I cried, I raged, I nearly died.' She took a deep breath, opened her eyes and forced a smile. 'I lost my child. And then Linus found me. And then my life started again.'

Evie stared at her open-mouthed. She had been so caught up in the knowledge that her parents had been taken from her by the City, it had never occurred to her that she was not the only one; she was not alone in the anger that she carried around with her, the betrayal, the bitterness.

'I'm sorry,' she murmured. 'I'm sorry I said what I said. About the damaged ones. About you not caring.'

Martha reached out and grasped Evie's hand. 'It's okay,' she said, 'I understand. We all do. Most of us have lost people. But they *are* lost, Evie. They are no longer who they were. We can look after them, but we can never find them again. We can never . . .' She sniffed, wiped her eyes. 'But all that happened a long time ago. You and Raffy . . . you seem to make each other so happy. It's a shame to see you so miserable.'

'It's that obvious?' Evie asked. Martha nodded.

Evie sighed heavily. 'It's my fault. I kept something from him. Something I did. He trusted me, and . . . and I betrayed that trust. And then I told him. And now he hates me.'

Martha appeared to digest this. 'He hates you? No. He's angry with you, I suspect. He wants to punish you. But he doesn't hate you. I can see the love in his eyes when he looks at you. He adores you. He needs you.'

Evie felt a strange sensation in the pit of her stomach. 'You think? Really? Because I love him – so much. I always have.'

'I know he does.' Martha smiled. 'Look, we're

nearly finished, aren't we? Let's get these labels changed and go and see him and Linus. Tell him how you feel and I think he'll forgive you. I'm sure he will.'

Evie felt a smile wend its way onto her face, and she realised what the feeling in her stomach was. It was hope. 'Okay,' she said, highlighting the last few names with a flourish, changing them to A's, then standing up, her eyes shining. 'Okay, let's go.'

23

They made their way silently up the stairs to the sixth floor, a floor that Evie had never been to before, had had no authority to go to. But she knew her way around; the floors were all set out in the same way and Raffy's directions led her straight to the room where she and Martha found him hunched over a computer.

'Nearly done,' he called out when the door opened. 'Did you find what you were looking for?'

They walked into the room and Raffy looked up. If he was pleased to see them he didn't show it. 'Oh, sorry. I thought you were Linus.'

Evie felt her heart sink. This was a bad idea. She couldn't talk to Raffy. There was nothing to say.

'Where is Linus?' Martha asked.

'He went out,' Raffy said, his attention already

turned back to the computer, his forehead wrinkling as he typed. 'To get something.'

'To get what?' Martha asked, her tone rather abrupt.

Raffy looked up impatiently. 'I don't know. Something. He said he'd be back soon.'

'And when was that?'

Raffy sighed. 'I don't know. A few minutes ago. Twenty minutes. Does it matter? I'm nearly done here. I just need to concentrate for a few more minutes . . .'

Martha looked at the clock on the wall. 'Twenty minutes? Where could he have been for twenty minutes?'

Raffy banged his fist down on the table in front of him. 'I don't know, okay? He'll be back. But if I don't get this finished . . .' He raised his eyebrows meaningfully and Martha sat down. Evie followed suit, her eyes travelling around the room where she knew Lucas had worked, as though he might have left something behind, as though some part of him might still be here somehow. Every so often she would shoot little looks at Raffy, wondering what he thought, what he really thought; wondering what he would say when she told him that she loved him, that she was sorry. She wondered if she would even get the chance, but it was as though he was completely unaware of her presence. Then, finally, he looked up.

'Okay,' he said with a sigh. 'Finished.'

'Finished?' Martha jumped up and walked over to the computer. 'You've rewritten the programme?'

'Did exactly what Linus told me to. It can't track any more. It's disabled. It can't do much, actually.'

Martha was quiet for a moment. 'I'm going to look for Linus,' she said after a brief pause. 'Wait here for me.' She slipped out of the room, leaving an awkward silence behind her.

Evie took a deep breath and stood up. 'Raffy,' she said quietly.

He turned to look at her, his expression not entirely hostile but not far off. 'Yes?'

'Raffy, I'm sorry. I need you to know that. I'm so sorry. About what happened with Lucas. I . . . I never had feelings for him. Not at all. It was just that night . . . He seemed so . . . broken. So fragile. And I was scared and I don't know how it happened, but I need you to know that it's you I love – only you. You I escaped with, you I want to be with. Always. And I'm sorry I hurt you and I hate myself for it.'

'Yeah?' Raffy said. His voice suggested a complete lack of interest, but his eyes told Evie otherwise and it gave her hope. His eyes were full of pain and defiance – those same eyes that had tugged at her heart when he'd been hounded, rejected, after his father was taken away. Eyes that made her want to weep because this time it was her fault.

'Yes,' she said firmly, slowly moving towards him. 'Raffy, I've been so miserable. I only told you because I needed you to know the truth, because I didn't want you loving a lie. I want you to love me, Raffy. All of me. Even the me that does stupid things.' Her eyes were filling with tears but she brushed them away because she didn't want pity, didn't want to be comforted.

Raffy didn't say anything for a few seconds. 'You really mean that? I saw him look at you. When we were with him just now. Were you looking at him?'

Evie felt her heart stop for a second. 'Of course I wasn't. Raffy, it's always been me and you. Always.'

'So why did you have to kiss Lucas?' he said, his voice cracking then, finally. 'Why the one person . . . Why Lucas?'

'Because he wanted to save your life,' Evie whispered. 'Because I realised that he'd been on your side all that time. It was you, Raffy, not him. I feel nothing for Lucas. Nothing. You have to believe me. You have to . . .'

She looked up at him, her vision blurred by the tears filling her eyes, and suddenly Raffy was close to her, holding her, kissing her – her mouth, her nose, her wet eyes . . . And she was clinging to him and kissing his neck, his mouth, and for a moment they could have been anywhere, could have been far, far away from the City, from the System, from everything that had held them back for so long.

'I love you,' Raffy murmured into her ear. 'I've always loved you.'

'I've always loved you too,' Evie whispered. 'Always.'

And for what felt like hours but could only have been seconds, they clung to each other, as though trying to merge their bodies, as though they were scared to let go.

Then the door opened and they pulled apart, slowly, reluctantly, but they didn't let go of each other completely. Evie wasn't sure she'd ever be able to let go of him completely again.

But when they turned to greet Martha and Linus, they stopped, their eyes widening and their hearts both quickening, but for different reasons.

'Lucas.' It was Raffy who spoke, Raffy who saw him first. Then she felt him leave her side in a blur as he lunged forward without warning, and suddenly he was pulling Lucas to the floor and hitting him.

'You bastard! You couldn't let me have anything of my own, could you?' he raged. 'You took my father from me, then all my friends. And you had to take Evie, too. You had to try.'

'Raffy, stop,' Lucas said through gritted teeth as blow after blow landed on him. Then Evie watched, startled, as he grabbed Raffy's hands and forced them behind him. The move was seamless, almost effortless, exhibiting a strength that Evie had seen just once before, against Mr Bridges' attackers. Raffy was pinned down on the floor, kicking like an upside-down beetle, helpless and frustrated. Lucas pressed his knees onto Raffy's legs, making him stop.

'Are you done now?' he asked, his voice low.

Raffy shook his head, seething. 'Never.'

Lucas looked down, his eyes clouded over. He seemed tired suddenly. Raffy noticed too, and tried to take the opportunity to wrest himself loose from Lucas's grip, but Lucas was too quick for him, turning him over to his front so Raffy's chin pressed into the ground.

'You have to listen to me,' Lucas said to him, his voice low. 'I wasn't responsible for Dad being taken away. He knew he was about to be made a K. He knew the Brother wanted to get rid of him. He trained me up. He told me I had to inform on him so I'd be beyond suspicion. He told me how to work my way up, how to get into the System so that I could continue his work. He made me promise, Raffy.'

'And that's why you kissed Evie? You pretend to be helping me, but you're not, Lucas. I don't know what your game is, but I see through you even if no one else does,' Raffy spat.

'I kissed Evie because . . . because . . .' Lucas looked up, met Evie's eyes, and she felt a jolt of something – pain, fear, desire – that made her shrink back and lower her eyes once more. 'I don't know why. It was stupid.'

Evie felt a stab of disappointment, which she immediately suppressed. She watched Raffy warily as Lucas let go of him, but Raffy didn't move; he stared at Lucas insolently.

Lucas sighed. 'I'm sorry,' he said. 'Okay? I'm sorry for everything. Truly, Raffy. Is that what you need to hear?'

Raffy rolled over, stood up and staggered back towards Evie. 'Yeah, well I'm sorry too,' he said. 'Sorry for you.'

Lucas nodded silently. His eyes were avoiding Evie; she knew because she was avoiding his, too. She didn't trust herself to look at him, didn't trust the emotions that would be conjured up. Instead she reached out for Raffy's hand, squeezed it, held it tight. Had it been stupid? She closed her eyes. Of course it had. Stupid was exactly the right word for it.

Lucas stood up, slowly. 'So where are Linus and Martha?' he asked. 'Everything's ready for you to leave.'

'Where indeed?' Martha said, walking into the room suddenly. 'I've looked everywhere and I can't find him.'

Lucas swung round in alarm. 'I don't understand. Everything's running like clockwork. Where could he have gone?'

Martha pulled a face. 'He could have gone anywhere. That's the thing with Linus. You never really know what he's thinking behind that smile of his.'

Lucas frowned. 'You want me to take you to the gate instead?' he asked, but Martha shook her head.

'We're not going without him,' she replied. 'So, everyone's in the Meeting House, right?'

Lucas nodded.

'And the Brother?'

'He's there too. Locked up in the back room. I've left Mr Bridges to keep an eye on him, but . . .'

'But you need to get back. I understand. I think we should all go with you.'

'To the Meeting House?' Raffy asked uncertainly. 'But we're meant to be leaving. If they see us . . . If the police guard know we're here . . .'

'Yes, but if I know Linus, and I think I do, then the Meeting House is where he's headed. And if he's there, then that's where we must go.' Martha turned to Lucas. 'Can you get us there without anyone seeing?'

'Sure,' Lucas nodded.

'Then let's go,' Martha said, a determined look on her face. 'Let's go and get him.'

The streets were deserted, but still they crept along the pavement, close to the wall; still they looked around furtively, flinching every time they heard a sound. The damaged ones had left, presumably secreted out safely by Angel; now an eerie silence had descended on the City. Everyone was in the Meeting House – everyone except the police guard, who were still patrolling the streets. No one spoke as they crept further into the City, towards the people they had all, in their different ways, escaped from.

Evie's throat felt tight with fear as she walked. Raffy was to her right; every so often he took her hand, shot her a look and squeezed her shoulder. And she would return the look, offer him a smile and nod to let him know that she was fine, that everything was good. And every so often Lucas would look back to whisper to Martha and his eyes would catch Evie's and she would hold his stare for a second or two before forcing her gaze away and looking anxiously at Raffy to see if he had seen, if he knew.

But Raffy would be looking ahead, always straight ahead.

'Okay, we're here,' Lucas said finally as they approached the back of the Meeting House on a path that Evie had never used before. 'You all wait here. Don't leave the shadows. I'll go in and see if I can find Linus.'

'I'll come with you,' Raffy declared, and Lucas looked at him cautiously, then shook his head. 'It's not safe,' he replied. 'You have to stay hidden.'

'Because I'm a K? I heard that you're a K now, too. Why is it safe for you to go in and not me?'

'Because . . .' Lucas cleared his throat, apparently lost for words for a moment. Then he put his hands on Raffy's shoulders. 'Because I have no one to miss me if I die. I have done what Dad asked me to do. You . . . Evie is depending on you. You have to look after her.'

Raffy opened his mouth to speak, then turned and looked at Evie, who stared back at him desperately, not wanting him to go but not wanting to stop him, either.

'I'll be no time,' Lucas said softly, breaking the silence, then he slipped away on his own. Just like always, Evie thought to herself.

* * *

The Meeting House was packed, just as Lucas had known it would be, the entire population of the City within its cavernous walls. Everyone was talking in worried voices and the result was an almost deafening hum of noise, questions and uncertainty. It took Lucas all his strength to block everything out as he slipped into the room at the back where he had left the Brother. Where could Linus be? With the Brother? Checking that Lucas had done his job properly? Elsewhere? If Linus was in the crowd, he would never find him. Lucas sighed; he realised as he approached the room that he barely knew Linus, that for years he had confided in and trusted a man he knew hardly anything about. But, he told himself, his father had trusted Linus, and that was enough. That would have to be enough.

He reached the door where Mr Bridges was waiting. 'Thank you,' Lucas said gravely. 'Thank you so much. You can go now. You have done enough.'

Mr Bridges looked around fearfully. Lucas put a hand on his shoulder. 'The Brother didn't see you; he doesn't know who has been guarding him. No one knows that you helped me in any way. Go, sit with the congregation – and know that tomorrow your label will have changed for good, just as everyone's labels will have changed. They will not change again. The System has been disabled. There will be no more labels. You're free. Do you understand?'

Mr Bridges nodded, his eyes still full of anxiety. 'And you?' he asked. 'What will happen to you?'

'I'll be fine.' Lucas smiled. 'I've just got some unfinished business, that's all. But thank you again. I cannot tell you how much—'

'It was nothing,' Mr Bridges cut in. 'It was the least I could do. When I told you that day that I would repay the debt I owed you, I meant it.' He held out a shaking hand and Lucas clasped it. 'You're a brave man,' Mr Bridges whispered. 'A good man. I hope that one day you'll be free to be a happy man, too.' And with that, he walked away, slipping into the shadows, towards the main room of the Meeting House; back to his community, back to where he belonged. Lucas watched him for a few seconds, wondering if he would ever belong anywhere himself . . . Then he pulled himself together. He belonged here, now. He had to find Linus. He had to finish what he had started. Taking a deep breath, he took out a key and opened the door.

But instead of being greeted by the scene he was expecting – the Brother, gagged and tied to a chair, just as he had left him – he found something else. An empty room. No sign of the Brother; no sign of anyone.

He swung round to call after Mr Bridges, to ask

him what had happened, but it was too late – he was long gone, impossible to find now. He wouldn't have let the Brother go. No one else knew where the Brother was. Lucas ran over to the high, single window and stretched up to tug at it; it had been unlocked. So the Brother had left without Mr Bridges knowing. But how? How had the Brother untied himself when Lucas himself had secured the knots? His mind raced, his pulse quickened and a sheen of sweat covered his body. Then he started, because he could hear shouting – and he recognised one of the voices. He jumped up to the window but it was too high; there was no clear view of what was happening below. Instead, he left the room, racing back along the corridor towards the door he had come in through. The voice he had heard was the Brother's. The other, he suddenly realised he knew as well. And he knew that he had to do something, quickly, before people heard, before everything they had planned so meticulously was ruined. Barely caring who saw him, Lucas hurled open the door and ran around the building to where he'd heard the voices.

'Lucas.' It was the Brother who spoke. He was standing with his back to the building, and in front of him was Linus. For a few seconds, Lucas studied the man he'd known remotely for so long; at the hospital he'd been too dazed to take much in. Linus was tall and muscular, more athletic than Lucas had imagined, with short grey hair. And his face, when he turned around to greet Lucas, reminded Lucas of an overripe peach, with its creases and lines like a landscape dried by the sun. Full of warmth, but tough, strong – used to surviving where others might give up.

'Lucas,' he said, breaking out into a smile that etched its way into every corner of his face. 'It's good to see you. Have the others gone?'

Sam stared at the wall in front of him. Was he going mad? Had he really seen who he thought he'd seen? Quickly he approached the front of the Meeting Hall. Still no sign of the Brother in spite of his clear instructions to meet him here half an hour ago. And now Lucas. It had been Lucas. He knew it. He'd recognise that upright posture anywhere. And if Lucas was here, and the Brother wasn't . . .

He turned and marched to the back of the building where two police guards were standing sentry, reassuring the City's inhabitants that they would be safe inside, that the Evils would not trouble them in such a sacred place. 'I think you might need some back-up,' he said.

'Back-up?' One of the police guards frowned.

'There's no back-up. Everyone's out hunting down the Evils. Why? What's going on?'

'The Brother is missing and I just saw a K in the building,' Sam said, his eyes narrowing. 'So please call for back-up or I shall have to talk to your superior.' He turned slightly, just enough to make sure that the guard saw his label and the gold inflection on it that told him Sam was one of the Brother's chosen few.

The guard blanched, then nodded. 'Yes, sir,' he said. 'I'll get on to it right away. You can leave it with me, sir.'

'Good,' Sam answered, and swept away.

24

'Linus, this isn't what we agreed.'

Lucas turned to see Martha behind him, walking towards them, her arms folded. Behind her were Raffy and Evie. Lucas forced his eyes away from Evie and turned back to Linus.

'Ah,' Linus said. 'So they're still here.'

'They wouldn't leave without you,' said Lucas. 'Please tell me what the Brother is doing out here? The plan was to leave him in the Meeting House. The plan—'

'Plans change,' Linus declared with a grin. 'The Brother and I were just having a little chat. A little catch-up.' Linus smiled again – a thousand smiles caught up in one face, Lucas found himself thinking.

'We're not safe,' Lucas told him. 'We need to leave.'

'Lucas, my friend,' Linus said, his eyes twinkling. 'You're right, as always. But it pays to be adaptable, wouldn't you say? And the Brother and I are nearly finished anyway.'

The Brother looked at him as though he were a rodent. 'We were finished a long time ago, Linus.'

'Really?' Linus looked nonplussed. 'Huh. Maybe I'm wrong then. Maybe this was a wasted trip.' He started to walk away, everyone watching him, then he stopped, turned and smiled again.

'Ah, you're teasing me, aren't you? We both know there are things we need to discuss. And since we're here with nothing much better to do, why not talk?' He walked towards the Brother until he was just inches away. 'So, let's talk,' he said then, his voice low and threatening.

Lucas looked at Martha, wondering whether to intervene, but she shook her head and stepped back. Lucas followed suit, his eyes inadvertently travelling to where Evie stood, her white skin almost luminous in the moonlight, her intelligent eyes fixed on Linus, no fear on her face at all. Next to her stood Raffy, his face the same as always, his emotions right there on the surface so you felt like you could touch them. His body taut, ready for action; his hair curling around his face, as unruly as he was.

'So, Brother. Still peddling your lies, huh? Still wrecking people's lives?'

The Brother regarded him stonily. 'You know and I know, Linus, that in difficult times, difficult decisions are needed. Courage of convictions. A plan. You never understood that. You were too idealistic. But idealism has no place in the real world.'

'The real world,' Linus said thoughtfully, moving back, taking a few steps to the left, then returning to where he'd stood before. 'And this is the real world?'

'Yes,' replied the Brother. 'We have a community. Mouths to feed, children to raise, products to supply, a City to protect. My people are inside. Let me go to them.'

'Your people?' Linus looked at him incredulously. 'You really think that lying to everyone, telling them that the System can see into their souls and give them the right label, is the best way to look after people?' Threateningly, he moved closer still, but the Brother didn't flinch.

'The System works,' he said. 'My System. Not yours.'

'Works in that most people are miserable and hate themselves? Works in that people think the scar on the side of their head is where the evil bit of their brain was removed, when really it's where a chip has been inserted to keep track of where they are and what they're doing? Interesting.' Linus smiled again, but this time his face barely crinkled and his eyes were cold. 'You're a cheat and a liar. You took my dreams and you turned them into a nightmare. But now it's over, Brother. Your System has been disabled. And now I'm going to disable you.'

He reached into his coat pocket, then froze, trying his other pocket, his trouser pockets, patting himself furiously.

'Lost something?' asked the Brother, a little smile of his own creeping onto his face. 'Oh dear. You never were very good at practicalities, Linus. And now, if you'll look behind you, you'll see that my police guard are here.'

Everyone swung round to see a man approaching with ten police guards, all carrying batons. Lucas's stomach lurched with fear and anger.

'Linus!' he shouted. 'Linus, what have you done? We should have left. We should have—'

'My gun,' Linus said, apparently not hearing Lucas. 'Where's my gun? Where's—'

A police guard lunged forward and grabbed him; another grabbed Raffy and Martha.

'Let them go.' Lucas's eyes widened as he saw Evie step forward, arms outstretched, and he saw a glint at the edge of her hands and for a moment he couldn't breathe, couldn't think, couldn't understand. Then she swung around and he saw the hate in her eyes, and he flinched. 'Let them go,' she barked again; the police guards immediately backed away.

There was a scream; people had begun to file out of the Meeting House behind the police guards; word had evidently spread that the Brother was outside, that there was something going on. They came tentatively, cautiously, surrounding Linus, the Brother, the police guards, Lucas, Martha, Raffy and Evie, but several feet back, strength in numbers as they huddled together. They cried out in fear as they recognised Lucas, Raffy and Evie, screaming every time Evie turned to look at them. But Lucas barely saw them, barely noticed that there was nowhere to run now and no way of escape. All he could see was Evie, holding a gun in her hands, her face serene, cold and angry. Like his, he thought with a start. Satisfied that her friends were free, she turned the gun on the Brother. His eyes were fixed on Evie, too. 'Evie, put the gun down,' he said. 'That is an implement of evil, of torture. It has no place in your hands. Put it down.'

'I don't want to put it down,' Evie said, her voice not wavering, not showing any fear at all. 'I am evil, remember. I helped a Killable escape. That makes me a K too, right? Right?' She swung round, her gun pointing briefly at the police guards, at the crowd; there were more screams as everyone stepped back, cowering fearfully. She turned the gun back on the Brother, who forced a smile.

'Evie,' he said carefully. 'Evie, you are young. You don't understand. You are not a K. You need help, Evie, that's all.'

'Like the help I needed for my dreams?' Evie asked.

The Brother blanched. 'Evie, we resolved your dreams. We realised that—'

'That it was the City I was dreaming about?' Evie asked, her tone biting. 'So not my real parents, then? The parents that you let the Great Leader mutilate before kicking them out of the City again? The parents that you allowed to be brain-damaged, to be turned into Evils?'

There was a gasp from the crowd; the Brother's face drained of blood. 'I don't know where you heard such a thing, Evie, but it's lies. Lies. It's—'

'I remember them,' Evie said, walking towards him. 'I remember coming here. I remember the hope they had. And you . . .'

'I always knew she was no good!' A shout came suddenly from the crowd, a woman rushing forward. Lucas recognised her as Evie's mother. 'We took you in, gave you a home, treated you as our own daughter, and look at you. You're just like your real parents. Evil. Worthless.'

'No!' Evie yelled, turning the gun on her. 'No, they're not worthless. You are. You stole me. You lied to me.'

Her mother stared at her for a moment, then ran back into the crowd, leaving Evie to turn back to the Brother. 'My real parents were never worthless. They loved me for who I was. They loved me. And you . . . you lied to me,' she said.

'We protected you,' the Brother answered forcefully. 'Your parents weren't able to join the City. They were beyond the New Baptism. They were—'

'The New Baptism doesn't work!' Evie screamed. 'No one here has had it. Admit it! Tell everyone.' She turned, her eyes shining in the moonlight, looking around at the crowd of people in front of her. 'The New Baptism doesn't work. It never did. It just damages people. That's who the Evils are. They're the only ones who've had the New Baptism. That's why they're like they are. It's not their fault. They're not evil. They're just damaged. Like my parents were. Damaged and then kicked out of the City, used to make us all afraid. But I'm not afraid, Brother. You're the one who should be afraid. Because I'm going to kill you, just like you killed my parents.'

'And then everyone will know just how evil you are. They will know that everything you've said is untrue,' the Brother said levelly.

She walked towards him again, her hands beginning to tremble just slightly. 'No,' she said. 'You are the evil one. You are the one who has ruined so many lives, taken so much life away. You are the one who must be stopped. And I'm going to stop you.'

The Brother stared at her, and as she approached, his round face lost its steel, its arrogant stance and he started to tremble. 'No,' he snivelled. 'No, Evie, don't kill me. I'm sorry.'

'You're sorry?' Evie asked icily. 'Not good enough. Not nearly good enough.'

'Please,' the Brother begged her. 'Please don't do this. Let's talk. I can change your label. Change Raffy's label. I can make things better. I can . . .'

'There are no labels,' Evie said. 'Not any more. The City doesn't need you. Doesn't want you.'

'Noooooooo,' the Brother cried out, a guttural sound that seemed to come from the depths of his round belly. 'Someone, do something!' He stared at the police guards, standing a few feet back. 'Take out your guns,' he shouted. 'Kill them. Kill them all!'

A murmur went up from the crowd. 'There are no

guns in the City. Guns are evil. Guns represent violence and corruption and . . .'

'Guns are only evil in the hands of evil,' the Brother said breathlessly, before turning back to the police guards. 'Stop being so pathetic and take out your guns!' he screamed. 'I don't care if everyone sees them. You have to shoot these people otherwise they're going to kill me.'

But no one moved. No one except Linus, who stepped forward. 'Everything you've told these people is a lie, isn't it, Brother? You have one rule for them and one for you. No one else is allowed riches, but you live in splendour. Guns are evil, yet you furnish your own police guard with them secretly. The City is a safe place, yet its citizens are continually under threat from you and your corrupt System. The Evils are violent criminals, yet in reality they are innocents, violated by you, by this place. You deserve to die. The City deserves better. But not by Evie's hand.' He touched her gently on the shoulder. 'Evie,' he said quietly, 'you've got your whole life ahead of you and if you kill someone it will haunt you for ever, even if that someone is a lowly worthless man like the Brother.'

'I have to kill him,' Evie said, her eyes not leaving the Brother. 'I owe it to my parents.' She looked around the crowd. 'My real parents.'

'Let me do it,' Linus said. 'Give me the gun. Let me do it.'

Evie shook her head.

Lucas watched her, watched Linus, watched the Brother, his hand poised.

Evie stood in front of the Brother, her hands shaking as she moved her finger to the trigger. Then suddenly a shot rang out and people were screaming and the police guard rushed forward and Evie stood, motionless, her mouth open, the gun still in her hands.

'But . . .' she said. 'But I didn't . . . I didn't . . .'

Raffy ran towards her and pulled her to him and the gun dropped out of her hands. Linus picked it up.

'I didn't . . .' she said again.

'I know,' Linus replied as they both looked behind him to where Lucas stood, holding the gun he'd just grabbed from one of the police guards. He held it up, pointing it at the guards, at the crowd. The Brother was moaning on the floor; Lucas looked down at him in disgust.

'It's only your leg. You'll survive,' he sneered.

'You should have let me kill him,' Evie said bitterly. 'You should have let me.'

'No,' replied Lucas, as Linus took Evie's gun and between them they held back the guards, the crowd. 'I couldn't let you throw your life away,' he said. 'Don't be bitter. Don't hide your emotions and hide behind a mask. Let it go, Evie. The alternative is too painful. It hurts even more. It takes your life away from you.' He looked over at Linus. 'You go,' he told him. 'I'll hold the guards back until you've got time to get out.'

Linus shook his head. 'I'm having fun here,' he said, his eyes crinkling softly. 'You go. Take the others. Angel will meet you outside, take you safely to Base Camp. I'll catch up. Just get out and keep running.'

'Linus!' 'Martha rushed towards him. 'What are you saying? You have to come with us. We need you.' She grabbed at him, but he gently pushed her away.

'Someone has to stay,' he said gently. 'I can hold them here, buy you enough time to escape.'

'And what about you?' Martha asked, tears in her eyes. 'How will you get out?'

'I'll think of something,' Linus said, smiling at her. 'Go. Go now and start your lives again. Know that the System that ruined your life is gone, that the veil has been lifted. What we did was worth it. And don't worry about me.'

'I'll stay with you,' Martha insisted, her lip trembling, but Linus shook his head. 'Lucas, take her. Look after her. Look after everyone. I'm counting on you.'

Lucas nodded. 'It's been good . . . almost knowing you,' he said.

Linus grinned. 'Likewise,' he said, swinging round to point the gun back at the Brother. 'Come near and the Brother dies,' he shouted, then winked at his departing friends. 'One of you follows my friends, and the Brother dies. Anyone moves and the Brother dies. Got it?'

'Come on. Let's go,' Lucas declared, looking at Martha who nodded reluctantly. He turned to the others. 'Raffy? Evie?'

Raffy nodded and took Evie's hand, then they started to run, back the way they had run that first time, disappearing behind houses, along hidden paths, heading east. No one said a word, no one was ready to talk about what had happened, what would happen in the future, what they had achieved, what they hadn't. They just moved forward, past the cottage, across the muddy swamps.

And then they were at the gate. But when Lucas went to open it, it stayed shut. 'Angel,' Martha called. 'Angel?'

'He can't hear you,' Raffy said bitterly. 'Ten inches, remember.' He ran towards it, pulling back every bolt. Still the gate wouldn't open. They heard shots in the distance and looked at each other in alarm.

'We'll have to go over,' Lucas said.

'Over? How?' Raffy looked at him incredulously.

'Like this.' Lucas clambered up the gate, grabbing hold of the top and swinging his feet up, twisting so that they stood awkwardly between the large metal spikes. 'You climb up on me and assume the same position on the other side. Then the others can climb up me and and climb down you.'

Raffy hesitated.

'Or we can wait here for the police guard,' Lucas said, his voice low.

'Fine,' Raffy relented. He jumped up, following Lucas's lead and in spite of losing his grip several times, he managed to get to the top. Evie started to shake – it looked treacherous, fifteen feet high with spikes covering the top. They'd never get over it alive. If Raffy fell, if he missed his footing . . .

'Watch out for the barbed wire on the way down,' Lucas said, handing Raffy some pliers. He took them, his eyebrows raised.

'Think of everything, don't you?' he said under his breath.

'I've learnt to,' Lucas replied lightly. 'It's something Dad taught me. Something I wish I'd been able to teach you.' He met Raffy's eyes for a moment and Evie saw something on Raffy's face, but it passed so quickly she couldn't be sure what it was, and already he had started to climb again. Evie watched, feeling like her heart was barely beating as Raffy disappeared over the top.

'Are you okay?' she called out, and got a muffled reply that told her nothing but at least reassured her that he was alive.

'You next?' Lucas asked.

Evie shook her head. 'Martha,' she said.

Martha nodded reluctantly and started to climb. She was more athletic than Evie had expected, ably shinning up over bolts and locks to where Lucas was perched. He lifted her up to where Raffy had clipped back the barbed wire and held her feet as she scrambled to reach the top. Evie couldn't look, couldn't contemplate the climb herself. She would falter. She would fall. She would ruin everything.

And then Martha was over, and Lucas looked down at her. 'Ready?' he enquired, his eyes suddenly so full of kindness it made Evie feel strong, like she could do anything. Wiping her hands on her clothes, she started to climb, not looking down, not thinking about what would happen if she lost her grip. And then Lucas's hand was reaching out to her and she took it, and he pulled her up, and she was resting on him, next to him, so close she could feel his breath on her cheek.

'Give this to Raffy,' he said, taking the watch off his wrist, the gold watch that he had been so proud of.

'Why?' She looked at it uncertainly. 'Why would Raffy want a watch that the Brother gave you?'

Lucas smiled sadly. 'It was our father's,' he said. 'I told Raffy the Brother gave it to me because . . .' He sighed. 'I told Raffy a lot of things. Dad wanted Raffy to have it, but it was too dangerous. So I looked after it for him. But now it's time to hand it over. I want him to remember Dad like he deserves to be remembered. I want him to know how much Dad loved him. How much I . . .' He trailed off again, his eyes shining.

'You can give it to him yourself,' Evie said. 'When we get over.'

Lucas shook his head. 'I'm not coming with you,' he whispered.

Evie stared at him, suddenly feeling chilled to the bone. 'What do you mean?' she asked.

'I mean I need to stay here. People are going to be lost. Confused. They'll need direction. They'll need hope. And anyway, someone's got to help that creepy guy Linus get out of the City.'

Evie shook her head violently. 'You have to come with us. You have to . . .' She could feel tears pricking at her eyes, anger and desperation and indignation surging through her veins. She didn't want to lose Lucas again. 'You have to come,' she said again, using her sleeve to wipe at her eyes and nose.

'I can't,' he said softly. 'You know that really. You go with Raffy. Go to Base Camp. Find one of the other civilisations. Make a life together.'

'And what if the police guard kill you? What then?' Evie demanded.

Lucas laughed. 'I'm not going to walk back to the Meeting House, if that's what you think,' he said, before his face went serious again. 'Evie, I just need to know. I have to know that what you and Raffy and Linus came here to do . . . that it worked. I have to make sure. For Dad's sake. For Linus's.'

Evie closed her eyes. She knew he wouldn't change his mind, knew that she'd lost him, knew he was right, but it felt so very wrong.

'I'll . . . miss you,' she whispered, not letting herself think too much about what she was saying.

'Evie?' It was Raffy's voice.

'She's coming,' Lucas shouted. Then he put his right hand around her face, cupping her jaw, and brought her to him, kissing her tenderly on the lips. 'The reason I wanted to be matched to you is because you're beautiful,' he whispered. 'Because you're insightful and intelligent and independent. Because I fell in love with you the first time I saw you. But I always knew you would never be mine. Be safe, Evie. Look after Raffy for me.'

'Thank you,' said Evie. 'For shooting the Brother. For . . . for everything.'

'I'm going to miss you, too,' Lucas replied, his voice soft and so full of emotion that she could see his lips trembling.

And with that, he hoisted her up so that her hands could reach the top of the gate, and held her as she pulled herself up and over. And as she went over the top, she lost her grip for a second and began to fall, and she was sure it was over, and for a second she didn't care . . . But then she felt two arms wrap around her, holding her, squeezing her to him, and she could smell Raffy, feel him – the boy she had loved all her life, the boy who had loved her, and she held him back, tears cascading down her cheeks, and together they climbed down to the ground.

'Lucas?' Angel asked when she landed. 'Where is he?'

'He's going back,' Evie said. 'He's going to stay for a bit.'

And if Raffy wanted to protest, wanted to ask why, or to know what else Lucas had confided in her, he didn't.

'Does he know what he's doing?' Angel asked, frowning.

'I think so,' Evie told him. She turned to Raffy, to

give him Lucas's watch, but then stopped herself. Now was not the time. And she wasn't ready yet. Instead, as they started to run, she held it in her hand, pressing it tightly against her fingers, as though it were Lucas himself that she was holding. As though she were protecting him, as though he had somehow left part of himself in the gold timepiece that had symbolised so much – that had turned out, like Lucas himself, like the City he had appeared to love, to be something so completely different to what she'd thought.

To what they'd all thought.

Epilogue

Dirt, dust and grime in her eyes, in her nose, choking her. A hand around hers, pulling her on, reassuring her. A rock catches her unawares and she falls, her face pressed into the ground; she lifts her head and wipes her forehead – there is blood on the back of her hand. Her lip begins to quiver but before tears can come she is swept up; her arms wrap around a familiar neck and she hears his laughter.

'Look where you're going, you idiot,' he says, grinning. 'Here, hold my hand.'

She takes it gratefully as they continue their journey. The rhythm of his walking calms her; she feels safe. 'We're nearly there,' he says, squeezing her hand. 'Nearly there, my darling.'

She walks beside him, walks towards their new life. Soon she will be somewhere else, somewhere new, somewhere better. Raffy grabs her playfully and she smiles, reaching out to hug him. 'I love you,' he murmurs. 'I love you . . .'

END OF BOOK ONE

Acknowledgements

I am very grateful for the support and counsel of Dorie Simmonds, my agent, and for the enthusiasm, energy and brilliant ideas of Kate Howard, my editor, whose attention to detail is really awe inspiring. I also want to thank everyone at Hodder who has helped to bring this book to life. And finally, thanks to everyone at The Old Clinic – I miss you!

Meet Gemma Malley . . .

'So, where to begin? School? Hmmm. School was okay. Great in some ways, not so great in others. I'm someone who likes to do things my own way, rather than following rules and that's not so easy in the regimen of the classroom. But I loved English – I had a wonderful teacher, Miss Pitt, who got me super excited about Chaucer. I really looked forward to those lessons.

Then university. I studied Philosophy, which I loved too – it's basically about arguing your point. Not just arguing your point; it's about challenging assumptions, asking difficult questions, having to come up with cogent reasons for things you've always just 'known' to be true. And I joined a band, too. Lots of fun. We toured Japan, toured France, had an album in the indie charts . . . I edited the university newspaper, too. If you want to write, I always say that the best thing to do is . . . write. Don't talk about it, just do it, and if you wind up writing about something that doesn't entirely fascinate you then great – writing is hard and you have to work at it. My first job in journalism was writing about pensions – if you can make them interesting, you can make pretty much anything interesting. Going for the hard option is often the best way to learn in my opinion.

So anyway, that's a bit about me. But

'If you want to write, I always say that the best thing to do is . . . write.'

you're probably not really that interested in what I got up to years ago. Maybe you're more interested in why I wrote my books? If you are, read on . . .'

Which children's authors most inspire you?

My favourite children's authors are those who, in my opinion, make the most of the genre with great story-telling, extensive imagination, and who aren't afraid to tackle difficult and complicated subjects. Philip Pullman is certainly one, as are Meg Rosoff, Jennifer Donnelly and Jacqueline Wilson. I think that Oscar Wilde's fairy tales are also absolutely wonderful.

Tell us the best thing you've ever written.

Probably the letter to my agent, Dorie Simmonds.

Do you have any particular habits or rituals when you write?

I don't have too many rituals when it comes to writing — I sit looking out into the garden, which is lovely and I can't even start thinking about writing until I've had a cup of hot, steaming tea. Other than that, I try to clear my mind completely, think about my characters, and then write as much as I can before my next tea break!

What career path would you have taken, if you hadn't become an author?

I'd like to say an astronaut or an adventurer, but I think I would have

'My favourite children's authors are those who aren't afraid to tackle difficult subjects.'

ended up writing in some way — perhaps as a journalist, or perhaps working in education. I might even have become a teacher — I think working with young people and getting them excited in a book, a subject or the world around them is about the most rewarding thing you can do.

Does it take a long time to write a novel?

It really depends — it can take weeks, months or even years! Sometimes a book just flows out of you; other times you have to wrench it out.

What first inspired you to write *The Killables*?

The idea for this novel sprung from a few different places, but the genesis came from an article I read in an academic journal about the amygdala and how some scientists were identifying it as the root of evil in the human brain.

I find neuroscience fascinating but worrying too; just because a certain part of the brain is activated when we fall in love, or because another part is activated when we think bad thoughts, does that mean that the love/evil resides in that part of the brain? That our brain, not us, is responsible for what we do? Some scientists think so and it has huge implications for morality and free will – are we distinguishable from our brains? If we have no control over our brains, then how can we be blamed for our actions?

'Sometimes a book just flows out of you; other times you have to wrench it out.'

It also got me thinking about what a world would be like if we managed to remove the 'evil' bit of our brain. Would we all be good? Can goodness exist without its counterpart? What is goodness anyway?

What inspired you to choose the dystopian setting?

I love to think of a utopia – in this case, a world without evil – and turning it on its head, looking for the flip side. Because the truth is, I don't think that utopia exists. Humans are fallible and that's what makes life such a roller-coaster ride. I like the ups and downs; without them things would be very dull. And don't we all appreciate the summer more after a long, cold winter?

Tell us about the sequel to *The Killables*

The Disappearances is set a year after the end of *The Killables*, and Evie and Raffy are living in a Settlement in the North, which couldn't be more different from the City and which is, to Raffy's relief, as far away from Lucas as possible. Meanwhile, Lucas is back in the City, where the System no longer tyrannises its people and labels no longer exist. But the City has been plagued by a new threat: the Disappearances – young people who have gone missing from within the City walls, apparently vanishing into thin air. And then Lucas discovers the truth . . .

'It's easy, when reading dystopian novels, to close the cover and thank our lucky stars that it isn't true, that it's just fiction, that nothing like that would ever really happen. That's why Anne Frank's diary is such an important book. Because things like that do happen. Did happen. And we should never forget it.'

A sneak peek at the next book
in THE KILLABLES series

THE DISAPPEARANCES

Chapter One

'Morning.'

Evie looked up to see Raffy next to her with two steaming hot cups of tea and she quickly sat up and took one from him. 'What's the time?' she murmured.

'It's early,' Raffy said, getting back into bed next to her. 'I couldn't sleep.'

Evie moved aside for him and took a sip of her tea. 'How early?'

'4.30am.'

Half an hour before their usual wake-up time. Evie tried to open her eyes properly, but they were rebelling, resisting her request. Instead, she allowed them to close again and let her head loll back against her pillow.

'Still, exciting day today. We're being fitted,' Raffy said. He was bearing down over her; Evie knew he was expecting her to open her eyes, so she did so, managing a little smile before closing them again.

Fitted. For her dress. For his suit. Next week would be their Welcome Ceremony, their formal acceptance into the Settlement.

And it was also going to be the day of their Wedding.

Available March 2013

H
HODDER

3 3132 03503 0303